Dear Reader,

A North Dakota blizzard blew Carly Austin closer to my doorstep than I ever imagined I'd find her. I knew who she was when I pulled her out of her car and took her into my cabin to thaw her out, but I didn't expect her to remember me. We hadn't exactly run in the same crowd when we were in high school. She was the hometown golden girl, and I was the "outlaw" from the reservation. But times had changed. Since I'd last seen her, I'd *become* the law, and she'd taken a teaching job in Indian country. Carly Austin was on my turf now.

Carly thought we ought to be friends. I told her I wasn't a friendly man. The woman had a lot to learn about outlaws and cops and guys who like to keep a tight rein on their hearts. But she had a few things to teach me, too. And I wasn't counting on that!

Yours truly,
Rafe Strongheart

KATHLEEN EAGLE

A Class Act

North Dakota

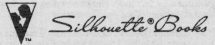

Published by Silhouette Books New York

America's Publisher of Contemporary Romance

For dedicated teachers everywhere;
For all my students—past, present, and future;
And for those who share with me
in having fond memories of the Employees' Club.

SILHOUETTE BOOKS
300 East 42nd St., New York, N.Y. 10017

A CLASS ACT

Copyright © 1985 by Kathleen Eagle

All rights reserved. Except for use in any review, the reproduction
or utilization of this work in whole or in part in any form by any
electronic, mechanical or other means, now known or hereafter
invented, including xerography, photocopying and recording, or in
any information storage or retrieval system, is forbidden without
the permission of the publisher, Silhouette Books, 300 E. 42nd St.,
New York, N.Y. 10017

ISBN: 0-373-45184-9

Published Silhouette Books 1985, 1993

All the characters in this book have no existence outside the
imagination of the author and have no relation whatsoever to
anyone bearing the same name or names. They are not even
distantly inspired by any individual known or unknown to the
author, and all incidents are pure invention.

® and ™ are trademarks used under license. Trademarks recorded
with ® are registered in the United States Patent and Trademark
Office, the Canadian Trade Marks Office and in other countries.

Printed in the U.S.A.

Chapter One

The little blue hatchback pitched its nose into another pillow drift, shuddered with the impact, and plunged ahead into the next one. Carly's shoulders ached from the battle with the steering wheel. The barrage of white flakes battered her vision, and the mesmerizing motion of the windshield wipers threatened her sanity. With each swipe of the blades, the wipers lost ground.

Carly took a deep breath and closed her eyes briefly, desperate for some relief from the awful burning. The hot air blasting from the defroster had dried them out completely. And the sight of white dots pelted at her even through closed lids.

Whoa! Steady. There was no yellow line anymore. No more shoulder on the right. There was only straight ahead. Straight into the wind. Straight on till morning. She had to be almost there. She'd been bucking drifts for three hours now, crawling against the wind. Each one seemed to drag longer under the car. It wouldn't take much more to high-center the little beast in the middle of the road. Then what?

Caught by a sudden broadside gust, the compact car reeled. The steering wheel, trembling beneath Carly's steady hands, was useless as the wind sent the car off on its own wild tangent. The grating underneath culminated in a *thunk*, and then it was still. The wind roared on. Carly's heart sank.

"Well, Old Blue, you've really done it this time." She reached across the pile of books in the middle of the seat and fished for her crocheted hat. "I thought sure you'd make it, but you've let me down." The hat drooped over her face. She drew on her thick mittens. "If I can't get you back on your feet, I may have to put a bullet between your headlights and strike out on my own."

Fighting the force of the wind against the door, Carly managed to push her way out into the night. She peered up the road, the icy blast cutting into her face. Her headlights split the dark, illuminating white whorls of snow. She turned her back to the wind and looked down the road. Dark and windy white. The car was undeniably stuck. And undoubtedly low on gas. Not the best planning she'd ever done.

Hopefully, there'd be other adventuresome souls on the road tonight. Otherwise she'd have to do all the digging out herself, God forbid. Had she put the shovel back in the trunk after Donna borrowed it last? She did have a blanket. Carly knew all the cautions—stay with the car, use the heater intermittently, don't let the tailpipe get plugged up. Unfortunately, she hadn't taken many *pre*cautions. The headlights and the flashers would attract attention, and someone would come along. Someone always did.

* * *

Nights like this always meant trouble. Somebody usually couldn't report for his shift, and even though people should have been snowed safely into their houses for the duration, there was always some fool willing to risk his fingers and toes for a quart of milk or bottle of aspirin. Nights like this brought out the crazies and the cops.

Rafe Strongheart had just about decided to leave the blizzard-prowling to the crazies when he spotted two fading beams of light a few years ahead. He pulled up beside them, dragged the zipper on his parka up to his chin, and let himself out into the driving wind. God, it was cold! An Alberta clipper. His grandmother would have said the hawk was out. Sixty below with the wind-chill, easy. The Bronco's door blew out of his hand, slamming shut.

He knew the car; he knew every car on the reservation. But this one in particular always caught his eye. It had moved to town in August, claimed a parking spot by the curb at the Employees' Club, and took a jaunt up to Bismarck every third Saturday. He'd run a check on the plates once just for the hell of it. Registered to Carly Austin, sure enough, the all-American girl. Excellent credentials. Rafe knew them well.

He reached for the car door and wondered why his heart still thudded like a scared kid's every time he faced a moment like this—hoping for the best, expecting the worst. The door was pushed open from the inside just as he pulled from without.

They both shouted at once into the roar of the wind.

"You okay?"

"Thank God!"

"How long have you been—"

"Hours! Please...I've been trying to shovel—"

"Get in the Bronco."

"I can't just leave it."

He reached past her and punched the lights off before jerking the keys from the ignition. Carly staggered back a step as he slammed and locked the door. "Come on," he shouted, lifting an arm in the direction of the Bronco as he turned his face away from the buffeting wind. Stiff with cold, Carly waddled alongside her rescuer, the blanket she'd wrapped herself in flapping around her legs.

The Bronco blazed its own trail as Rafe swung it through an S turn, reversed its direction, and headed back. Shortly he turned off the highway, taking what was, underneath the snow, an unpaved access road. Sheets of snow whipped in front of him, and he was driving on instinct. He must've been crazy to leave the house in the first place.

"Where are we going?"

Her voice was small and thin, not at all what he'd remembered. Was it from cold or fear? Surely she hadn't lost her stage presence, not in a drama of her own making, as this certainly was. He spared the shivering bundle in the passenger's seat a glance. She had a blanket pulled up around her ears, a floppy hat slouched over her face, and he'd yet to see whether she looked as he remembered. "My place. It's just up here, less than a mile off the road."

"I'm f-r-r-e-ezing. I can't even feel my hands and feet anymore. I hope your p-place is warm."

"If you're frostbitten, you'll need more than shelter from the storm. Can you move them?"

Carly's brain sent the message, but her extremities hesitated in their response. "I don't know whether they're moving or not,'' she mumbled, silently telling herself not to panic.

"I suppose there was a good reason for you to be traveling in weather like this,'' he said as he pushed the Bronco along the curve that flanked his house.

"School tomorrow'' was her only answer. "How about you?''

"A very good reason, as it turns out.'' After securing the vehicle, he pushed himself back out into the wind.

Rafe mounted the back step ahead of her, maneuvering the storm door toward Carly as he bent to the lock on the inside door. But the storm door flew out of control somewhere between their hands, knocking Carly off the step and smashing its glass panes as it crashed against the side of the house.

Cursing into his upturned collar, Rafe jumped over the side of the stoop and dragged Carly out of her cushion of snow. Supporting her under one arm, he managed to get them both through the door and into the house.

"You okay?'' he asked after he'd taken several deep breaths. "I'm sorry; it blew right out of my hand.''

"I'm...just cold,'' said the small voice in the dark. Rafe found the lamp switch and his jacket zipper at the same moment. Using them both, he turned quickly to find her leaning against the wall by the door.

"Listen, the best remedy for this is a tub full of warm water,'' he suggested. She was shivering visibly, her chalky white face a startling contrast to the bright blue floppy brim of her hat. Her lips matched the hat. Rafe moved her away from the wall and began to unwrap her clothes. Fifteen years ago he'd have welcomed the opportunity to tear at her buttons this way. Carly Austin.

She always did think the massess would step aside for her. Obviously she extended her expectations to the elements as well.

The blanket, coat, hat and mittens made a pile at her feet. "I'll make you some coffee and get the wood stove going in here while you..." Her eyes lacked understanding as they stared up at him, wide and trusting. He took her hands in his and squeezed gently. Her fingers felt icy, and his heart beat out the rhythm of some formless fear. "Feel anything?"

"I don't feel much like getting into any water." She looked down, watched his hands for a moment, and then groaned.

"It hurts? Good. That's a good sign."

"Ohhh. Sadist," she accused, trying to pull away from the source of her pain. But when she got away, the pain came with her. "They feel like they're going to fall off."

"Come on," he insisted, steering her through the small living room toward a hallway. "I'll run the water for you and we'll get you undressed."

"That part I can handle."

"I figured you'd be good for that part. You need to stay in the water for a good half hour." He flicked the light switch in the bathroom and leaned down to start the water. "This is what they do for chilled calves," he explained over his shoulder. "Should work for chilled chicks just as well."

Carly couldn't manage any appreciation for his attempted humor. Her bones were knocking against one another and her hands and feet were throbbing now. She knew it would hurt to get in that water. She was so cold.

Moments after leaving her alone in the bathroom, Rafe heard an agonized yowl and shook his head. Flames from the tinder licked at the short log in the firebox. He added another log and closed the door. If she came out of this with all her fingers and toes, she'd be lucky. She couldn't have been out there very long. But it didn't take long at sixty below. If he hadn't taken a crazy notion to see if he could make it to the police station before the roads drifted shut...

A fourth measure of ground coffee went into the basket. Rafe jammed the plug into the wall and turned to watch Carly, wrapped in a thick Pendleton blanket, pad into the living room and take a seat at the end of the sofa. He'd left a set of his longjohns and a pair of socks for her on the bed. Incredible. Carly Austin was wrapped up in *his* blanket and sitting on *his* sofa in front of *his* fire. Even more incredible, her clothes were in his bedroom, and she was wearing his.

Months ago, when he'd heard her name mentioned following an understated description of the latest in a never-ending parade of new English teachers, he'd had a fleeting mental picture of running into her somewhere and of her remembering him. Then he'd envisioned the image seen so often in the past—the girl in the fanciful dress, the girl who had all the right lines, all the right moves, and who made his heart act funny every time he saw her. These revived fantasies brought half a smile to his full lips. Carly Austin. She wouldn't remember him, but he remembered.

"How do you feel now? Any warmer?" Rafe turned the handle of a steaming mug into the hand sticking through the small slit she allowed in her drapery. "This is very hot."

"Thank you. What I really could use is a little brandy."

"Sorry. None in stock." He joined her on the sofa with a mug for himself.

"I'd even take whiskey, though I can't stand the taste."

"No booze in the house. I wasn't expecting company. Coffee's my best offer."

Carly slurped a little as she tried to sip the coffee and hold the blanket closed at the same time. After several scalding sips she set the mug on the end table and lay her head back, exhausted. "I sound ungrateful, I know. It's just that I'm chilled to the marrow, and I hate being cold." She felt heavy, every part of her heavy and sinking. Rolling her head toward him, she had a fleeting thought she she should be alarmed, but that would take too much energy. "I find myself in sort of an embarrassing situation," she said. "I'm not sure whose underwear I'm wearing at the moment."

"A cop's," he said simply.

"Oh." She sighed, closing her eyes. "Then I must be safe. Do you have a name, cop?"

"Mm-hmm." He sipped at his coffee and swallowed, disappointment dropping to the pit of his stomach like a rock. What was the matter with him? He damn sure hadn't expected her to greet him like a long-lost friend. "What color are your fingers and toes?"

"Blue, I think. Why?"

"If they're gray or yellow-looking, you might have frostbite," he told her. "If they turned pink when you got them in warm water, they're probably going to be all right."

She took this more seriously. "I think they were pink. I just know they hurt." Something about him niggled at her from the dark depths of her brain but she didn't feel like being bothered with it. "Don't I know you?"

"Probably not."

"I think I do." She sighed, closing her eyes again. "I know you...from somewhere. What's your name?"

Give her a chance. "Rafe."

"Think I could sleep over tonight, Rafe?"

"I think our options are limited."

Her head slid toward him, and the speed of her conversation was shifting into very slow and very drowsy. "Don't wanna put you out. Couch is fine. Just don't let my students hear...about any of this. Ruin my... reputation."

She was asleep on his shoulder. The situation would have been laughable except that bundling on the sofa with Carly Austin wasn't his idea of...wasn't a funny idea. Nevertheless, he thought, looking down at the face that nuzzled his collarbone, he seemed to be stuck with her, and she didn't even know who he was. But he wouldn't let that bother him. He'd prove it didn't while he indulged in something of a boyhood fantasy. For old times' sake, he would sit and hold her awhile. The man could satisfy what might be left of the boy in him at least that much.

It was some time later when Rafe Strongheart leaned against the doorjamb, the lamplight from the living room at his back, and simply looked at the woman asleep in his bed. He brought the cigarette to his mouth, pulled on it slowly, and then observed her face under a soft gray cloud of smoke. Carly Austin. Fifteen years. *Don't I know you?* Hardly.

Carly awoke slowly, not quite sure of her surroundings. She could smell coffee, and water was running

somewhere. Beyond that was the wind. She was adrift
in the eye of a storm, safe and snug and warm, and all
around her was the raging wind. Her nose ducked beneath the covers. It was good to be warm.

It was from that cover she took stock of her situation. The room, her snug little eye in the storm, though
perfectly neat, was a statement of bachelor simplicity.
The open-beam ceiling and varnished log walls were a
stark source of beauty. A closet door on one side of the
bed was open just a crack. A nightstand with a lamp
and an alarm clock stood on the other side. Blinds hung
on the single window, and the slats were open, admitting blizzard-gray light. No picture or mirror hung on
the wall, but there was a tall oak chest. Next to the chest
was a door that opened, and a cloud of steam rolled into
the bedroom.

Recollections of the night before darted piecemeal
through her mind as Carly tried for a mental image of
the person about to come through that door. *A cop.* She
didn't know any cops. He'd have to be a policeman with
the Bureau of Indian Affairs. She knew she'd crossed
the state line between North and Sound Dakota before
she'd run aground, and she was south of Fort
Yates...south of Fort Yates in a log house in some
man's bed. She propped herself up on her elbows and
watched the bathroom door swing open.

She couldn't see his face, but what she could see was
breathtaking. His long, lean torso was brown with a
dewy sheen, and his muscular legs were covered by a
long-legged pair of blue jeans. Above that a white towel
was being applied vigorously, presumably working over
wet hair.

He dropped the towel around his neck and returned
Carly's stare. There was not a hint of a smile in the

dark, hooded eyes nor about the full-lipped, wide mouth. A pure black mop of hair gleamed slick and wet under the bathroom light. He was carved flesh, chiseled planes, the edges unsanded, the angular lines inflexible. He was an unexpectedly powerful male presence, and his gaze penetrated her, electrifying her brain with the incontrovertible message that she had no secrets anymore. With a look, he disassembled her and knew every cell of her being.

For Carly, there was no looking away. He held her pinned in place with his eyes. Rafe exercised this power for an interminable moment, and then turned away, drawing the towel from his neck and draping it over a towel bar by the sink. He didn't spare her a glance as he walked by the bed on silent bare feet, pulled open the closet door, and reached for a red-and-black buffalo-plaid shirt. She watched him slip the shirt over broad shoulders. He didn't bother to button it. He took a pair of black cowboy boots from the closet, then moved to the bureau and took a pair of neatly rolled socks from the top drawer.

The bed could well have been empty. He sat at the foot of it and began to put on his socks. Carly hadn't moved from her pose, elbows propping her shoulders above the pillow. "Good morning," she finally said to his back.

"You thawed out, then," he said without turning around.

"I think so. I feel like somebody beat me up. You didn't, did you?" She pushed the pillow back against the headboard and slumped against it.

"Not yet." He turned to look at her, riveting her with those black-as-pitch eyes again. "Maybe I ought to. I can't arrest you for what you did."

"What did I do? I didn't hit anything, did I?" The night before was still a white haze. She'd been cold and afraid, but she didn't remember doing any damage.

"You had no business being on the road. Anybody who goes out in weather like this ought to have her head examined." His voice was quiet and lacked emotion. He enumerated the instances of her stupidity as though he were listing the flaws in her golf swing. "Blizzard conditions, you're out in the middle of nowhere alone at night, your car's built too low to the ground, and you had no—"

"I know you from somewhere."

He stared for a moment. *Try again, Carly. Take all the time you need.* But her perusal of his face turned up nothing, and he turned his back again and put his other boot on. Then he stood and buttoned his shirt. "How do you like your coffee? Your body could probably use a little sugar."

"My mouth likes cream and sugar. I'll fix it myself if you'll just tell me where I can find my clothes."

He was tucking in his shirt as he headed for the closet again. "I hung them up. The little stuff is on top of the bureau." A wide leather belt was threaded through the loops on his jeans. His hips were slim, and the belt settled at the base of a low-slung waistline.

"I'm sure I know you," she mused, watching him. "Where do I know you from?"

"You give it some thought while I get us some breakfast."

He moved toward the door, his long-legged stride restricted by the confines of the small room—a Thoroughbred in a box stall. "Hey," Carly said quietly, and he surprised her with a pause at the door, a questioning glance. "Thanks for being out last night where wise men fear to tread."

"Wise men? Hell, what do they know?" The smile he gave her wasn't much, but it was a beginning.

Carly listened to the clicking, rattling and sizzling in the kitchen while she dressed, trying to place that ruggedly handsome face. She'd known him before—before she ever came to Fort Yates. She felt as if he had been on the fringe of her life before. So many places, so many faces...and yet, those eyes....

Carly found eggs, bacon, toast and coffee waiting on the little kitchen table. "Oh, boy, this is great," she declared, gratitude flashing in her eyes. "I'll keep this resort in mind for my next vacation."

"You might find the rates a little higher in season," he quipped as he opened a cupboard door.

"Oh? What are they now?" Carly slid into a chair and crunched into a corner of toast.

"Depends. If you know the management, sometimes you can get a pretty good deal." He eyed her over his shoulder. A challenge.

"I'm sure I know the management. Just let me stare at you a while. It'll come back to me...Rafe? You did say Rafe, didn't you? Last night?" Rafe. Rafe. She was on the verge. She sipped absently at the coffee and then wrinkled her nose at the bitter taste. Black coffee, the color of those eyes.

A bowl and a jar were plunked in front of her. "Cream and sugar," he announced. "Staring is rude. You people do that a lot."

"Mm, you're right. It's rude." Her mouth was juggling eggs over her tongue. "Wasn't that a stare I got from you back there in the bedroom?"

One side of his mouth suggested smiling, but the other side refused to go along with the idea. "I think you'd call that eye contact. An unspoken mutual agreement to size each other up."

The agreement was made again as he sat across the table from her, but this time she looked at him and saw a much younger man—a boy, really—tall and gangly, a gaunt face with sharp angles along the jaw and chin and under the eyes. Riveting, coffee-colored eyes. "Rafe...Strongheart. High school. I knew you in high school. Of course!"

"We went to the same high school," he confirmed. "To say you knew me would be stretching it." But he had an odd sense of relief. Perhaps she hadn't known him, but at least she'd known of him.

"Well, you were so quiet. Nobody knew you except that wild bunch you ran with."

"When I felt like running, wild was the only way it seemed worth the effort." He dipped into his breakfast, aware that she was watching him, and granted her a moment or two before he paused with a questioning look. "Are your eggs okay?"

With the little flutter of one caught staring, she turned her attention back to her plate. "Yes, fine. Eggs never tasted so good." Then, settling back into herself, she gave him an apologetic smile.

"So what are you doing here, Carly Austin?"

Carly's smile brightened as she stirred her coffee. She felt more comfortable now. "Enjoying the role of damsel postdistress. You do a first-class rescue number."

"What are you doing *here*—on the reservation?"

"You seem very much the efficient cop. I'm sure you knew the minute I ventured into your territory last August. I came to teach English.'' His eyes were compelling. She wanted to study him, to draw some connection between the boy she remembered only vaguely and the man who sat across from her, but the look he returned made her glance away.

"It's usually the kids, fresh out of college and full of big ideas, who come to the reservation to share their newfound knowledge with us. A woman your age should be comfortably situated with tenure and seniority somewhere."

She gave him her best scowl. "A woman *my* age? What am I? Methuselah?"

"How long have you been teaching? Ten years?"

"Nine and a half terrific years." She was proud of that number, and she always let it show. She knew she was good at what she did. "I've taught in Puerto Rico, on Guam and the Philippines in the Air Force schools, and in Alaska. I came here to be closer to home because my grandfather's been ill."

"So why not teach in Bismarck?"

"Why not teach in Fort Yates? There was a position open here, and I knew I could do the job. I take it you don't work for Welcome Wagon."

Rafe replied with a little shrug. "I work for the *paddy* wagon. I've reported your situation in case anyone calls Law and Order about you. You can use the phone if you want to tell somebody you're all right."

"Tell you a secret; you're the first person who's worried over me in a very long time. Everyone who knows me knows it's pointless. God seems to keep an eye out for me, and only He knows why."

"Come up to the police station sometime, and I'll show you pictures of fools who've tempted His patience once too often."

"Ah, but I'll bet you'd have twice as many stories of people you've rescued from terrible fates if you wanted to look at the bright side." She hesitated, frowning a little. "I never would've expected you to be a cop, Rafe."

He amended that with half a chuckle. "I don't imagine you formulated any expectations on my behalf."

"I guess not," she agreed. "You were—what—two years ahead of me? We didn't cross paths very often, did we?"

"No, not very often."

They considered each other wordlessly for a moment, but for Carly there was admittedly little to remember. For Rafe there was more than he felt comfortable with under the circumstances. There was the tawny hair falling past her face as she bent to pick up the purse she'd dropped on the floor. And when the hair was tossed back, there were the blue eyes, laughing as always.

The howling wind claimed Carly's attention. Wind and snow on the prairie. If you were smart, you didn't quarrel with them. She reached across the table for his empty plate and set it on top of hers. "I don't suppose I'll be able to move my car today," she said.

"We're not going anywhere for a while. The whole western part of the state is paralyzed, along with most of South Dakota."

"It didn't look bad at all when I left Aberdeen last night. I didn't even think about listening for a weather report."

"There's more coffee," he said. He gestured with his chin, puckering his lips toward the pot, and Carly smiled at what she'd come to regard as a peculiarly Indian gesture.

"I'll get it." Refilling both mugs, she continued. "I spent the weekend with a friend, but I had to get back for—"

"Boyfriend?"

She laughed. "No. A girlfriend. Married, two kids. Funny you'd ask that."

"Yeah," he agreed, suddenly impatient with the conversation. "Funny." The chair scraped the floor as he pushed it back from the table. "You still look pretty tired. Maybe you should get some more rest." Leaving only the coffee, he cleared the table with one trip to the counter.

"I'm fine," she assured him, joining him at the sink. "Let me do this. You did the cooking."

Her offer was rejected as he plugged up the sink and ran the water. "You don't look fine. Those circles under your eyes are very large and black."

Left standing behind him, she looked down at the coffeepot in her hands and wondered what she'd said. "I think I've got enough strength left to help with the dishes," she offered again quietly.

He took a step back and gestured toward the rising cloud of bubbles with an open hand. "Be my guest."

She hoped her smile was conciliatory. "I'll wash, you'll dry, and we'll talk."

The look he gave her lacked patience. "What would we have to talk about, Carly Austin?"

"Any number of things. The weather..."

"Which is bad."

"Teaching."

"Which I know nothing about."

"Police work."

"Which you don't want to know anything about."

Carly's lips tightened as she folded her arms in front of her. "Are you mad at me or something? Was it something I did last night? Or did I insult you years ago? Either way, jog my memory with the details, okay? Then we can get down to the serious business of becoming friends, which would seem like a good idea since we appear to be stuck with each other for a while."

Rafe lifted a very straight, black eyebrow. "Friends? That's a pretty radical idea, Miss Austin."

"Not really. I've bathed in your tub, worn your thermal Skivvies, and slept in your bed. Those are pretty radical ideas. I'd say we could expect to be friends after all that."

"How about lovers?"

She looked directly into his impassive eyes. "That would be easy, wouldn't it? Friendship might take a bit more effort." Deliberately, she turned back to the job at hand—the sink full of dishes.

"Between you and me, anything would take effort." *Remebering who I was took considerable effort on your part.*

"Why?"

"Because you're Carly Austin."

"And who do you think Carly Austin is? Girl most likely to get a car from Daddy for making the honor roll twice in a row?"

"Girl least likely to teach school on a reservation."

"There, you see how ridiculous those predictions are? I'm not *Carly Austin*," she emphasized, attacking a plate beneath the water. "I'm just Carly Austin, *woman*, who wants to be your friend."

"Why?"

"So I can get my traffic tickets fixed. You're awfully suspicious, Rafe Strongheart. Did I turn you down for a date or something way back when?"

"I never asked you for a date. I wasn't a basketball player, and I didn't have a car. Those seemed to be prerequisites."

"Wrong. I expected a sense of humor and some semblence of a brain." Then, with half a smile, "And, of course, I couldn't be serious about any man who wasn't a virgin."

Rafe chuckled. "I'd have failed on at least one count."

"Which one?"

"You'll have to discover that for yourself." He took the frying pan she handed him and toweled it dry, a little smile sneaking across his face. "Now that you've earned your keep, why don't you get some rest? I've got a few chores to do outside."

Carly nodded in agreement, but she formulated other plans as she watched him walk out the door. He'd issued an interesting proposition, and she intended to take him up on it. Not the one about being lovers. He'd obviously tossed that out to find out whether she shocked easily—or perhaps to hide some reaction of his own. What interested her was the prospect of discovering more about him. She hardly remembered who he'd been as a boy, but the man was certainly attractive, a bit enigmatic, and fascinating.

When Rafe came in from his chores, Carly had hot chocolate and molasses cookies ready, and the kitchen was filled with delicious air. She watched him peel a brown wool scarf away from his face and fill his nostrils with the aroma of freshly baked cookies. There was something in his eyes just then—a pleased look she hadn't seen before—and, for some reason, it tugged at her heart.

"My grandmother made molasses cookies in the winter," Carly said. "Yours, too?"

"I'd forgotten that smell. We'd come in from sledding on those big inner tubes, and the kitchen would smell just like this."

Carly slipped a cookie from the pizza pan she'd used to bake them on and slid it off the spatula into her hand. "Here's a fresh, hot one for you." He still had his gloves on, so she offered it to his mouth. Beautifully even, white teeth claimed half of the round, brown cookie. Carly bit off half of what was left. "*Very* hot—mmm. I'm a pretty good cook, no?"

"So far, so good," he said through the cookie.

"My cookies have made me many friends in the past. Island children and igloo children. Thought I'd try them on a prairie policeman." She fed him the last bite, ignoring the fact that his hands were free.

His high cheeks had been brightly russeted by the wind, and the snow in his eyebrows and in the hair over his forehead was melting quickly into tiny beads of water. The sweet offering had made him smile, and he almost looked like a boy come in from sledding. "For a few more of these I guess I can be had," he admitted, unzipping his snowmobile suit.

"You're easier than I thought you'd be," Carly judged, luring him to the little living room and the warmth of the wood burner with mugs of hot chocolate and a plate of cookies.

"Now you know which of the requirements I was lacking." He knelt in front of the wood burner, reconsidering. "Actually, I was probably lacking all three at the time."

"Like most teenagers," she mused. "I'm sure my personality left a lot to be desired, too."

You were desired, Carly Austin, your personality notwithstanding. "There's no way out of here as long as this wind keeps up," Rafe told her, changing the course of the conversation. He replaced the cast-iron door on the firebox with a screen before joining her on the sofa. He stretched his long legs toward the stove. "The access road is drifted over, and you still can't see your hand in front of your face out there."

"They've already called school off for tomorrow, too. I heard it on the radio. So here we are."

"I thought you'd be asleep when I came in," he said quietly.

"In a few minutes I may be. This is nice."

Yellow flames licked the black firebox, their tongues hissing and crackling against their confines. Outside the cozy log walls the wind howled. Wind and fire, Carly thought. The howling wind and crackling fire, the taste of hot chocolate, and the quiet company of the man who'd come along at just the right time.

"I would have accepted, you know," Carly said thoughtfully, as though considering a recent proposal. A flash of orange flame rose from the center of a split log as it broke open, and, unaccountably, she shivered as she watched it. "If you'd asked me for a date, I'd have accepted."

"Dating was one of the many social activities I wasn't involved in as a kid. More than my personality left something to be desired by the folks uptown." Rafe stood quickly, disappeared into the bedroom for a moment, and came back with a red plaid blanket, which he draped over Carly's shoulders from behind.

When he sat on the sofa again, he was shaking a cigarette out of a pack. He offered, and she declined. He slipped the package in his breast pocket, then struck a match and lit it, inhaling deeply. "What would your father have said when I came to the door?" he wondered, plucking the cigarette from his mouth with a thumb and forefinger.

Carly smiled at him, pulling the blanket around her shoulders. "My father would have greeted you politely, offered you a chair, and then dragged me into the kitchen for a little talk. Meantime, my grandfather would have come downstairs to check you out. *His* approval was the important one, and he'd have approved."

Levering the heel of his right boot on the toe of his left, Rafe pried his foot free, wondering, almost as an afterthought, "How do you know?"

"You and my grandfather are two of a kind, and he'd have seen that within five minutes."

"Really?" The other boot came off as a result of similar footwork. "What makes you say that?"

"That you're like my grandfather? He'd have brought me a blanket a moment ago, too, the same way you did—without any ceremony."

Rafe laughed. "We don't do many blanket ceremonies anymore. Don't take the gesture as a proposal. I just don't want you getting sick on me."

"My grandfather would've tossed off some face-saving remark, too. Admit it, Strongheart—you're a nice man." She grinned at him, pleased with her analysis, but the grin faded when his eyes caught and held hers. God, he was handsome.

God, she was beautiful. She was all the beauty he remembered, polished to a glowing luster, refined by the years of early womanhood. Rafe dragged the last of what he needed from the cigarette without taking his eyes from her. Unerringly, his hand found the ashtray on the end table and crushed the remains of the cigarette. The smoke from his mouth blended into the late afternoon grayness of the room. Her round, wide eyes stirred warmth in him—stirred him and drew him to lean closer to her—and if he didn't pull his eyes away, he'd have to kiss her.

Yes, kiss me, she thought. Her lips parted slightly. *I'd like the taste of your lips. I know I would.* Her own pulse throbbed in her ears, and she couldn't expel the last breath she'd taken. *Yes, I want you to....*

Rafe straightened himself abruptly, as though he'd just remembered something. His eyes released her, and he reached for his boots. Surprised, Carly watched him pull his boots back on. He left the room without a word, and she heard the kitchen door slam shut only a moment later.

Carly shivered again, her mouth quivered slightly, and her eyebrows crinkled a bit as she stared into the yellow glow of the firebox.

Chapter Two

The wind drove tiny snow pellets into his face as Rafe Strongheart slogged through thigh-high drifts of snow. One gloved hand anchored the cowboy hat he'd jammed on his head, and the other clutched the lapels of his sheepskin jacket together under his chin. He hadn't bothered with his snowmobile suit nor the sensible pile-lined cap. When he reached the shelter of the pole barn, he dragged the sliding door shut and flipped the light switch. The wind whistled through little cracks in the steel building.

Rafe folded his arms over the tubular steel gate of one of the stalls he'd made from a set of portable panels. He was breathing heavily, thinking that plowing through snowdrifts shouldn't leave him that winded. He'd have to quit smoking. But he knew the quick thudding of his chest wasn't from working his way through the snow. It was that damned Carly Austin.

A big, fuzzy, sorrel horse shuffled through the straw bedding in the stall and stood on the other side of the gate, waiting. The two stared at each other for a moment, one equine eye to two human ones. Then Rafe literally cracked a smile in a face already stiff from the cold as he rubbed the red-brown muzzle with a black leather glove.

"I suppose you think I came out here to feed you and your buddies again." The horse bobbed his head against Rafe's hand, and Rafe laughed. "I thought so. You see me, and all you think about is oats. Some friend. Hell, I came out here to talk. What do you think of that? Huh, Rusty? I came out here to stand around with you guys and freeze my ass off." He eyed the other three stalls down the line, each penning a horse—a paint and two bald-faced sorrels.

Rusty had no markings. He was just a plain sorrel, homelier than sin with the thick coat and heavy whiskers winter had put on him. But Rusty was Rafe's favorite. They'd been together a long time—ever since Rafe had seen him, a wild-eyed, half-starved yearling scratching around some farmer's bare pasture. He'd paid more for the colt than the farmer would've gotten from a canner, and then Rafe had brought Rusty back to life.

"Tell me something, old man, what do you do when you want a woman you can't have? You oughta know." The horse snorted and lowered his head to sniff near the toes of Rafe's boots.

"Yeah, I know. I've got it coming after what I did to you. But it was the only way to keep you from going after Brave Bull's palomino. Ol' George got all bent outta shape every time he caught you in his pasture nosing around his fancy filly. And you. Look at all the proud flesh you ended up with from those wire cuts."

Rafe snickered at himself and hoisted his right boot up on the lowest rail of the gate. "*Proud flesh.* Where'd they ever get that term? It's scar tissue, right boy? Tough and hard and ugly, but it covers up those old wounds."

Rafe shed the glove from his right hand and reached under his jacket for matches and a cigarette. With the cigarette in one corner of his mouth, he mumbled out of the other, "Just said I oughta quit smoking, didn't I?" The match flared between them, and the horse's head jerked, ears pricked forward. Rafe blew out the match and stuck it in his pocket. Rusty took a step back, one large round eye popping warily at the source of fire in his barn. "Makes you nervous, huh? Yeah, me, too. You don't have an ashtray out here, either, do you? Of course not—I don't let anyone smoke in the barn.

"So what do you do, Rusty? Walk away, right?" He plucked the cigarette from his mouth and examined it. "Right. Walk away from a warm house—nice, cozy fire—come out here in the middle of a blizzard and talk to a horse." Giving the animal's jaw a consoling scratch, Rafe dragged on the cigarette again and then spat smoke with his words. "Damn that woman. Just looking at her does funny things to my insides. Always did. Now I'm stuck with her in my bed for another night.

"And what's wrong with that, you ask? I'm on the sofa; that's what's wrong with it. I've got Carly Austin in my bed, and I'm on the sofa. You know, I used to watch her in those school plays. She was in every one. She always seemed..." Unimpressed, the horse tossed his head and bumped the brim of Rafe's hat. "Okay, okay. You'll get your oats." He adjusted the hat before he headed for the door to extinguish the cigarette, muttering, "Ungrateful nag."

She'd filled the kitchen with aroma again, this time of tomato and garlic. The minute he walked in the door, she started chattering about the spaghetti sauce, the weather report, and what a wonderfully tight structure the little log house seemed to be. *Until the storm door broke,* he thought. *Before you came it was closed tight, completely self-contained.* He walked over to the pot on the stove and peeked in.

Carly extended a spoon in his direction, assuming he was after a preview of his supper. "That hamburger is really lean and smells sort of funny. It was frozen, though. I don't see why it wouldn't be—"

"It's deer," Rafe said, letting the lid clatter back down on the pot rim as he ignored the spoon.

"Oh. Deer." She studied the rejected spoon for an instant before she shrugged. "I've had venison sausage, but not ground...deerburger? A new treat. No one in my family hunts. Yours must—"

"*I'm* my family."

"My, my. Exclusive, aren't we? I was sure you'd come in from your walk in a better mood."

"I did. This is as good as it gets. This ready?"

"If you are."

Carly told Rafe of the phone messages she'd taken for him from the police station, and he told her that the food was good. After that they ate in relative silence. They washed the dishes together, Carly weighing the advisability of tossing out another bid for conversation.

She was putting him out. The man was obviously a very private person, and she was intruding on that privacy. The living room had shelves and shelves of books, a nice stereo, which he'd yet to play since she'd been there, but no TV. He led a quiet life at home—maybe because he had enough noise in his work. She probably made him uncomfortable with all her chatter. Carly dried her hands on a towel, mentally resolving that he would have his bed back that night, and she would try not to disturb his peace further.

But she did disturb him. Her presence was a disruption, and Rafe didn't allow any disruptions in his private life. Anticipating calls from her family and friends, he'd informed the police dispatcher that she was safe, but he hadn't discussed her whereabouts. Now she was answering the phone, taking messages for him. And people never had any trouble putting two and two together when it might add up to some hot gossip. Gossip disturbed him. Speculation disturbed him. And Carly Austin disturbed him plenty.

Rafe followed Carly to the kitchen door. He flicked the kitchen light off just as she remembered leaving her watch on the counter. She did an about-face and collided with Rafe's chest in the near-darkness. He caught her shoulders between his hands, and this time she was too close, her upturned face too inviting to be resisted. Their eyes met in the shadowy firelight. There was no mistaking the unspoken questions and answers that passed between them before he lowered his head and took the kiss he'd wanted so many times and years before.

Sliding his arms around her shoulders, he gave the kiss she'd expected earlier in the afternoon. She expected his full lips to cover hers completely and his tongue to seek hers out immediately. She hadn't expected her own blood to surge so violently at the first touch of his lips to hers. She hadn't anticipated reaching her arms around his back to pull herself closer to the hard wall of his body. She hadn't known she'd open her mouth and groan with pleasure when he responded by twisting his head to reaffirm his mouth's claim.

He lifted his head slowly and looked down at the soft mouth he'd just tasted, the slightly parted lips glistening with moisture from his own mouth. Her hair fell away from her face, dusky in the shadows behind her back. It was long, plush, silky-looking hair, parted over her left eye and dipping to wave over her right. He watched his hand settle over the curve of her head, trembling slightly like some hesitant bird fluttering over an untried perch. His fingers steadied under that irresistable wave and traced her hairline.

When she opened her eyes, the first thing she saw was his smile, and it surprised her. She'd expected anger or hunger or even lust, but not this gentle smile, not this careful hand, certainly not this genuine...affection.

"Sorry, sky-blue eyes. You flew too close to the flame this time," he said softly. There was no apology in his eyes.

"You're lying, Rafe. You're not sorry."

"No, but I probably will be. I thought I'd get through this little visit without doing that."

"I'm glad you didn't. It was nice. Maybe now you could turn on some music, and we could sit by the fire and talk. The sound of that wind makes me shiver inside."

"I see you shivering outside once in a while, too." He got a grateful smile out of her as he rubbed his hands along her upper arms and generated some pleasant friction. "And you didn't get any sleep this afternoon, did you?"

She shook her head. "I don't suppose you'd have a pair of flannel pajamas you could lend me tonight?"

He laughed. "Never owned a pair. How about a flannel shirt?" She nodded. "I'll go see what I can find. You pick out some music."

Carly watched him disappear through the doorway to the short bit of a hall. The door to his bedroom was just around the corner to the left, and at the opposite end—just around the corner to the right—was another door. Carly decided it must be a spare bedroom.

"Rafe," she called, following him. She heard a bureau drawer slide open as she reached for the doorknob to the other room. "Is this another bedroom? Couldn't I sleep..." The room behind the door smelled of paint and linseed oil, and the light from his bedroom crept in behind her. She saw an easel with a darkly mottled canvas on it, a stool, what appeared to be a workbench, and a good deal of unidentifiable clutter. She'd come to believe he was the most meticulous person she'd met, but here was real clutter—and something more.

She turned and found him watching her from the doorway of his bedroom. "I...thought maybe it was another bedroom."

"As you can see, it isn't. Close the door," he said quietly.

"You paint?"

"It's something I do just for myself."

She wanted to turn around and look again, but she didn't dare. "I wasn't prying, Rafe, but I'd love to see your work. I do a little amateur photography myself, although I'm not very—"

"I asked you to close the door."

It was not an angry command, but it was an insistance that she respect his privacy. She complied without further comment on the subject. "I'll sleep on the sofa tonight," she offered.

"It's up the the host to decide on sleeping arrangements. Here's a nightgown for you." He handed her a blue and white long-bodied baseball shirt. "And here's a robe." It was a blue plaid flannel shirt. "I'm not big on nightwear."

Carly took the items gratefully and headed for the sofa. "I guess you don't throw many slumber parties, huh?"

"Do you?"

"Used to." She dropped the jersey over the arm of the sofa and slipped the flannel shirt on over her sweater. Then she flashed him a pair of high eyebrows and a conspiratory grin. "But they were never coed."

"What kind of music do you like?" He stood before an impeccably shelved collection of tapes.

"Anything." But she was surprised when the click of a lever was followed by "Rhapsody in Blue." "Everything about you is unexpected," she concluded.

"Willie Nelson goes on after this. Is that more what you'd expect from me?"

Carly settled on the sofa. "Let's make a pact. From this moment on, we'll erase all preconceived notions about each other from our minds. We'll resolve to get to know the people we've become in the past fifteen years. Deal?" Her hand was positioned for a handshake as he approached the sofa and took a seat beside her. His warm palm slid against hers, his fingers curving lightly around her hand.

"Come on, Rafe, give me a good, firm handshake," Carly protested with a grin, taking a grip on his hand. "Show me you really mean it."

"Like this?" He squeezed her hand and pumped. "Is this the sign of honest intentions?"

"Yes, a good—"

"Who says?" Her hand was caught, motionless now in his powerful grip. "You people try to wrench each other's hands off, pumping like you expect to get water. You're always trying to outdo each other's sincerity act. Haven't you noticed by now that we don't shake hands that way?"

"Well, I...*had* noticed the handshakes I'd been getting were usually limp. I thought my hand was distasteful in some way."

"No, you didn't. You just thought we weren't doing it right because we hadn't caught on yet. You were going to give me a little pep talk on the value of a firm handshake just then, weren't you?" He hadn't released her hand, and his tone was gentle. "Weren't you, teacher?"

Carly shrugged, her smile apologetic. "In a way, I suppose I was."

"Our gestures of respect have always been too subtle for you people. You want everyone to be as bold as you are. You can forget the pep talk, teacher. I've heard it."

"So what kind of gesture is this?" Carly wondered, nodding at their clasped hands.

"This," he explained, switching her hand from his right to his left, "is a friendly attempt to warm an icy hand. We call it holding hands. What do you call it?"

"Truce."

It was an easy truce with music and popcorn and firedreaming and not-very-serious conversation. They exchanged occasional wistful glances between shared smiles and laughs. When Carly finally took herself to Rafe's bed, leaving him to the sofa, she felt sure he had come to like her, and somewhere down the road there might be a modicum of trust. At this point she knew she wanted his trust.

She had no idea how long she'd slept. Not long, it seemed. The wind's hollow howl nagged at her dreams, and she couldn't feel warm. Whenever she moved, a new expanse of cold sheet shocked her skin. She tried to keep herself in one spot, but the cold crept along her sides, and the darkness pierced her with chills. Carly curled into a ball. Shivering, she remembered the warmth of the wood stove.

Rafe woke with a start, wide-eyed and momentarily terror-stricken. It was a few seconds before he had the presence of mind to tell himself that he was in his own home. He hated that feeling—one he still faced in the dark on too many occasions—that sensation of not knowing where he was. He was in the living room, he reminded himself. He was on the sofa because Carly was...Carly was huddled under a blanket by the wood stove.

Propping himself up on his elbow, Rafe peered past the haze of his own grogginess. She'd opened the stove's door to get closer to the fire, and the outline of her hair glowed with hints of copper.

"Carly?"

She swung her head over her shoulder and presented a pretty profile in silhouette. "I didn't mean to wake you," she whispered.

"What's wrong?"

"Nothing. I can't seem to get warm. I think I was even dreaming cold dreams."

"You don't feel sick, do you? You want me to—"

"No, I'm all right. Just cold. The fire feels great."
She offered long, slender hands in fire-worship and then
pulled the blanket over her shoulders, hugging herself.
For a moment Rafe was mesmerized.

Catching himself, he settled down again, wondering
what bent posture he could try sleeping in. He watched
Carly shove another piece of wood on the fire. The
blanket slipped off her shoulders and down to the floor,
baring her long, white legs below his thigh-length shirt.

"What I'd like to do is sit on this stove," Carly
mumbled, staring into the fire. Fingers of flame curled
around the chunk of wood. "Rafe?"

"Hmm?"

"I really wouldn't mind sleeping on the sofa."

"Might get a little crowded."

"I thought you might like to have your bed back. It's
kind of a cold bed."

"But it sounds like a hell of an idea," he groaned,
moving over. Removing the back cushions had given
him a bit more room. He looked up to find her standing beside him.

"That isn't what I had in mind," she said. "I
thought, if you wouldn't mind, we'd trade beds."

Rafe braced himself up again and crooked a finger at
her. "Come down here," he said. "I don't like talking
up to you." Carly knelt beside the sofa, bringing them
face-to-face. He reached for her hand, which gripped
the edge of the blanket just momentarily before allowing itself to be taken slowly to his chest. His warmth was
a balm. "You really are cold," he admitted.

She studied the two hands—his holding hers against
his chest. "You're not," she managed in a small voice.

"No. I tend to be pretty hot-blooded." She glanced up at him, and he enjoyed the hint of wariness in her eyes. "I'm not moving. But I'll share the fire with you." He lowered his eyes to the space beside him and then raised them to hers. A dare.

"What are you wearing?" she asked, hesitating.

"Jeans. I'm decent. Come on, Carly, let's get some sleep." He held the blankets up for her, and she crawled under them. Snuggling against him followed irresistibly. He groaned again. "Hell of an idea."

His smooth chest was like a warm brick, and he smelled of spicy soap and wood smoke. The sleep that had eluded her now settled into her bones, stilled every muscle, and convinced her brain that this was safe haven from the wind.

Rafe needed sleep, which was probably why it wouldn't come easily. He'd never been a glutton for punishment before, and wondered what had come over him. He could have been stretched out comfortably, alone in his own bed. Instead, by his own choice, here he was—cramped and hot and tired. There was one consolation, however; Carly Austin lay here in his arms.

The following day the wind stopped blowing, and the sky turned blue again. The sun's gems, scattered on the snow, dazzled the eyes. Digging the chief of police out seemed a high priority for the BIA Roads Department. Carly's car wouldn't be coaxed into starting, and Rafe finally towed her into town behind his Bronco. The town was busy digging itself out, but the familiar white four-wheeler with the little blue hatchback in tow stopped several shovelers. Pairs of eyes peered over mountains of snow along the route to one of Fort Yates's two gas stations. Rafe knew he wouldn't have drawn any more attention if he were towing a dinosaur and had a caveman sitting in the seat beside him.

The owner of the station emerged through the frosty glass door and squinted against the sun. Adjusting the earflaps of his olive-drab cap, he plodded toward the tandem vehicles, dragging the soles of his flapping galoshes against the packed snow. He grinned down at Rafe, who was removing the tow bar clamps from Carly's bumper. "You going into the wrecking business, Rafe? Weather like this, we could use two more trucks, easy."

"Ordinarily I wouldn't cut into your business, Pete, but I knew you'd be busy today." The tow bar was detached from the Bronco's hitch and deposited in its cargo area.

"Busy ain't the half of it. No, sir, weather like this..." He shook his head as an expression of real futility.

Rafe shut the Bronco's rear hatch and turned as Carly joined them. "And this woman was an especially pathetic case. The battery on this thing is dead. Won't even take a boost."

"Say, your little friend Donna was in this morning," Pete told Carly. "Said she was worried about you. All the police knew was you were stranded on the highway, picked up by somebody, and you were okay. She wondered where you ended up."

Obviously Pete wondered, too. "Captain Strongheart helped get me out of a snowdrift," Carly explained.

"You're one lucky lady, that's all I got to say." But it wasn't. "Remember that carload of kids got stranded a few years back? You remember, Rafe." Pete reconsidered. "No, don't think you was here then. Got stranded with one o' the coaches in his car—blizzard near as bad as this one. Had to burn the back seat to keep warm. Made it out okay though, 'cept for a little frostbite.'' Pete shook his head again, giving Carly a serious look. "Bad business. You gotta be real careful. A car's just a machine, you know. Can't tell when—"

"I've got to get up to the police station," Rafe put in. This was a good time for a fast break. "Business is probably pretty good up there, too."

"Oh, yes," Carly said quickly. "I've taken up too much...you've been..."

Their eyes met, and he willed her not to say what he'd been, not to thank him, not to comment further. "No problem. Hope it's nothing serious," he offered, tipping his chin in the direction of her car. In another moment he was gone, and, feeling that too much had been left unsaid, Carly only half heard the rest of Pete's commentary.

Reassured that her car could be repaired, Carly walked the two short blocks to the Employees' Club. She tracked snow through the communal living room and ignored a three-handed card game as she passed. Then she took herself upstairs to the landing shared between her apartment and one other and let herself into the room. She fell on the bed, exhausted.

Apartment was a presumptuous word for what served as Carly's living quarters, but she'd had worse. Her teaching positions had never been plums by most other teachers' standards. They had been adventures, and she regarded them in just that way. All she needed was a bed and some way to get meals. At the Employees' Club she had any number of extras.

The common kitchen, dining room and living room were shared by the tenants, though not without some disagreements about the ownership of the moldy cottage cheese and whose turn it was to vacuum. The club had once been a dormitory, a two-story brick structure built in the 1930s. As the number of boarding students declined and the need for staff housing became more acute, it had become the small town's version of an apartment building. Each room was furnished with an eclectic assortment of contemporary dorm-style beds and bureaus juxtaposed with some older oak reproduction pieces in remarkably fine condition.

Fort Yates was, indeed, an eclectic town. Having once been an army post and the seat of the Indian agent, it was now the hub of the Standing Rock Sioux Reservation and the home of the Bureau of Indian Affairs, the tribal offices, the Indian Health Service, Law and Order, and headquarters for a network of service agencies for the reservation. The boarding school system, though dying in the midwest thanks to improved transporation and the availability of public schools, still provided for Indian students who, for various reasons, could not or did not live with their families during the school term. In Fort Yates, the public school and the BIA school operated cooperatively as one.

It was the kind of teaching position Carly continued to seek, and she made no apologies to anyone—including Rafe Strongheart—for that choice. She was a fine teacher, and she knew what she had to offer. She chose to offer it in places where she felt she was needed and where she counted on no two days being exactly the same. So far, she had not been disappointed.

The knock at the door would be Donna, and Carly was in no mood to explain where she'd been to sweet Donna McFarlan. There was another quiet knock. Carly swung her legs over the side of the bed and sat up. Generally Donna wasn't so hard to take. She meant well, but she was just so young and... *So what am I? Methuselah?*

"The door's open, Donna."

Donna McFarlan approached Carly's stature at five-seven, but, outweighing Carly by more than fifteen pounds, Donna looked soft and round. Her hesitant entrance into the room was, by its very nature, an immediate apology for her being there. "Oh, you were resting. I won't...I was just worried. I mean, you're okay, aren't you?"

Carly smiled. *Young in years, this girl, but aging fast from worry.* "I'm fine. I've just had a real adventure. Have you heard anything about school tomorrow?"

"The busses won't be running, but we'll have school for the town kids. You sure you're okay?"

"Sure."

"Maybe we could have supper together later. Pizza."

"Sounds good."

The door closed quietly, leaving Carly to herself. The shades were drawn on afternoon's dimming light. Reminders of past adventures surrounded her, and she looked on them with personal satisfaction. Her baleen baskets and little ivory carvings came from Alaska, her ebony carvings from the Philippines, and her coral and conch shells from the Pacific. She'd traveled to places most people only read about; she'd gone to work; she'd pitched right in and done her job as she knew it needed to be done.

At each of her teaching posts there had been a fraternity of the single teachers. This was a companionship of people who, under different circumstances, might not even have been friends. Here, however, an important common denominator drew them together. They were imported teachers. They were a minority of outsiders. They were there for different reasons—not all for the love of teaching—but inevitably they came together socially because of the common denominator. Eventually they would go their separate ways and wonder what they'd ever had in common, but, for now, they were friends.

Carly joined the group in the kitchen, where Todd Johnson leaned against the sink watching Maxine Wounded Soldier exchange an uncooked pizza for the bubbling brown one in the oven. Maxine was the bridge among the club dwellers. She was a teacher, but she was a Standing Rock native.

"Weeell! The ice woman cometh," Todd quipped, shifting his weight from one leg to the other and flashing a boyish, blue-eyed smile at Carly. "We heard you got stuck on the highway and some cop made the rescue. Where've you been? At a farm or something?"

"At his house," Carly supplied, opening a cupboard to take out a stack of colored plastic plates.

"Whose house?" Donna asked, standing behind Carly like the mother who wanted the whole story.

"The cop's. I was rescued by the chief of police, no less. I ran aground near his place."

Without looking up from the grid she was scoring in the pizza, Maxine asked quietly, "Rafe Strongheart?"

Carly turned to the small, dark-eyed woman, who went right on cutting the pizza, affording Carly a view not of the dark eyes, but only of the short, black hair and busy hands. "Do you know Rafe well, Max?"

"No, not well. My sister knows him."

"It took me awhile to realize where I'd seen him," Carly said. "He went to my high school. I think he graduated when I was a sophomore. Kind of hung out with hell-raisers, but in school he seemed pretty much of a loner.''

''I'm sure there weren't many Indians in your school in Bismarck,'' Maxine said.

''No, not many. Funny I didn't know he was here before this. I probably heard the name and didn't make the connection.''

''He's still a loner,'' Maxine said. ''The BIA brought him here to straighten out the police department a couple of years ago. Before that he was at Pine Ridge and Crow Creek, and I don't know where all. He's from this reservation originally, though. Bullhead, I think.''

''I know who he is,'' Donna put in. ''He stopped to help me change a tire once last summer. I got a flat on the gravel road between Kenel and Wakpala.''

''What were you doing way out there?'' Todd asked.

Donna made the mistake of assuming that Todd was interested in an answer to his question. ''The cemetery down there is just full of history. I may take my first graders there this spring. Chief Gall—you know, the one who rode with Crazy Horse at the Battle of the Little Big Horn—he's buried there.''

When Todd stuck his head in the refrigerator, Donna turned back to Carly. ''Rafe Strongheart came along in a pickup—pulling a horse trailer and everything—but he stopped to help me. He had a hydraulic jack. You mean you've been at his house since Sunday night? He's really nice.''

Todd was opening a big green jug of wine. ''Leave it to Donna to be impressed with a man's hydraulic jack.''

''I was impressed with *him*. He's great looking. He's bound to be married or something, right Carly?''

Carly had gathered napkins and glasses and was headed through the doorway toward the nearest of the three dining-room tables. "He's not married, but I don't know about 'or something.'"

"Not married or anything," Donna reflected. "And to think I was worried about you."

"I wasn't," Todd mumbled. "Now I am."

Carly sat across the table from Maxine and watched for her reactions to the conversation. There were none. Maxine used a fork to eat her pizza, while Carly used both hands to slide the floppy crust, stringy with white cheese, into her mouth. Swallowing the initial tangy bite, she asked, "Your sister knows Rafe well?"

Maxine's dark look told Carly that she didn't care to discuss her sister's business, but she answered, "He was at the university when she was there. She sees him occasionally."

I shouldn't have asked that, Carly told herself. It was rude. She remembered Rafe's gentle scolding. You people. You want everyone to be as bold as you are. She regretted being considered part of a group he thought of as *you people*, and she wondered whether there was a woman in his life whom he connected with himself as part of *us*. But she and Rafe had been together for a time in the calm eye at the center of the wind, and there'd been no hint of anyone else. Now she would resume her routine, and he'd go back to his. She wondered what that was—his routine. Whatever it was, she wanted to be part of it—occasionally.

Carly taught one section of sophomore English that comprised twelve boys. Every girl scheduled into the class had run directly to the counselor's office for a schedule change, refusing to be grouped with the "Dirty Dozen." The boys had informed Carly from the outset that they had no intention of studying anything, especially not English. She could flunk them if she wished—indeed, most of them had taken sophomore English before—but they hastened to point out the advantages of passing them. Those included keeping her car, her apartment and her sanity intact.

Carly had a surprise in store for the Dirty Dozen. She'd seen their kind before. In fact, she'd seen worse. Like a pied piper of letters, she lured them into reading and writing without letting them realize they'd been had. Not that they produced great masterpieces—Carly wasn't able to turn water into wine. But they did read *Julius Caesar*, and when no one was looking, they did a ghastly murder-in-the-capitol scene. Carly took the female roles, for none of the Dozen was about to play the part of a woman.

They had gotten into mystery now. They'd read screenplays by Hitchcock and scenes from Agatha Christie, and now, in a joint effort, they were writing a mystery. Carly decided that a field trip to the police station was in order.

It had been three weeks since the blizzard, and she'd not seen nor heard from Rafe Strongheart. She found, remarkably, that her heart thudded in her ears and the receiver felt slippery against her palm when she asked to speak with him.

"Hello, Rafe? This is Carly."

Pause. "Hello."

"I wonder if you would do a favor for me?"

Pause. "Are you going to tell me what it is?"

A little laugh. "Yes, I am. Some of my students would like a tour of the police station."

"Some of your students have already seen the police station—from the shady side of the cell bars."

"I'd like them to see it from another point of view. We're doing a unit on mystery, and we thought—"

"I'll arrange for someone to show you around. When do you plan to do this?"

He sounded bored with the whole idea, but he sounded like Rafe—his low, quiet, unruffled tones—which, Carly noted, sounded good in her ear. "At your convenience. I'd like you to give the tour personally, if you would, complete with the grisliest true-life stories in your repertoire. This is a difficult bunch to impress. The class meets at two twenty."

Pause. "How about Friday? I'll do it if I'm free. Otherwise, I'll assign someone to take care of it."

It wasn't the most receptive response she'd ever gotten when she'd shown interest in a man, she thought after she hung up. She stared at the black receiver cradled in the black phone and took deep breaths. Cleansing breaths. It was foolish to be angry, or indignant, or hurt, or whatever it was that had left her face burning. She'd asked for a favor, and he'd said he'd arrange it.

Rafe considered arranging to be too busy to accommodate Carly and her students himself. When the time came, however, he found that he'd allowed himself to be free, and he met them in the entryway. This tour wasn't a bad idea, and he recognized several of the boys as having been former "guests" at Law and Order. Maybe they would profit from a look at the other side. He'd be the friendly policeman for her today.

Frankie Fire Cloud filed in last, and he looked Strongheart straight in the eye, just as cool as you please. Strongheart shot the same look back. The challenge registered mutually. *Yeah, we've met. How long before we meet again?* Frankie didn't drop his eyes until Strongheart looked away. That gave Frankie a point in his perpetual match between himself and the "big shots" in this world.

Frankie had seen these cells many times. He knew why they were empty at the moment. The jailbirds—the "trustees"—were out working somewhere. They were shoveling snow or cleaning out some warehouse. It made a nice display, Frankie thought as he followed Albert Many Bear at the end of the line, shuffling by the cell block and listening to the cop impress Austin with all his damned facts and figures.

Frankie was big for his fifteen years, and the coach kept telling him he was a natural athlete. But he wouldn't go out for sports. None of these guys was likely to play the high-school hero. The Dirty Dozen touring Law and Order. That was a laugh. Well, it was better than sitting in class—even Austin's class, which wasn't too bad most of the time.

Rafe ended the tour in his office, where he leaned against his desk, his left thigh balanced along the edge. He wore the BIA policeman's uniform of Air Force blue with a navy stripe along the side seam of his trim pants. He seemed to enjoy answering questions about running license-plate checks and dusting for fingerprints. The boys were most interested in weapons, and Rafe hauled out a mounted collection of them.

"This looks like an ordinary can opener," Rafe pointed out, "and it was—until a man used it against his girlfriend to plow furrows in her back. This," he said, pointing to a small, pointed instrument clipped to the long white board, "is one of those things you use to put ear tags on calves. We arrested a young man who'd palmed it, used it in a fight against another young man, both of them about your age. The first young man is in the state training school, and the other lost an eye in that fight.''

"Don't give them any ideas, please," Carly warned.

"Some of these guys have ideas I haven't seen tried yet. We aren't fooling each other. Right, boys? You guys have a choice to make. You can exercise your right to life, liberty and the pursuit of happiness without denying anybody else's, and we'll get along fine. Or you can decide to hurt somebody, and then you deal with me.''

"They're not going to—''

"They haven't had time to make up their minds yet, Miss Austin. Some of them think they might be able to beat the system. I know that for a fact because I damn sure thought I could when I was their age.''

"What made you decide to become a cop?" Frankie asked.

"A dead boy." Rafe's ominous tone broached no further questions on the subject.

"What was that tire iron used for?" Carly wondered.

"Glad you asked about that one, Miss Austin. A young woman was beaten to death with that weapon. Her car stalled late at night, and the man who stopped to help her also helped himself to the use of her body and then beat her to death with her own tire iron." Rafe gave her a laser-beam stare. "Driving these country roads late at night is risky for a woman.''

"My experience has been that people who stop to help are generally good Samaritans," she said.

"Your experience is limited.''

In the quiet seconds during which Rafe and Carly held eye contact, not a person in the room missed the

electrical crackle between the two stiff-backed princi-
ples, each grounded in self-righteous stubbornness.

"Miss Austin, I have to catch my bus."

Carly swung her head in Ralph Steiner's direction and
then let her eyes follow suit. "The time got away from
me. You boys go ahead. Behave yourselves this weekend, and I'll see you Monday."

A fire bell couldn't have cleared the room any faster.

Rafe pulled a file from a drawer and sat behind the
desk with it before he gave Carly the benefit of his
heavy-lidded glance again.

"I appreciate your taking the time to do this, Rafe."

"It happened that I did have the time this afternoon.
It was no problem." He opened the file and seemed to
study it. She didn't move. Without looking up, he
asked, "Is there something else I can do for you, Miss
Austin?"

"You can stop calling me Miss Austin and stop being so damned stuck-up."

"I haven't heard that expression in a long time."

"I haven't used it in a long time," she retorted, coming to stand in front of the desk. His chair creaked as he
leaned back in it and looked up at her.

"What's the matter, Carly? Didn't I play the role
right just now? I thought you wanted me to do my
policeman-is-your-friend routine. I'm sorry if I wasn't
as charming as you'd like, but I'm not from Mr. Ro-
gers' neighborhood."

"You were fine with the boys, but your manner with
me leaves a lot to be desired."

"What do you desire, Miss Austin? A lusty buck who
can't keep his hands off the pretty school marm? Next
time you want to stage a production for the boys, let me
see the script in advance so I'll know my part." He was

on his feet now, and they were nearly head to head over the desk.

"I would love to know just what it is you hold against me," Carly said, effecting a stiff calm.

Rafe managed to resist laughing and telling her what he'd *like* to hold against her. He remembered too well what it had been like that night on his sofa. Instead he sighed and decided he was better off sitting in the chair, keeping the desk between them. "I have nothing against you personally. But you're one of a species of bleeding hearts who come to the reservation looking to ease mankind's collective conscience with a personal sacrifice. Apparently you're bent on making a career of it, which is of no consequence to me, but I'm not interested in playing along." Rafe reached in his pocket for his cigarettes.

"I didn't ask you to play anything. I asked for a tour of the police station. And I suspect I was hired for my job for the same reason you were hired for yours. We both have good track records in, shall we say, difficult situations."

"Don't flatter yourself, lady." He sucked smoke into his chest and then snatched the cigarette from his mouth. "The BIA doesn't hire teachers for their 'track records.' They take what they can get—veterans with civil service preference points, jocks who want to coach Indian ball teams, evangelists of all kinds and do-gooders like you."

Carly gave him a Cheshire-cat grin and cold eyes. "I don't work for the BIA, Mr. Strongheart. I work for the school district. We have a cooperative school here, you know. And I'm not a bleeding heart any more than you are. I'm here because I like to take on jobs that other people have made more difficult by bungling. You do, too. That's why *you're* here." Carly turned to the wall next to his desk, where a collection of framed certificates was displayed. "I've been eyeing these while you were talking. Your credentials are impressive. You seem to have more than your share of special training. Looks like you can shoot pretty straight. And this—how many cops around here have a BS from the university?"

Rafe shifted uncomfortably in his chair. "They insisted on hanging all that stuff there to impress God know's who," he mumbled.

"Probably the do-gooder teachers and their hardcase students who dream of great careers in crime." When he looked up at her this time, there was a twinkle in Rafe's eyes, and Carly took that to be a hint of a smile. She smiled back. "I think I've got you pegged, Rafe Strongheart. You've seen every movie Clint Eastwood ever made."

"Some of them four times," he admitted. He'd tried his best machine gun onslaught, and she hadn't wilted like the typical do-gooder. "Listen, Carly, be careful around those boys. A couple of them are well on their way to realizing their dreams."

Carly reached for the down-filled nylon parka she'd tossed over the back of the chair. "I know they're hellions, but they're still kids. You see them at their worst. I see them with possibilities."

"There's a good possibility that Frank Fire Cloud will work his way into the state training school before another year is out. If you've decided to mother hen this brood, make sure you have someone else along when you take these little jaunts." He watched her long-fingered hands ply her zipper up to her pointed little chin and remembered unbuttoning the coat she'd worn the night she'd insinuated herself back under his skin.

"Care to come along on the next jaunt I plan?"

"No, thanks. Most of these boys aren't too fond of me."

"I can't imagine why. I'm very fond of you. In fact, I'll probably find some way to pester you again very soon. See you later, Chief."

Rafe's ears followed the staccato clicks of her boot heels until they faded completely down the hall.

Chapter Three

Within a week she'd found a way. Carly reported a theft of her property and asked Rafe to investigate the situation personally...if he could find the time. He had no time for her games. She obviously intended to be courted by a native while she was doing her *noblesse oblige* bit for the reservation. He wasn't captain of the basketball team, but at least he was captain of something. Carly Austin was due for a hot news flash, however. Rafe Strongheart didn't *court*. He'd set her straight with a very brief visit.

A shaft of bright winter sunlight fell on the book in Carly's lap. It was Saturday, and the club was deserted. Everyone had either gone to Bismarck for the day or away for the weekend. But Carly had work to do. Donna McFarlan's cat basked in front of a crackling fire in the fireplace, and Carly sat in a steel frame chair with big, gray vinyl cushions, part of the government-

issue look of the club's common rooms. She peered out
the window at the campus quadrangle, having forgotten her rereading of the *Odyssey* for junior English and
wondering instead whether any of the innocent-looking
passersby had stolen her boots. They were sealskin
Alaskan mukluks, very warm, and irreplaceable.

The spring on the back door squeaked. Year-round
the screen door announced all entries. Carly heard the
inside door close quietly, and heavy boot heels traversed the hallway in her direction. He was a dark
shadow in the hall, and she smiled at him before she
could see the expression on his face. When he stopped
and stood framed by the doorway, she knew immediately that Rafe was not in a sociable mood.

Carly crossed the big living room with a buoyant step,
talking rapidly as she approached him. She would put
him at ease with her charm. "Thank you for stopping
by, Rafe. I know how busy you are, but I thought you
might combine my investigation with a cup of coffee
since you probably—"

"No, you don't," he said, unzipping his parka. Carly
saw now that he wasn't in uniform.

"I don't what?"

"You don't know how busy I am, and you aren't interested in knowing how busy I might be."

"I'm sorry. Weren't you on duty?"

"No. I had some paperwork to do." He glanced to his
right toward the dining room, left at the fireplace, and
then looked at Carly again. "Your room's upstairs?"

She nodded. "I guess there wasn't any real urgency,
but I thought the sooner..."

His one-sided smile betrayed the cynic in him. "No
urgency? How persistent are you when you are desper-

ate, Carly? I guess the sooner I satisfy your curiosity, the sooner I can get back to work. Which room?''

Carly stiffened and leveled her glare. ''I'm not going to ask you what you meant by that since I'm not that naive. I'm just going to tell you that you're way out of line. Someone stole my boots out of the back entryway this morning, and I want them back. I got them in Alaska, and they're—''

''I'm the chief of police here, Carly, not your personal—''

''I didn't ask you to drop everything and come over here. I said 'when you have time,''' she returned defensively. Then she reached down deep for control. ''I thought we'd have coffee, talk about my boots and your paperwork—a friendly break away from your desk. I guess I...misread the signs.''

''I guess you did.'' He failed to stir the reaction he'd hoped for—the one that would affirm the conception he chose to harbor. He wasn't even sure what he was looking for—a little hissing, maybe—certainly a ladylike leap into the saddle of a very high horse. But so far she'd kept her feet on the ground, set him straight without relegating him to his ''proper'' place. ''How do you know the boots were stolen?'' his policeman's voice asked.

''I heard someone open the door, and when I looked out the window from my room upstairs, I saw a darkhaired boy with a blue jacket running away with my boots.''

''There are a lot of dark-haired boys around here,'' he reminded her.

''I couldn't see much of him. He jumped in the back of a beat-up green station wagon—Chevy, I think. The front door on the driver's side was bashed in.''

"You people all have keys to the outside door here?"

"Yes, but we never—"

"Start using them. The kid's probably sold your boots by now, but I'll see what I can do." He allowed his eyes a few more seconds with hers before he turned to leave.

"I did make coffee," Carly said quietly.

"I don't take coffee breaks."

The *whack* of the screen door reverberated in Carly's ears. She heard a car engine turn over, and though she didn't move from the spot where she'd stood talking moments ago, her mind's eye watched Rafe's Bronco pull away from the curb. Pins and needles worried her throat, and she couldn't seem to swallow them away. She'd set a cup of friendship out for someone she liked, and he'd left it sitting there like a bad brew. He was attracted to her; why didn't he *like* her? And why had it become so important to her to make him like her? The rejection hurt her, and she would have preferred to be angry.

"I don't take coffee breaks," she said to the empty hallway, mocking his tone. The emptiness was still there, but she tried to fill it up with a rejection of her own. "Fine. I don't take insults from unfriendly cops, either. Just do your job, Chief. Find my boots."

Rafe glanced at the sealskin boots in the seat beside him. He'd had to squeeze a little to get Frankie Fire Cloud to admit he'd sold them to Carol White Horse. Frankie hadn't had any money, but he'd borrowed some from a friend when Rafe gave him an ultimatum: boots or jail. Frankie gave Carol her money back, swearing all the while he'd been nowhere near the club. Someone had given him the boots. No, he wouldn't say who. And he hoped Rafe wouldn't tell Miss Austin, because he didn't want to fail English again.

A lousy ten bucks. Frankie would eventually end up behind bars over a handful of change. He was a "court-order case," placed in the dorm by the court for want of a better situation. Rafe had been a court-order case, too, but that had been a long time ago, and he'd found a better situation. Not an easy situation—living uptown in a foster home was difficult for an Indian kid—but it had turned out okay. You couldn't dwell on the fact that when they drew lots for parents, the luck of the draw hadn't been on your side. You had to pull yourself up by your bootstraps and make something of yourself. No one else could do it for you. He wanted to shake some sense into Frankie. Of course, it wasn't *just* Frankie. Frankie was one in a long parade of hardcases who'd passed through Rafe's files.

Deliberately trying to remind himself of the broader picture, he was working up to his mental tirade against the whole juvenile system when the image of a tawny-haired woman with quiet outrage in her eyes clouded his focus.

Carly Austin, get out of my mind.

Rafe made his hands take the turn that brought him to the little trailer near the clinic. He told himself he hoped Carmen wasn't working the night shift. She wouldn't ask for friendship or conversation or complications, but she'd satisfy whatever this itch was he couldn't seem to alleviate with ordinary scratching. An evening with Carmen would do the trick, he told himself. When she came to the door, his heart iced up a bit. He'd told himself a lie. Seeing Carmen wouldn't change anything, and he didn't much like himself for standing here under the pretense that it would. He'd lied to himself a lot lately. It was beginning to disgust him.

"I need a cup of coffee," he told the small woman, whose long fall of raven hair didn't even draw his attention as he walked past her and sat at the little kitchen table.

"Is that all?" she asked.

"That's all. Just a cup of coffee."

The chocolate-eyed nurse drank her coffee in a silence that matched Rafe's. He'd carried another woman in his heart ever since she'd known him, and now the woman was back in his life. He'd avoided love the way most people avoided pain, and Carmen understood that Rafe regarded the two as one. She hadn't the means to help him separate them, but maybe the other woman would find a way.

When he finished with his coffee, he left her as abruptly as he'd come. And Carly was still on his mind.

It had been a week. He'd begun to measure the passage of time in units since he'd seen Carly. There'd been two accidents and one exposure victim—an old woman who'd been found frozen in her tiny two-room shack. Rafe needed a day off. He also needed a couple of fifty-pound bags of horse feed from the grain elevator.

It was Saturday and one of those rare and wonderful North Dakota winter mornings—windless, with a wispy layer of heavy frost covering every twig and branch of every tree, every strand of fence wire and every stalk of old grass that managed to poke through the snow cover. Where they'd been blown clear, the rolling hills sported a white froth of winter foam. Nice morning for a drive.

When he spotted Carly's little blue car, Rafe groaned audibly. It was parked beside the road only a couple of miles south of the turnoff to his place. He slowed the Bronco as he approached and looked around. No Carly. What was she up to now? He parked behind her car and followed her tracks in the snow. They led past the No Trespassing sign tacked to a fence post, down into a ravine, along an old roadbed and into the trees that lined a frozen creek. He found her photographing frosty trees.

She turned at the sound of his boots pushing prints into the drifts, and she brushed her hair back from her forehead as she lowered the camera to let it hang from her neck. She filled her nostrils with air that frosted them inside, and she thought, *This time I didn't call him.*

"I saw your car parked by the road. Wondered if you were in some kind of trouble," he announced.

"Hello, Rafe," was all she offered him.

"You're all right then?"

"Fine. But thank you for your concern. And thank you—" she glanced down at her feet "—for my boots."

"No problem." He thrust his hands in the pockets of his jeans, and he looked at her with all the innocence of a boy who'd retrieved her kitten from a tree. "Those kids'll take advantage of you if you let them, Carly. Don't let yourself be an easy mark."

"It was just a prank. I'm sure they'd have brought them back. I shouldn't have bothered you with it."

"No, you did the right thing. If you hadn't called the police, you'd never have seen those boots again."

"But I shouldn't have bothered *you* with it."

He shrugged, glancing away uncomfortably. "A lot of people think they have to take their complaints straight to the top. I should be used to that, I guess, but I get a little testy."

"You suggested that I had an ulterior motive, as I remember."

His disgust with himself was evident in his slow, quiet sigh. "I owe you an apology for what I suggested about your reason for calling me," he said.

"You really thought—"

"I guess I misread the signs."

"Not entirely," she said, offering him a smile that was meant to let him feel comfortable with her. "I did want to see you. But pay up anyway."

"Pay up?"

"You said you owed me an apology."

"Yes. I'm sorry."

"Apology accepted. And I'm sorry for all the curses I laid on your head after you left."

"You taking pictures of the scenery?"

She nodded, laughing, and he smiled. "I love to take pictures. One of these days I'll be good at it. Wanna see my slides sometime?" His smile widened. "It's a three-day show, no intermissions. So you thought I was in trouble again, huh?"

"I don't like seeing your car on the side of the road." He shrugged, and Carly would have liked to have seen the expression behind his dark glasses.

"*My* car? Do I detect a note of personal concern, or is my car more of an eyesore than most?"

"I've gone to a lot of trouble for you lately. Maybe it's becoming a reflex."

"Probably just a professional instinct." She pulled off a fur-lined glove and held her hand out to him, eyes brightly inviting. "Come on. I've got something to show you."

There was a quick warmth that passed between hands and startled them both. They stood still, just looking at each other, and for the moment there seemed to be no harm in letting her lead him by the hand.

A derelict car of undeterminable age rested at the foot of a stand of frosty cottonwoods. The roof was mashed, the front end, including hood and engine, almost completely gone, and there was no glass where the windows should have been. Rafe glanced up at the hill to his right, and he imagined the kids who must have rolled the car off the hill with the same delight they might have found in throwing eggs at parked cars.

"I hope you didn't find a body in this thing," Rafe mumbled.

"Shh," Carly warned, advancing on the wreck more slowly. "You'll scare her away. I think she's wild." Carly pointed at the space that was left between the roof and the body of the car where the windshield would have been. Rafe peered in. Stretched out on the front seat a big calico cat fed her litter of newborn kittens. Her eyes glittered like broken bottle glass as she hissed at the intruder.

"Everything serves its purpose, doesn't it?" Carly said quietly. "She let me take a family portrait, but I don't think she likes you."

"She probably knows how I feel about feral animals. They're notorious troublemakers."

"Then I shouldn't have given away her hideout. With seven mouths to feed, I'm sure she has enough on her mind without having to worry about the cops bringing her in on a feral charge."

"I'll let this one slip by," he promised. "I'm easier to get along with when I'm off duty."

"Is that so?" She showed him an arched eyebrow. "Prove it. Lend me your artistic eye. Help me find great visual moments."

They walked along the creek bank together, and Carly snapped a picture once in a while. They talked, and it was like the easy conversation they'd finally had at his house during the blizzard. Once when she laughed, he caught the joy in her eyes and tried to absorb it through his own eyes into himself. He wanted to make that joy his own—an old feeling he remembered having about her years ago. He shook his head, glancing away.

"What is it?" she asked.

"A foolish notion," he said, intending to leave it at that. The question in her eyes drew him out. "You've always had laughing eyes. I remember seeing you surrounded by people and thinking the color of laughter was sky blue."

"You were so quiet, so aloof. You never seemed to notice me. . .except that once."

"When I fixed your purse," he recalled.

"And then how could you help but notice? The strap broke, and everything spilled on the floor."

"I stepped on your pen and broke it."

"And then you took the purse to the shop and put a rivet in the strap. I was surprised you'd do that."

"Why?"

"I thought you were pretty tough. You hung out with Chuck Morris and those guys."

"I didn't hang out with them. I got drunk and raised hell with them once in a while because they were the only show I could get a ticket to. But I didn't hang out with anybody." He unzipped his jacket and reached inside for cigarettes and matches. They stopped walking while he cupped the match in one hand and lit his cigarette.

"Maybe you didn't give anyone a chance," she suggested.

"I didn't see any point in it."

"You still don't." Again Carly wished for a glimpse behind those dark glasses. He started walking again, and she fell in beside him. "Do your parents still live in Bismarck?"

"My parents never lived in Bismarck."

"How did you—"

"I was living in a foster home." He still couldn't say it aloud without a bitter edge, even though the Smiths had helped him turn his life around. He was surprised he'd said it at all. "The Smiths took me in when I was fifteen. He was a minister, and he saw something in me worth salvaging. Like Frankie Fire Cloud, I was on my way to the state training school. I had run away from the tenth foster home I'd had in about nine years. Anyway, the Smiths let me stay until I finished high school, when I was almost twenty years old."

"What happened to your parents?"

Rafe blew a cloud of smoke, which dissipated quickly into the crisp air. "My mother died when I was four. I stayed with my grandmother until she died. I was seven then."

"And your father?"

Rafe shrugged. "He's around."

She sensed that he'd told her all he was going to, and she asked no more. They walked in silence until Rafe stopped again to drop his cigarette into the snow. There was a quick hiss, and then he stepped on it and looked across the creek. Spotting a coyote, he dropped a hand on Carly's shoulder and pointed in the coyote's direction.

Carly snatched the camera to her face and screwed the telephoto lens in place at the same time. Another coyote appeared at the top of the hill beyond the first. "A rabbit!" Carly whispered. She focused and clicked, clicked and focused again. The rabbit was trapped. Tail sailing straight out behind him, the first coyote darted in for the kill. The rabbit froze, and the coyote pounced on it.

The camera fell to Carly's chest. "I should have warned her," she said. "I could have shouted and scared the coyotes."

"Why should the rabbit be a *her*?" he asked. "The coyote may be a mother with a litter of mouths to feed."

His hand still rested on her shoulder, and she looked up at him with the intention of nodding, but she lost the thrust of the gesture when she saw his eyes. He was slipping the glasses into a pocket, and his plans were in his eyes. He lifted the camera strap from her neck and hooked it over his own shoulder. "You can't scare a stalking coyote anyway. Once he's made up his mind…"

"He?" She tried to fasten her attention on his full, sensuous mouth as his thumb traced her jawline.

"That one may be a *she*," he murmured. "This one's a *he*. You should never have let me get a taste of you, Carly. You taste too good…too damn good."

She tilted her chin and slid her arms around the down-filled puff of his jacket as he pulled her against him. He kissed her gently, nourished by the warm, wet taste of her. His hunger excited her, as did the smoky taste of his tongue and the slow caress of his lips. She clutched the back of his jacket, and he buried his fingers in her hair. Then he closed his hand tightly around the back of her head, held her still, and willed all the hot desire he felt to be fulfilled just in the taking of her mouth with his.

Kissing her this way was deliciously bittersweet. For just a moment he let his lips linger near hers, mingling the mist of his breath with hers. It was all the mingling he dared attempt with this woman, but even the little stab of regret that came with his reluctance to draw away felt good. It was the perverse need to play with fire or push the accelerator to the floor; eventually it would bring you down, but the thrilling rush in your stomach was irresistible. He dipped his head again and helped himself to another kiss.

The old-fashioned radiators in her classroom clicked and clinked. They blasted uncontrollable heat through the open window at the back of the room. Carly brushed her thumb back and forth across the tips of her fingers, banishing the chalk dust. "This is the assignment for Monday, people," she announced, indicating the yellow scrawl on the board behind her. A deep choral groan followed. "Try Sunday afternoon. Great time for reading." The clanging of the bell signaled day's end, and Carly dismissed her class. Frankie Fire Cloud was the only student who didn't dash for the door.

"Got a problem, Frankie?" Carly asked as she slipped a pile of papers into a zippered vinyl envelope.

"Yeah, I got a problem. I got a lot of problems." Frankie slid his booted feet forward along the floor and stretched theatrically, pressing his back against the desk chair's backrest.

"Care to tell me about any of them?"

"Strongheart's after me."

Carly frowned. "What makes you say that?"

"He's always making trouble for us—me and my dad. I can't afford any trouble before the end of the school year if I wanna go back with my dad. Me and him both gotta stay out of trouble."

"Does your father have custody of you?"

"Not now. The court does. That's why I'm stayin' at the dorm." Frankie beat his fingertips lightly on the desk for a moment, considering. "You're friends with Strongheart, aren't you?"

"I know him," Carly said carefully.

"Know him pretty well, from what I hear."

"You're overstepping, Frankie."

"Okay, but you *do* know him. Look, Miss Austin, I been tryin' pretty hard in your class. I flunked English last year, and now I'm pullin' a C."

"It's always better the second time around," Carly said with a smile.

"I'm doing pretty good this year." Frankie punctuated his next statement with an unwavering look at Carly. "I don't want any trouble. I was hoping you'd tell Strongheart that."

"Did you tell him that?"

"Yeah, but he don't believe me."

"You're probably overreacting, Frankie. Rafe Strongheart strikes me as a fair man."

"Will you tell him I didn't do nothing?" Frankie persisted.

"If the opportunity arises, which is unlikely." Her smile was neither indulgent nor patronizing. It was that of a friend. "Now get on out of here and behave yourself this weekend."

In the office Carly was tossing her attendance report in the box when she heard Rafe's deep, quiet voice. She peered around a corner and recognized his back as he stood just inside the doorway of the boarding school principal's office. Carly decided not to go home quite yet. She stepped back in the main office's little anteroom and waited by the wall of teachers' mailboxes.

Rafe rounded the corner on a firmly planted boot heel, his momentum bringing him head to head with Carly in the anteroom. Their eyes locked in the first second, Rafe's surprise facilitating an unguarded moment. Stiffening then, Rafe muttered, "Hello, Carly."

"If you have a few minutes, Rafe, I'd like to talk to you."

"Another time, Carly. I'm pretty busy...."

"I know. You've put the fear of Strongheart into one of my boys."

"One of *your* boys?" He refused to reflect her smiling expression. "Are you taking responsibility here or just possession?"

"Let's talk in my classroom," she suggested, turning to lead the way. She unlocked the door to her classroom and let them both in the room, then closed the door behind her.

"What's this about, Carly?" Rafe hooked his hands at his slim hips and looked the part of the teacher himself, preparing to receive a wild homework excuse. "I don't have time for a visit."

"How about just a 'Hello, Carly? How are you?'" she recited with mock enthusiasm.

"Hello, Carly. How are you?" His tone was as flat as the expression on his face.

Carly moved to the desk, pushed a thick textbook out of her way, and sat at the edge of the desk top. "What is it with you, Rafe? Why do you run hot and cold with me? My instincts can't be so completely off base."

"And what do your instincts tell you?"

"That you don't really want to like me, but you do. And that you don't find me totally unattractive. Our last parting was on friendly terms."

"We're wasting each other's time, Carly. I'm sure there's a telephone book full of men who don't find you unattractive. Pick a number."

"I picked yours, but I keep getting a busy signal."

"You got a wrong number," he corrected quietly. His gaze was black granite, and she gave him blue crystal. He dropped his hands at his sides and took a step toward the door.

"I want to talk to you about Frankie Fire Cloud," Carly said quietly.

Rafe stopped and turned to her. "You've got a roundabout way of leading up to it. What about him?"

"He stayed after school today to talk. He's worried. You've been coming down pretty hard on him."

"That's it? That's all?" Rafe took two slow steps in Carly's direction as though edging toward a questionable reality.

"I've been teaching a long time, Rafe. I'm not easily fooled. Frankie stayed after school because he's worried. He's hoping the court will let him go back with his father, and he thinks you're out to get him for something."

"What is this?" He indicated the room with a wave of his hand as he came to stand over her at the desk. "Some sort of academic confessional? You figure you've got some kind of sacred trust with your students? Think again, lady. That kid's a troublemaker. He's been trained by the best of them. The last thing he needs to do is go back with his old man."

"The kids have their rights. Frankie was very upset, Rafe. You shouldn't be able to come into the school and put the squeeze on them or whatever it is you do."

Rafe allowed himself a short laugh. "I like to use ant hills and wet rawhide, but that's only good for summertime interrogations."

Taking Carly's shoulders in his hands, Rafe emphasized his point with quiet, measured words. "He's in trouble, Carly, he's always in trouble. And you can't protect him from himself. He's got himself in a pressure cooker, and he's been looking for the chance to blow off some steam."

"You sound like you just want to get him."

"I want to get him off this treadmill he's got himself on." He meant that. It was there in his eyes—the burning sense of responsibility—an intense obsidian glow. And there was more because he kept looking at her, and because his fingers kneaded her shoulders very slightly, and because she couldn't take her eyes away from his.

"I do, too," she said finally.

"Then be his teacher. If he ever needs an attorney, the court will appoint one."

"He just…he just asked me to tell you he didn't want any trouble, so I did. I believe him, Rafe."

Rafe dropped his hands. "That's fine. You believe what you want. Why do you think he came to you?"

"Maybe he trusts me."

"Or maybe he has you figured for a do-gooder. A do-gooder who has some pull with a cop. Everybody in town knows I pulled you out of the freezer during the blizzard. I'm sure your boys have done some locker room speculating about the time you spent at my house."

"I'm a professional teacher. That means I'm very good at reading teenagers, and this one's not lying to me."

"Then I'm sure Frankie will feed your ego with the right flattery—gratitude for your faith in him for starters. He'll know just how to keep you on his side." Rafe took three strides toward the door before turning back to her with, "I'm a professional, too, Carly. And I know Frankie Fire Cloud."

As he closed the door the thud echoed in the dark hallway. *I know Frankie Fire Cloud, Carly. I've been Frankie Fire Cloud. He'll chew up all your good intentions and drop them on the ground like an old wad of gum.*

It was Carly's turn to listen to footsteps retreating down the hall. She had to remember Rafe was a policeman, and he saw the kids in a different light. His perspective had to be different from hers. He couldn't be overly sympathetic. She, on the other hand, had a finely tuned empathetic nature, and her students sensed that. When no one else would listen, they often opened up because they knew she could be trusted.

And Frankie Fire Cloud seemed a special case. He was one of those kids whom everyone on the staff warned you about the first day of school. Troublemaker. No motivation. Can't turn your back on him. It was all true; yet in Carly's class he did well. Maybe he thought he was doing Carly a favor, but in doing so, he did himself one. Carly had her own tricks of the trade.

Frankie, too, had his. Carly was working in her room that night when Todd Johnson rapped on her door. "Hey, Carly, you wanna talk to Frankie Fire Cloud? He's at the back door."

Frankie waited in the entryway, head down, hands in his pockets. He looked up at Carly, his eyes bright with desperation.

"What's wrong, Frankie?"

"I need a favor, Miss Austin. I need a ride to Mobridge. You're the only one around I can ask."

"I'm not authorized to check you out of the dorm, Frankie. You know that."

He pulled a yellow card from his pocket and thrust it in Carly's direction. "I've got a pass. I just have to find a ride. Please, Miss Austin. My kid brother...he's in the hospital with a busted appendix. I've gotta be there with him."

"Now? Tonight?"

"They took him in on emergency. He asked a nurse to call me, so she did."

Carly shifted her eyes to the ceiling, looking for an excuse. "Oh, Frankie, I don't think—"

"Please, Miss Austin. I wouldn't bother you, but I don't know what else to do, and I've gotta hurry."

Carly sighed. Another look at those desperate eyes beneath the diagonal slash of untrimmed black hair weakened her. He wore neither hat nor gloves, and that look told her that he would walk the fifty miles if he had to.

"Miss Austin, the kid's only ten, and he's got nobody but me."

That did it. "I'll get my purse."

Mobridge was an hour's drive with long stretches of deserted highway. Frankie fidgeted all the way, nodding when Carly assured him that an appendectomy was a very routine operation and his brother would surely be fine. As they approached the hospital parking lot, anxiety pitched Frankie forward on the seat, as though he were ready to leap through the windshield.

"Maybe you'll want to ride back with me, Frankie. They may have him sedated or—"

"No. I'm staying with him."

"I'll wait until you find out what the situation is. Or I could go in with you and—"

"No, thanks. I've taken up enough of your time as it is. I just wanna be with him. He's just a kid...probably real scared."

"Yes, he probably is," Carly agreed. "He'll be glad you're here."

"Uh...Miss Austin...could I maybe borrow ten dollars from you? In case he needs something or...in case I can't find a ride back."

Carly gave him the money and watched him spring between banks of snow and disappear behind double glass doors. She felt good; she'd done a good deed.

In bed that night Carly thought about Frankie. She only wished that Rafe could have seen the boy as she had—the fear in his eyes, the desperation, the love he must have felt for the younger child. As a teacher, she'd seen the price so many children had to pay for their parents' mistakes. Rafe's heart had been hardened by his job, but surely he remembered what it was like from his own experience, which must have been difficult in its own right. Frankie was no model child, but he was no criminal, either.

There was that racket again! Clanging and banging, the old heating system's pipes rattled their demand in the middle of the night. Somebody would have to go down to the basement and drain them or there'd be no heat. Carly was the only somebody in the building who wouldn't lie there shivering until morning. She turned over and looked at the clock. One thirty. In five and half hours she'd have to get up. *Clang, clang, clonk!* No, she'd have to get up now.

The only entrance to the basement was via an outside stairwell. The last time she'd called Plant Management about the heat, the man had shown her what had to be done, and she'd taken possession of a key to the basement door. After shoving bare feet into her mukluks and tying the sash on her velour robe, Carly tossed a white blanket over her shoulders and made her way down the stairs. In the kitchen she found the flashlight she'd stashed in the broom closet and headed out the door.

It was a bright, white night, piles of snow gleaming like a moonscape. A little network of shoveled pathways led from building to building, and one, fortunately led from the back door to the basement stairwell. Carly lifted the edge of the blanket over her head and rounded the corner to the entrance.

She closed the door behind her and thumbed the light switch. No lights. One thing she couldn't master in this place was its fuse box. The flashlight would have to get her around.

The club's basement served as a fallout shelter and community library. Homemade shelves were stocked with donations of used paperbacks and library cast-offs. Carly had agreed to put in her voluntary three hours a week to keep the library open until she discovered no one ever came. No wonder. The place was a musty dungeon. Now she scanned the shelves with her flashlight until she found a title that seemed to fit the occasion: *Deep Caverns, Dark Secrets*. Then she turned the wheel to let the pipes drain and settled in the back room near the furnace to wait. *Chapter One.*

The basement door creaked on arthritic hinges. One foot slid softly against the cement floor, and then another. The hinges creaked again, and the door clicked closed. Carly doused the flashlight, slipped her boots off, and toe-danced to the far corner of the room, pasting herself to the wall next to the furnace room's open doorway. Her eyes became saucers in the dark as she listened to slow, quiet footfalls. A shaft of light shot through the doorway and fell on the white blanket she'd dropped over her boots. More slow footsteps crossed the cement floor, the intensity of the light increasing.

Carly's heart was a kettledrum. The intruder reached the doorway, took one step beyond, and met Carly's outstretched leg. It was as though she'd brought down a tree. A flashlight clattered across the floor as the intruder's bulk thudded at Carly's feet.

Get out of here and don't look back.

She was not quite fast enough. An arm clamped her knees together and brought her to the floor with a thud of her own, knocking her breath from her lungs. Face down on the gritty cement, she heard her own small wheeze and the intruder's oath at the same time. And then she fought for air as the hands that had brought her down moved to her hips, stilled, then gently moved along her back and to her hair.

"Carly?"

She managed a shaky gasp.

"My God! Are you hurt?"

The hands that lifted her face away from the floor, brushed her hair back and gently held her head were Rafe's hands.

Chapter Four

"I'm okay."

Her words were windless. With great care, Rafe rolled Carly into his arms, grimacing as the knee he'd just bruised slid under her back. She shuddered and gulped a chestful of air.

"Did you hit your head?" The flashlight beam was turned to the far wall, throwing dim light back to the doorway. He could see tears in her eyes. "Oh, God, I've hurt you. Tell me..."

Her chest heaved with another blessed breath, and she shook her head. "I'm okay. Can't catch...my breath."

"Are you sure? You came down pretty hard. You didn't hit your head?" His fingertips grazed her cheek, touched her hair, then gingerly cupped the back of her head.

"No, really..." A couple of deep breaths brought the depth of her voice back. She exhaled a little laugh. "You take my breath away."

Rafe's shoulders sagged as he wiped the moisture from the corner of her eye with the back of a finger. "Damn. You scared the life out of me."

She smiled. "I got you down, didn't I?"

"Yeah." He chuckled at the thought of how it must have looked. "You got me down, all right. I may need a new kneecap."

Carly sat up, and they helped each other up from the dark floor. "You fell on your knee? Do you think it's—"

"No, it's okay. I should've—"

"I thought you were—"

"I didn't—ow!" His right knee buckled, and Carly reached for his waist.

"You *did*..."

"No, it's just—"

"Come sit down." Her arm went around him, and he leaned on her shoulder. "There's a chair over here. Is it bad?"

He looked down at her and enjoyed her anxious eyes. What the hell, he told himself, and he let his knee buckle a little more than necessary with each step toward the chair. "No, it's fine. You know how it is when you hit your knee."

"Oh, dear. When I was a kid, I kicked a boy in the knee and did permanent damage." She deposited him in the chair and reached for her blanket.

"I don't think this is that bad," he judged, kneading the area once before dismissing it completely. "You mind telling me what you're doing down here in the dark?"

Bundled in her blanket, Carly sat on the floor beside Rafe's injured knee, absently stroking it as she explained about the pipes and the lights. "I thought you were a burglar or something, although there's nothing down here anyone would want."

You're down here was the thought he tried to ignore. "One of the dorm matrons called. Said she saw a ghost go down the steps to the club basement. I thought it might be..." He'd thought it might be Frankie Fire Cloud, who'd been reported missing, "AWOL" from the dorm, but after their last run-in over Frankie, Rafe didn't even want to mention the name to her.

Carly smiled expectantly. "You thought it might be what?"

"I thought it might be a burglar or something." He shrugged, returning the smile.

"Wrapped in this blanket, I suppose I did look rather ghostly," Carly admitted. "You work nights a lot, don't you?"

"People seem to get into the most trouble at night. You're no exception."

"You could have sent someone else."

"I don't get to see many ghosts." Her slow, circular rubbing was soothing to his knee, but it was aggravating the other ache she'd planted in him long before. He covered her hand with his. In the eerie light that splashed up from the floor and rebounded off the wall, her face was a sultry black and white framed by dusky hair. His fingers curled around her slight hand. "They're as unpredictable as they say. And pale as moonlight."

His gentle fingers swept her cheek and brushed her lips, drawing Carly to her knees. His eyes pulled her into their dark shadows. "You haunt me," he said thickly, an admission of a truth he'd been trying hard to deny.

"I have no designs on your soul," she promised.

"What, then?"

She reached up to touch the hair over his temple, and her fingers sank into its dark, coarse thickness. "Your lips, I think. Maybe a kiss."

Rafe's mouth made a gradual descent. Carly watched his lips part, and then her eyes shuttered as she let all sensitivity gather in her mouth for a meeting with his. He was at once gentle and firm, taking her shoulders between his hands and pulling her up to meet him. The inclination of her body was to extend itself into his kiss, to stretch herself like the crocus, grounded in spring cold and reaching for summer-warm sun. Oh, yes—his kiss was summer-warm sun, stirring dormant roots in Carly's womb until they tingled with life.

Rafe rose from the chair, drawing Carly with him, and his lips delved more eagerly into hers, nibbling and massaging her dewy mouth. His arms encircled her, pressed her to his chest, and he let his tongue skim the oval outline of her mouth. The tight, crisp cotton of the shirt under his jacket felt cool and smooth under her palms. His hand slid over her bottom and brought her hip into his.

Rafe nestled his lips against the side of her neck and feathered her with kisses. "You're dressed for bed," he whispered.

"Yes. I was in bed."

"What's it like there? In your bed?"

"Solitary."

"I think it smells like wildflowers and musk." He nuzzled the hair line behind her ear and then ran his tongue under her lobe. "And it's piled high with blankets because you're always cold at night."

"Yes, I am."

He moved his hands to the tops of her shoulders and slipped his thumbs under the edges of her robe just below her collarbones. He found bits of satin straps underneath the soft velour. God! How he wanted to slide it all off and touch white shoulders and creamy breasts. But he was a damn fool for letting himself come this far, for responding automatically every time his brain flashed "Carly" in red neon letters.

He drew back and looked at her. "You'd better get upstairs and get under those blankets, then. It's cold down here."

"I'm not cold. Not at all, now that I've gotten my kiss."

"You sure went to a lot of trouble to get it."

"I knew better than to call the station and ask you to bring one over. You're a busy man."

Rafe slid his hands down her arms and dropped them to his sides. "I was on my way home anyway. You ought to get Plant Management to do something about this heating system."

"I did," Carly said, stepping into her boots. "I got them to show me what to do when it starts going off in the middle of the night."

"I'll bet they love you for that. They won't have to fix it as long as you're around."

They both leaned down to pick up the blanket. Rafe got to it first and peeled it off the floor. "Would you like some coffee?" Carly asked, accepting the blanket and swinging it over her shoulders.

"No, thanks."

"Maybe I could make you some breakfast?"

He shook his head slightly. "I don't think so. Are you finished down here? I'll just get my—"

"Your flashlight." Again the both started toward the object on the floor. Carly reversed her motion. "Mine's over here."

They stood, facing each other like two mechanical figures on a German clock, hesitating a moment, and then turning regretfully toward the door. Rafe's flashlight pointed the way.

"Oh." A quick about-face as she remembered. "I have to turn the wheel on the pipes back." His flashlight found the mechanism for her. "It would be no trouble to fix something," she said almost shyly as she twisted the wheel.

"You've fixed a lot already tonight, Carly—the heat, my knee..."

"Which seems to have recovered," Carly noted.

"Yeah." They'd walked to the basement door. "Thanks for the offer. I'll see you later, Carly."

She wanted to swallow the word, but couldn't. "When?"

"When?"

Was it a foreign word? "When will I see you again?"

"Next time I get a report that you're out prowling the night, I guess."

"Some people think they have to go straight to the top with every little complaint," she reminded him.

He chuckled. "I like to deal with repeat offenders personally."

She wondered if his attention could be worth going to jail for. "Soon, then, I imagine. I can't seem to stay out of trouble. I still think if you'd just ask me out it would make matters much simpler."

Rafe followed Carly's lead up the stairwell. "My life couldn't be any simpler. You're talking about complicating it. Just being your friend puts a strain on my patience."

She'd reached the shoveled walk. Whirling to face him, she was his mind's image of the Lakota's legendary White Buffalo Woman, opalescent in the moonlight. She smiled. "Are we friends, then?"

"I guess it's come to that."

She leaned closer and conspired in a low voice. "It's come to that now, has it? What next?" Trailing her blanket, she scampered around the rack of garbage cans and up the steps, quietly trilling a merry, "Good night, Rafe. And sleep well. If you can't have quantity, at least have quality."

The back door swallowed her up.

Carly didn't have to commit a major crime. Within a few days she had only to ignore a corner stop sign, and she saw the red light flashing in her rearview mirror. Craning her neck after she'd pulled over, she saw the Bronco with a portable light flashing on its roof. Rafe climbed out, looking grim behind his dark glasses. Carly heard his boots scrape against the pavement next to her car as she rolled the window down.

"The sign says *stop*, lady. It doesn't say roll on around the corner if nobody's coming."

Carly offered him half a laugh. "I knew you'd be one of those smart-aleck cops who has it in for women drivers."

"I'd like to see your driver's license, please." The request seemed to come from a silver belt buckle peeking out from an open jacket.

"May I see your identification first?" she said primly.

He flipped his wallet open over the car window, flashing a badge and a horrible ID picture. Carly's giggle bubbled in her throat. "Now may I see the face that goes with this picture?" The wallet was clapped shut, the unsmiling face appeared, and the dark glasses were slowly removed. "Yes, I see the likeness. You could stop a charging buffalo with that look."

"Your license?" His voice was patient but completely impersonal.

"Wanna frisk me for it?"

The corners of Rafe's mouth twitched as he tried not to smile. He draped his forearms over the car's window ledge and nodded at the far side of the street. "That carload of kids would get a charge out of that."

At her glance in their direction the kids gave Carly a show of hands and a toot of the horn. There must have been at least eight of them in the battered sedan. She sighed and pulled out all the documents he could want. They were in his hands only a moment before he handed them back and started writing on a pad.

"We'd like our teachers to set a better example, Miss Austin. These kids look up to you. They figure if you can get away with these things, they can, too. They're very impressionable." She watched his strong brown hands tear out the ticket and fold it in half. "You understand," he concluded, handing her the paper.

"Of course. Thank you for reminding me of the weight of my responsibility."

"No trouble at all, ma'am. Have a nice day."

Carly laid the ticket on the seat beside her and looked in her rearview mirror as she rolled the window up. He was taking the gumball light down from the roof of the

Bronco. You are supremely difficult, Rafe Strong-heart. Oh, yes. You are that.

Pulling away from the snowbank at the side of the street, Carly resolutely left him behind her, waving at the carload of teenagers as she drove by. She caught a glimpse of Frankie Fire Cloud and noticed he didn't wave back. He hadn't said much since she'd taken him to Mobridge other than that his little brother was do-ing well. The car angled neatly into a curbside space by the club. Carly didn't want to worry about Frankie any more than she wanted to worry about Rafe. What she wanted was a long soak in a hot bath with a good book.

Reaching across the seat for her bag of groceries, Carly eyed the folded ticket for a moment. She'd have to pay his price, and she'd better take it upstairs with her before it got lost. She picked it up and spread it open with the fingers of one hand. The blanks weren't filled in and nothing was checked. She let the bag settle back on the seat, and she read the message scrawled across the printed ticket. *I'll fix the ticket if you'll come out to my place Sunday and fix dinner. Got any ice skates?*

Carly let her head fall back against the high-backed car seat, and she smiled. He'd finally asked her out.

An honest-to-God date with Carly Austin. He won-dered if she'd show up. As he poured two quarts of corn and oats into Rusty's feed box, he told himself he wasn't going to kid himself about this lady. Her "loves" and "hates" didn't run deeply, and her interest in him was bound to be short-lived. He was a diversion for her—nothing more. But, in all fairness, he'd had his share of diversions, too. He couldn't condemn her for that.

He'd just have to watch himself. As always, he would monitor his emotions. He'd developed supreme emotional control and found that skill to be invaluable in maintaining his self-contained life-style. Carly was a challenge who insisted upon being met head-on. It was good being with her, and she seemed to want to be around him, so why the hell not?

The high-pitched hum of a small car wound down and shut off outside the barn. Rafe's heartbeat tripped into high as he headed for the door. Damn—he would surely have to quit smoking. It was making his pulse erratic.

"I had to go to Bismarck yesterday for my skates. Where's the ice?" Carly unloaded a cardboard box from the car and shut the door. "I don't know what I'm fixing for dinner, but I brought dessert. You look like a pecan pie man. Am I right?"

"Sounds good." Rafe took the box from her arms. "I wasn't sure you'd come."

"And pass up a bona fide invitation from you? Never. You're not the kind of guy a girl can tell she's washing her hair."

"Washing her hair?"

"You know: 'Sorry, I can't tonight. I have to stay home and wash my hair.' Part of the dating game." He rolled his eyes in disgust, and she laughed. "So where's the ice?"

He cocked his head over his shoulder. "There's a dam behind that hill. Snow's blown clear, and the ice is like glass."

"I wouldn't have picked you for a skater."

"Thought I'd watch you."

"Think again," she retorted.

"Actually, I'm pretty good. Thought I'd *race* you."

"You're on."

The morning sun slanted across the log house's iced eaves and winked in the long icicle mirrors made by melting shingles of snow. Rafe and Carly mounted the steps together. He reached around her to open the swinging, glassless storm door, and Carly smiled up at him. "I should fix this for you, shouldn't I? It was my fault."

"It's almost spring," he said, and he smiled, too, as a drop of water splashed on her cheek. He reached out to brush the water away, and her eyes sparkled at the gesture. The unfettered storm door nudged Rafe's backside, and he suddenly felt awkward. What was he doing, having a woman over for dinner? This kind of thing was for other men—the kind who spent hours calculating ways to be witty and charming. Rafe would pit his *wits* against men like that any day, but wittiness was another ball game, and charm was out of the question. He was about to make a damn fool of himself.

Carly eased the moment by opening the inside door and stepping into the house. "Have I told you how much I love this little house?" She took the box from him and set it on the kitchen counter.

"I don't remember. Probably."

"It's very sturdy and sensible, and it feels sort of independent. You know—made directly from trees. No middlemen." She lifted a pie from the box and peeled back the foil, letting the smell of caramel and toasted pecans tempt his salivary glands. He raised both eyebrows. *Both.* He was impressed. "And I also brought you a double batch of molasses cookies. So what am I making for dinner?"

"Ham. I was just coming in to get it started."

"You really didn't think I'd come?"

"I was planning to eat whether you got here or not." He flipped the door open on a lower cupboard and squatted to look for a pan. "Now I'll eat better."

"I take that as a vote of confidence. Would it be a good day to ride your horses?"

"Sure. I'd have suggested that, too, but I wouldn't have picked you for a horsewoman."

"I have a lot of surprises in store for you, Rafe Strongheart."

He'd taken the ham from the refrigerator and was removing a network of string. "Why me?"

"Because you need surprises. I've never met anyone more in need of surprises than you are. What else is for dinner? Have you got any sweet potatoes?"

"I don't care for sweet potatoes. And cops don't enjoy surprises. You saw how I reacted the other night when you took me by surprise. Here." He got a box down from a high shelf. "I like macaroni and cheese."

"Don't you have any real cheese?" she asked, wrinkling her nose at the box.

"In the refrigerator. What's wrong with the stuff in the box?" he asked. The plastic container she'd set out on the counter yielded a cookie.

"It looks like chalk dust. I'll make you *cheese* and macaroni like you've never tasted before." She kissed her fingers to the air.

He folded his arms over his chest and leaned his hip against the counter, watching her lower the oven door and slide the pan of ham onto the rack as he snacked on the dark-sweet taste of molasses. The gentle curves under the back pockets of her jeans drew an unconscious smile from him. She had the willowy shape of a woman who'd not borne children. She should have children, he thought, and then pushed the thought away, voicing an abrupt, "Got anything on under those jeans?"

Half turning and popping up at once, corkscrewlike, she flashed the complete circles of her irises at him. "I thought we were just going to be *friends*."

"You're gonna be pretty cold if those jeans are all you're wearing, *friend*."

She smiled. "I have on the prettiest set of thermal underwear with little pink roses underneath these very jeans."

"What would you like to do first, then? Bust your buns in the saddle or on the ice?"

When he grinned like that, she wanted to hug him. It was a boyish grin that took the hardness out of his eyes completely. She knew he felt at least comfortable with her when he allowed himself that relaxed grin. "My buns will not touch the ice, Mr. Strongheart. I am an accomplished skater, as you shall soon see."

"It's a good thing, Miss Austin. You haven't got much padding back there."

"We'll see who needs the padding, *friend*."

Rafe had not exaggerated when he'd described the glassy ice. It was slightly wet—not as fast as the ice of a frigid day, but perfect for figure eights and little spins, which Carly loved to show off. Rafe did nothing fancy, but he was a good, strong skater, and she could never have bested him at any distance. They chased each other over the ice, grateful for the warm sunshine and lack of wind.

At last they simply glided. Rafe found her hand in his, and he wasn't sure when he'd taken it. But he wouldn't argue with anything that felt so natural—not now.

"Do you do this often?" Carly wondered.

"When I have time. I like to skate. The oldest boy at my last...where I lived when I went to high school...well, he played high school hockey. I used to play with him a lot—you know, one on one. I enjoyed it."

"Why didn't you go out for it?"

"Indians play basketball, Carly. They don't skate. You wouldn't have picked me for a skater, remember? In those days we played basketball, or we didn't play anything."

"Can you play basketball?"

"Damn right, I can play basketball."

"But you wouldn't," she concluded, sweeping a smooth curve beside him as they reached the earth mound that formed the dam. Just like Frankie, she thought.

"No, I wouldn't. I wouldn't go out for track, either. I had a good-sized chip on my shoulder. I'll admit that. I was supposed to be an athlete because I was built like one and my skin was the right color."

Deftly reversing herself, Carly put the breeze to her back and pushed the blades of her skates against the ice as she held both hands out to him. "You've turned the chip into a shell, dear friend. Swing me." Tethered by clasped hands, they spun like a two-seated amusement park ride, and Rafe forgot himself for the moment. His laughter echoed across the flat land, sailing freely in the clear, high plains winter air.

"Whew! I'm out of shape." Carly panted puffs of steam and cut a sharp arc at the edge of the ice next to their abandoned boots. Bending her knees, she prepared to drop her bottom in a drift of snow when Rafe glided to her side and caught her in one arm.

"You were about to bust your buns on the ice." His voice was a warm purr next to her ear.

"Purposely. That doesn't count."

"I'll get your laces," he offered, lowering one knee to the ice.

"How gallant! I am most grateful, sir," she drawled.

"I don't want you sitting on my furniture in wet pants."

Carly looked down at the top of his head, where jet-black hair caught white sunbeams. There was not a hint of red. She caught his shoulders for balance as he slipped her foot from the skate and slid a mukluk in its place. "I've worn your clothes before. Don't you remember?" His hands stilled a moment, then went to the other skate.

"Yeah, I remember." *It nearly drove me crazy.*

"The slipper fits, sir. I am indeed the girl you've been searching for these many years," she gushed with theatrical flourish.

"Just wanted to see that the slippers were returned to their rightful owner, lady." Unlacing his own skates, he added, "Would you hand me my boots, please?" One boot appeared at his shoulder. The other boot followed. And then a ball of ice slipped past his collar and down his back. "Ahhh!"

Carly jumped back grinning and loosed a peal of giggles as she watched Rafe dance on one booted foot while he pulled the other boot on, hooting as the ice slipped around inside his clothes. Once shod, he freed the back of his shirt from his waistband and shook the ice free. "Oh, God, that's cold! Gallantry be damned, lady. You're gonna get it now."

Carly let out a little shriek as she quickly spun around. She then bounded through a drift, prancing like an antelope in knee-high snow. She managed several yards before he caught her around the waist and pulled her over backward with him. Rolling quickly to reverse their positons, Rafe raised himself to his knees and loomed over her.

"You wanna play games? You're gonna be wet now, baby. Soggy right down to your pink roses." Carly shrieked again, trying without success to wrench herself away from his handful of snow. It shocked her neck, some of it slipping down between her breasts. She choked on a giggly shriek as he tunneled under the bottom of her jacket and sweater and smeared another cold shock on her midriff.

"Give up, Carly," he commanded, laughing. "Promise to behave or I'll pack you in snow."

"I promise!" She was released, and she lay quivering with laughter, gasping, "I promise...I promise."

Rafe sat back on his heels, still grinning. "Satisfied now? You made me blow my cool."

"Yes," she said, her eyes dancing. "I'm satisfied...for the time being. Shall we make snow angels?"

He watched her flap one arm up and down and swish her legs like a pair of windshield wipers. "You're crazy, you know that?"

"You're in the way of my other wing. No, here." She rolled to her feet and moved to another spot. "We messed up the snow there. Here's a better one." She repeated the swishing and flapping, then reminded him of a delighted toddler when she again rolled from her back to her feet and hopped off her creation. "There. Perfect snow angel."

Rafe stood behind her and brushed snow from the back of her head, his fingers disappearing in the mass of tawny brown hair. "Perfect snow angel," he muttered. "We'd better get back to the house before your teeth start chattering."

Turning, she looked up and found herself resenting the dark glasses that covered his eyes. She wanted to thank him for his concern with a kiss, but she let her smile be her message for the time being. He put an arm around her shoulders, and they picked up their skates and started over the hill toward the house.

Carly's pants were thoroughly soaked. Because Rafe was quite slim-hipped, she could resort to rolling up a well-worn pair of his jeans. Together they got dinner on the table and listened to Chopin while they ate. Rafe acknowledged the superior flavor of the macaroni and cheese, and Carly noted that he'd selected a fine ham. Carly's pie was caramelized heaven.

Since Carly's jeans and thermal underwear were draped over two chairs in front of the wood-burning stove, blocking the view of the fire, they had to look at each other while they sipped their coffee. A crescent of red waffle-weave undershirt was exposed by the two open buttons at the top of Rafe's black-and-red buffalo plaid shirt, which tapered from the broad expanse of his chest to his long, narrow waist. Built like an athlete, he'd said. He slouched in the corner of the sofa with his long legs stretched to the seat of the straight-backed chair that served as a drying rack for Carly's clothes. He looked comfortable, contented, sated.

"Why do you work such long hours, Rafe?" Carly tucked both feet under her bottom and hooked one arm over the back of the sofa. "You always seem to be working. At night, especially."

"I'm there a lot because I need to be on top of things. I've got some inexperienced men, I'm short-handed, and I'm dealing with a hefty crime rate."

"But you're working much more than a forty-hour week."

"Probably. I don't log hours." He sipped at his steaming black coffee, considering, and the shrugged. "I'm usually home by midnight, and I often take mornings off or afternoons, depending on what's happening. I like to work my horses in the morning." Shrugging, he added, "And do other things."

"Work, work, work. Why don't you just say you *ride* your horses? Horses are for fun, aren't they?"

"I do work mine. I break 'em and train 'em. Kind of a hobby, but a profitable one."

"So you even work in your spare time—what there is of it. No wonder you have such a cynical streak."

"The cynical streak has nothing to do with my work. I picked that up in the school of hard knocks and brought it to the job with me, and it keeps me from giving credit where it isn't due."

"And where it is?" she asked.

He hiked up one eyebrow and one corner of his mouth. "I've been telling you—you look good, and you cook good, and you skate just fine. I'll probably even compliment your horsemanship now that I'm on a roll."

"Tell you the truth, I haven't ridden much—recently not at all."

"Hope you brought something to wear on your feet besides those Eskimo things," he warned. Carly nodded and leaned over to test the condition of her jeans. They were dry.

Carly changed into her own clothes before she followed Rafe out to the corral. She watched him arrange the tack on a sorrel horse. His hands worked quickly, but not without pausing to rub the animal's furry chest and to pat its neck. As horses went, the sorrel was homely beside the one who stood nearby, already saddled. Irregular splashes of white on a brown coat made the paint stand out even under the thick coat of winter hair.

Carly didn't quite hear what Rafe said before he disappeared into the barn. Something about getting something. Carly's eyes were on the pretty paint. That was the horse she wanted to ride. She walked quietly to the animal's left shoulder and found the reins knotted together and draped over the saddle horn. Hands on the saddle, left foot raised to the stirrup, Carly levered herself up and swung into the saddle. The stirrups seemed short, and, oddly, the horse tensed. Its ears lay back, and every hair on the animal's body seemed to quiver just slightly.

Rafe emerged from the barn leading a bald-faced sorrel. When he saw Carly, he froze. She beamed and opened her mouth to speak, but when he held up his hand and shook his head, she hesitated. He dropped the reins on the horse he led and moved carefully in Carly's direction.

His voice was low and quiet. "Don't touch the reins, Carly. Put just the toe of your boot in the stirrup and ease yourself down from that horse."

Carly's eyes saucered. She swallowed hard and did as she was told. Once on the ground, one look at the paint's wild eye told her that this horse was not "broke."

Rafe grabbed her by the shoulders and moved her back several steps before he flung her around. "What are you trying to do, Carly? That's not a saddle horse. Nobody's been on her, and she's skittish as hell." His voice was gravely, and he spoke as though he didn't want the horse to know he was talking about her.

Carly felt utterly stupid. "They were both saddled. I thought...really? You've never been on her? Why didn't she buck me off?"

"I don't know," he sighed. "I've worked with her—gentled her some. But she's been a real live wire. This is the first time she's been saddled. She's just learning to carry it. My God, Carly. You could've gotten hurt."

"I'm sorry. Did I ruin the horse now?"

He tucked her under his arm. "No harm done. I try to break them without ever letting them buck, and I spend a lot of time gentling them before I ever get on them. This one wasn't ready, and that was a foolish stunt."

"You mean I broke a horse?" she asked, brightening.

"Not exactly."

"Let me get back on her and see if she'll just walk around a little. I'm like Snow White, you know. Animals just become tame in my presence."

"Yeah, right." He allowed himself a little smile.

"Really. I'd be careful."

"Not on your life. We're lucky she didn't bury your head in the dirt. C'mon over here. Rusty's the only horse I trust with you."

"Or trust me with?" Rusty got Carly's cocked-headed appraisal. He'd do, but that paint... "Just think, Rafe. I was the first one ever on that beautiful horse's back, and she didn't try to buck me off."

"She was thinking about it. She just hadn't figured out what you were yet. You know, you're a walking hazard—mostly to yourself. You should try a little thinking."

"I can't think when I'm being impetuous." She swung into Rusty's saddle and grinned down at Rafe. "I hate operating under conflicting impulses. Don't you?"

"Yeah." He took her foot from the stirrup and reached under the strap to adjust the length. The back of his hand brushed the front of her thigh, and his stomach tightened. "Which means I probably shouldn't hang around you."

It was a bright blue, wispy-cloud afternoon. They rode the hill crests and flats where the snow had blown clear. Carly admired the liquid flow of Rafe's body, moving in unison with the horse. After a time she felt herself bouncing in the saddle. Her legs were rapidly turning to jelly. By the time they returned to the corral, every muscle below her waist was in protest.

Rafe saw her drag her right foot over Rusty's rump, and he caught her at the waist and lowered her to the ground, chuckling in her ear. "A little wobbly, are you? I hope you've got a padded chair at your desk for tomorrow."

"Oh, dear. My legs seem to be molded to the shape of that horse." Carly laughed, surprised as she looked down that she didn't look as quivery as she felt. "It was worth it, Rafe. I won't mind being bowlegged for a while in payment for this wonderful day. Now show me how to unsaddle the horse."

"I'll get it."

"No, no, I want to learn. A good cowboy always sees to his horse first, right?"

"Right. I like you better all the time, Carly Austin. First, you hook the stirrup over the horn and get the cinch..."

Rafe carried both heavy saddles into the barn. At her request he showed Carly where to put the horses, and then he took care of the paint. Chores done, they walked back to the house together, laughing when Carly floundered on shaky legs in a drift of snow. Rafe hooked an arm around her waist. She leaned against him, feeling her breath catch in her chest.

Later, after ham sandwiches and molasses cookies, Rafe lit up a cigarette and joined Carly on the sofa. The warm coffee and the slow country music on the stereo had a lulling effect on her. She rolled her head along the back of the sofa and smiled as she watched the smoke billow away from his face.

"That's the first cigarette you've had today," she noted.

"Second. I had one when I was getting the horses saddled." He cocked an eyebrow at her, eyes dancing, and revised, "I *sneaked* one in the barn."

"Did you start smoking very young?"

He nodded, looking down at the cigarette. The corners of his mouth turned down a bit. "Like all bad boys, I got my bad habits started early. Picking them up is easy, but laying them down is something else."

"I can't see you as a bad boy anymore, Rafe. I can't believe you ever were. When I was a kid, I guess I thought you were bad, but kids never get beyond the shallows of one another. They look at each other and see reflections. They're totally self-centered. I know I was."

"You were the all-American girl." His eyes darkened inscrutably again, and then he took a deep pull on his cigarette, his eyes narrowing as he considered her through the smoke screen he'd put up. "You were Carly Austin."

"I hate it when you say my name as though it were an exclusive label in some fancy store," she said quietly, returning his measured gaze.

"God, how I wanted to be able to shop in that store. Sometimes I'd sneak into the projectionist's booth and watch you practice those plays you were in—watch you laugh when you flubbed a line, watch your occasional theatrical tantrum...watch the leading man kiss you."

"I didn't know." She imagined him sitting up there in the dark, and she felt a strange delayed remorse.

"If you had, you'd have locked your bedroom windows at night."

"I had no idea, Rafe. You never seemed to be—"

"I was damn near twenty years old and still in high school. You were years younger and everybody's darling. Even after I went to the university, I used to come back for those school plays."

"I wish you'd said something. We'd have been friends that much sooner."

Rafe crushed his cigarette into an ashtray and shrugged. "There were all those bad habits."

"Now you're down to one."

"You were way out of reach."

"How did you know that?"

His gaze betrayed no emotion. "I knew."

"I'm within your reach now, Rafe." Her plea was but a whisper, and he knew she'd offered more than he dared take.

But he reached anyway, pulled her to him, and ground his kiss against her lips. He relished the bitter-sweet taste of molasses on her mouth, swept his tongue against hers, and ran his hands over her back. Carly's hands sought the thick hair at the back of his head. She nibbled at his generous lower lip, and whimpered in answer to the opening of his mouth over hers. Rafe slipped warm hands under her sweater and rubbed little circles over her skin.

"I just want to kiss you, Carly," he whispered near her ear. The circles he was tracing on her back grew larger and heavier. "Like the leading man in your play. Don't let me do any more than that."

Her heart fluttered in her throat, and "Why?" became a dry rasp.

"Because I think I can handle kisses." He gave her lips a gentle one. "Yeah. I can handle that."

And while he was handling another one, Carly felt her bra go slack. "Damn it, Carly, that was one of the things I didn't want you to let me do," he groaned.

"I have news for you, my friend. I'm not very good at protesting too much. Don't you know—"

"No, Carly. I don't want to know." His voice was gravel hard, but the hands that moved tentatively to bracket her breasts were painfully gentle.

Carly ached. "What are you afraid of, Rafe?"

"You." He kissed her again and let this thumbs stray to her nipples, which he titillated into smooth, hard pearls. He lifted his head, letting his breath hover over her parted lips, and knew what he was doing to her. She quivered in his hands and he gloried in it.

But he stopped himself. His arms went around her, and he held her against his chest. "It's not going to work, Carly." He sighed, and she heard his swallow. "You were right. Becoming lovers would be so easy, but I've never been too good at making friends. I'm not a friendly man."

Carly made an effort to breathe normally, resting her forehead against his shoulder. ''I think we're having trouble reading each other's signals again. I took yours to be friendly.''

''Friendlier than I intended.''

Carly pulled back so that she could see his face. ''You don't trust me, do you, Rafe?''

He gave her a sad little smile. ''I don't trust anybody.''

Chapter Five

"Trust Carly to come up with a way, Todd. She'll think of something."

Donna was shouting her end of the conversation through the living-room doorway and down the hall as Carly skipped down the steps. Dressed in black tights and a long yellow-and-black rugby shirt, Donna had made the wings and antennae that rounded out her bee costume. It seemed somewhat unrealistic to see her buzzing from streamers on the ceiling to paper flowers on the tables. But on Carly's birthday, the bizarre became natural. It was Mardi Gras.

Carly's grandfather had started the Mardi Gras tradition. Her birthday was February 29, an elusive day at best, so Grandpa Austin had appointed Shrove Tuesday for Carly's birthday, and every birthday party was a Mardi Gras. There'd been no exceptions.

"A way to what?" Carly wondered.

Donna's attention and the pressure of her thumb were focused on a tack. "Todd thinks we should cover the dining-room windows somehow. I don't know, Carly, he might be right. Do you think we'll have any trouble with...Carly!" Jumping down from the step stool, Donna watched Carly float from the bottom of the stairs into the living room. As she walked layers of white froth fell from her shoulders and drifted behind her. She, too, wore wings. Large and white, they looked like something spun by a spider. A bit of gold Christmas garland encircled the top of her head, crowning her upswept hair.

"You're gorgeous," Donna breathed. "You look absolutely angelic!"

"Then I've achieved the look. Gabriel—or Gabriela maybe. Angels probably don't worry about gender. Trouble with what?"

"With people crashing the party. The dining room is all windows. We might as well have a party in a car dealer's showroom." Donna walked around Carly, tentatively lifting the delicate fabric that hung freely from Carly's shoulders. "This is unreal, Carly. Did you make this?" Carly nodded. "It must've taken yards and yards of material."

"Eight yards, to be exact. It's like the dresses I used to make for my dolls out of my mother's scarves."

"The whole town'll turn out just to see this outfit. What'll we do if we start getting gate crashers—especially kids?"

"We'll turn the kids away. Anybody else—as long as they behave themselves, I don't see any harm in—"

"Is your policeman coming?"

Carly frowned. "He isn't *my* policeman, and, no, he isn't coming."

"Didn't you ask him?"

"Yes, but he..."

The voice of the devil intruded. "Good. That means all dances with the heavenly hostess are mine." Todd drew his red cape before him with a flourish, smiling wickedly beneath his penciled mustache. There were horns and a tail and fiendishly slanted brows to complete the effect.

"Where did you ever get such awful red pants?" Carly asked, laughing at the outfit Todd revealed when he tossed the long cape back over his shoulder.

"They're golf slacks, of course. Wait till you see Al and Pete. They're Charlie Brown and Lucy."

"Allan's Lucy," Carly guessed, and she laughed delightedly when Todd nodded. She thought of tall, slender Allan Taft and short, stocky Pete Kohler, roommates who were a living cartoon as it was.

"And Mrs. Delaney's coming," Donna announced. "She said she wouldn't miss it." Sixty-five and still teaching fifth grade, stout Mrs. Delaney held her beer as well as she did her age.

The party grew quickly. They started with taped music, but Allan and Pete brought out guitars, and Mrs. Delaney, incredible as curly-locked Shirley Temple in a sailor suit, surprised the "young folks" with her fiddle music. There was rock music and polka music, and the dining room fairly jumped with dancers buffing up the shine on the newly waxed red linoleum. The punch Carly and Donna had made never seemed to run out, the color and flavor changing considerably with each new guest's contribution.

Ralph Steiner and Albert Many Bear, two of Carly's Dirty Dozen, tried to slip in with the crowd, but they didn't get past Carly's watchful eye. Charlie Brown and

Lucy turned the boys back out into the cold night despite the adamant assurances that they "only wanted to watch." Carly had had little time for food and drink until her birthday cake was served, and then there was toasting, most of it silly. Carly was beginning to feel a bit silly herself when Donna drew her toward the back door. Peering into the dark entryway, Carly recognized the tall shadow before she could see the face.

"Rafe! You decided to come after all."

"I told you I was working tonight, Carly."

"You're always working. You work too much." In a low, suggestive voice she added, "What time do you get off tonight, sweetheart?" Then she gave him a party smile.

The situation was distasteful to him, and he didn't like that bright-eyed smile. "This party is getting out of hand, Carly. I've had several complaints. You'll have to shut it down."

"Shut it down! It's my birthday, Rafe. You can't—"

"You've got this place lit up like a Christmas tree and packed with people."

"I didn't invite them all. They just showed up."

"You should have kept it closed. You're sitting in the middle of a boarding school campus, and it's Tuesday night." He listed the offenses with a cool tone.

"My birthday is always on Tuesday, and I always have a party," she said stubbornly.

"You've had your party." Her petulant pout gave him a fleeting pang of regret at having to play his usual killjoy role. Bracing one arm high on the doorjamb and cocking the other at his hip, he slipped into a softer attitude. "Look, I'm sorry, Carly, but I've had calls from a dorm matron and a school board member. We both know what's going to happen here if this goes on much longer.''

Carly sighed, glancing past the kitchen into the crowded dining room. He was right. ''Some of them are getting pretty loaded. Do you think they'll leave quietly?''

He straightened and gave her a quick wink. ''I think they can be persuaded.''

Carly followed Rafe into the crowd, watching him push past people as he headed for the stereo. After shutting the machine off, Rafe put his hand to his mouth and gave a loud, piercing whistle. The crowd wound down like an old-fashioned Victrola.

''I'm sorry, folks, but the party's over.''

''Hey, we're not causing any trouble,'' someone protested.

''That's the way I want to keep it,'' Rafe said. ''We have to comply with safety codes in these buildings, and I can see the walls bulging on this one. You folks'll just have to call it a night and move along now.''

Carly waved a few good nights and watched her guests file out. They looked like a group of scolded children. Rafe stood by quietly looking a bit too smug. She was embarrassed. She should have kept the party closed, but everyone had meant well, and she was only trying to be hospitable. She'd been pleased that so many people from the community had felt welcome to join the group. Rafe seemed satisfied with his night's work as he wished her good night and followed the crowd out the door.

He *was* satisfied. Parked at the curb not far from the club dining room's big windows, he let the Bronco's engine growl at the cold night air. He watched the residents make a halfhearted attempt at straightening the mess before, one by one, they abandoned their hostess in favor of warm beds. Yes, this was what he wanted to see—the fair-weather friends who disappeared when the fun was all over.

He watched Carly through the window as she stuffed crepe paper into a trash bag, and he thought about the way she'd looked standing by the fireplace in that crazy white outfit and watching her party break up. She was Little Bo Peep saying goodbye to her sheep. Even now he felt perversely triumphant at having taken her away from her flock. Triumph and some regret. Once again, he was sitting in the back of an auditorium, watching her on the brightly lit stage. He hated the admirers who imposed on this time with her but chided himself for being one of them. Conflicting impulses. He shut the engine off and headed back inside.

She looked up from her big green plastic bag, pleasure replacing surprise on her face when she saw him. "What did you forget?" she wondered brightly. "Your whistle?"

He stood in the dining-room doorway thinking that a casual reentry would be hard to affect at this point, but he gave it a shot. "I never forget my whistle. Just put my lips together and blow."

She laughed, delighted. "I wish I'd said that. A girl could make a name for herself with a line like that."

"Yeah," he agreed, unzipping his jacket, "and a guy could make a fool of himself making a big exit and then..." He dropped his jacket over a chair.

Carly's eyebrows elevated expectantly. "And then?"

"I don't know. I guess I hated to see you left with all this mess. Want some help?"

Carly looked around her. "Everything's going in the garbage. I guess I should take the stereo back upstairs.

The rest of the cake..." She saw that he wasn't sure why he was there. "How about some cake? There weren't any candles, and no one sang 'Happy Birthday, dear Carl-y-y.'" She sang the last off key and got a smile out of him. "Looks like that part's up to you."

He shook his head, his eyes obviously feasting on her. "Sorry, kid. I never sing when I'm out of the shower. What are you supposed to be in that outfit, anyway?"

"An angel. I had great wings, but they got in the way when I danced."

That image made his stomach do something that felt suspiciously like a cringe. He didn't want to hear about any dancing. "How can your birthday always be on Tuesday?"

"It's really February 29, so my grandfather decided it should be on Shrove Tuesday. You know—Mardi Gras. If he'd been here tonight, you'd have faced some stiff opposition."

"Not if he'd been manning the switchboard."

"Really? Did they get pretty huffy?"

Rafe shrugged. "The usual indignant pillars of the community. Wait till their kids have their graduation keggers. Then I'll be 'overreacting.' You said your grandfather hasn't been well," he remembered.

"No, he hasn't," Carly said, stiffening against the thought. "His health is fragile." Then she smiled. "But his spirit is indomitable. I'd like you to meet him, Rafe. Sometime when we're in Bismarck."

"When *we*'re in Bismarck? When would *we* ever be in Bismarck?"

"Whenever you get around to asking me for another date," she said lightly. Sobering, she asked, "Why didn't you come tonight? I really wanted you to."

"I was working."

"You could have rearranged your schedule."

His eyes flicked past her, taking in the scattered chips on the table, the discoloring remnants of dips, the punch bowl with half a bottle of gin standing sentinel beside it. "Not for a party."

"What have you got against parties?"

"I don't like crowds." *I don't like seeing you surrounded by people.*

"I suppose reformed hell-raisers make the best cops," she noted, reaching for a little paper plate. She cut him a piece of cake and watched him while he ate it. "Are you still on duty? We could toast my graceful aging. I can't vouch for the contents of the punchbowl, though."

"Genuine swill would be my guess."

"I'd offer champagne if I had any."

"I'd turn that down, too," Rafe said, finishing off the cake. "But a cup of coffee might be good."

"You really are a reformed hell-raiser."

"I came to the conclusion that booze doesn't mix well with my brain. It makes me drunk."

"It does that to most people when they drink too much."

She said that with such blithe innocence, as though the observation were elementary. He couldn't help laughing. "Yeah, well, when *I* drank, I usually managed to drink too much. So I don't drink."

"You have a lot in common with my grandfather." Carly watched Rafe shake a cigarette loose from a package. "Poor man. He had to give up smoking, too. With him it was cigars."

"I'll get around to quitting sooner or later." Rafe lit his cigarette and then held the burning match out to

Carly. "Here's your candle. Make a wish before I get burned."

Carly hesitated only a second and then blew. She smiled saucily. "Now you'll get around to it *sooner*."

"How soon do I get that cup of coffee?" he wondered, tossing the burnt match into a plate full of cake crumbs.

"Coming right up," Carly promised, backing toward the kitchen as she chattered. "If you don't mind cowboy coffee. I've had some sitting out here all night. Nobody wanted any."

Through the window, Rafe noticed the lights of a car slowing to confirm the identity of his vehicle parked outside. Somebody was taking notes. "Never mind the coffee," he said quickly, crushing most of his cigarette into an upturned jar lid on one of the tables. "Where does the stereo go?"

"It goes upstairs in my room." She moved toward him slowly, quietly adding, "It wouldn't take long to make a fresh pot."

The stereo components were already in his arms, all but one speaker, which Carly brought along herself. Though he'd never been to her room, Rafe went directly to her door at the top of the stairway. Following him, Carly indicated the spot reserved for her stereo. Together they bent to unload their burdens, then straightened, facing one another, aware of the hour, the room, the pervasive stillness, and their warm proximity to each other. Rafe's eyes transfixed her as they had a way of doing. Intimidating eyes, obsidian glass, they saw through to the soul, but betrayed no secrets of their own. Carly felt a sudden fear that he might stay, and then had a tightening dread that he might go. She was the one who broke the eye contact, glancing down to his belt buckle.

"I haven't seen you with a gun," Carly said, for no particular reason other than to prolong the moment. "Do you ever carry one?"

"Yes."

"Have you ever had to use it?"

"Yes."

"You must see so many terrible things."

"So many terrible things," he confirmed quietly.

"And the terrible side of people."

"I surely see that."

"That must be why you're so conservative."

"Conservative?" He laughed softly as he captured a piece of white angel froth between two fingers. "I used to be one of the bad guys, and now I'm one of the good guys. Don't you like good guys?"

"Of course I do, but I don't think I'd like doing what you have to do. I wouldn't want to put people in jail."

"Or break up parties?"

"Or break up parties. But I understand that. You probably saved us from a lot of embarrassment."

Rafe rubbed the soft cloth between thumb and forefinger. "I also save children from mean dogs, and get pregnant women to the hospital just in time. Although one time I didn't quite make it."

"You delivered a baby?" she asked, her voice reflecting surprise in response to the mental image of Rafe holding a slick, squalling newborn.

"The woman's sister delivered it in the back of my patrol car. I just drove. I delivered one myself once, though. I got there before the ambulance did. But that was a few years ago. Nowadays I push a lot of papers around."

"You rescued a teacher during a blizzard fairly recently," Carly reminded him. "I hear she's very grateful."

"Is she?" He tilted her face up to his with the length of his forefinger, and he brushed his thumb back and forth across her chin. "I don't need her gratitude."

"What do you need?" Carly searched his face as she waited for her answer, but there were only dark, unfathomable eyes.

"I don't need anything," he said finally. "I want her to understand that. I've found ways to meet all my needs." He watched her lips part, and he knew he didn't want to lie anymore right now, and he didn't want to hear what she was going to say, so he kissed the words away.

And Carly kissed the taste of his lie from his lips. She felt his hand slide down the side of her neck and along the top of her shoulder. The breath he drew seemed to fill her hand as it lay against his chest.

"This is some outfit," he murmured, toying with the folds of fabric that fell from her neckline. "You don't look real."

"What do I look like?" His hand had burrowed under the material again, and he found her waist.

"Something out of a Disney movie. *Fantasia.*"

"We must make quite a pair—you in your costume and me in mine."

He chuckled, lightly kissing the soft skin below her ear. "The Indian cop and the Sugar Plum Fairy."

"That's not *Fantasia*," she whispered, tremulous beneath his eager-gentle hands. "That's a different story."

"It's a fantasy, just the same." His fingers crept along her ribs by slow degrees. He found her breast, and she stopped breathing. "But this feels real," he whispered, and the kisses he peppered over her neck were as excruciatingly teasing as the fingertips that flickered over the thin fabric covering her swelling breast.

In the street below a car engine rumbled, lingering for a moment, then roared a taunting challenge, tires squealing in agreement. Rafe snapped to attention at the sound. "Damn kids," he grumbled over Carly's head. "They know exactly how long that Bronco's been parked there. This place is a giant aquarium, Carly." He drew back, smiling apologetically. "You might as well live in a zoo—sell tickets."

Carly sighed and shrugged. "There wasn't much choice. Housing's in short supply."

"Yeah," he began, taking a reluctant step back from her, "but gossips aren't. I shouldn't be up here. I'll take out the trash on my way out." He turned away, reaching for the door, and then stopped, his gaze fixed on the fistful of doorknob. "It wouldn't make any sense, Carly. It would be a mistake for both of us." Quietly spoken, those words hung in the air even after he'd left her.

Had she been adept at avoiding mistakes, Carly probably would never have initiated her research unit with the Dirty Dozen. The interview assignment yielded some interesting pieces of writing. Ralph Steiner interviewed his uncle about his beer can collection. In the one-hundred word article at least fifty were brand names. Duane Taylor wrote a fascinating piece on stripping abandoned cars. He'd interviewed his cousin, who, Carly was assured, was a real expert in the field— or by the road.

The next assignment would be conducting the survey. Carly explained that the class would choose a topic, design a survey tool, conduct the survey and tabulate the results. Above a chorus of groans, she asked the boys to brainstorm for topics while she wrote their ideas on the board. She's written their meager offerings: something about cars, popular music, drugs and alcohol.

"Come on boys, I said *brainstorm*. This is hardly a sprinkle here. What do you want to know about your fellow students? They'll be our survey population."

"How about sex?" Ralph suggested with a grin.

"You still havin' trouble with that one, Ralphie?" Frankie taunted. "Ralph couldn't figure out whether to check male or female when we took those SRA tests."

"When they ask for sex, he writes in 'Not yet,'" Duane chimed in.

"Maybe we could just survey the girls," Albert Many Bear suggested. "Ask what kind of guys they like." Ideas were rolling in now.

Frankie fired a flippant zinger from the back of the room. "If we included female teachers in our survey population, I'll bet cops would get at least one vote."

Carly responded with a good-natured smile and a gentle correction. "*Policemen* would rank right up there with poets and polo players, I'm sure." Her attention was drawn to the front row. "Duane, what are you doing?" It was a rhetorical question. She could see that he had a box elder bug tied to a piece of thread, and she knew he'd have been very disappointed if she didn't give him the chance to play out his joke.

"I'm taking my bug for a walk."

"Where did you find that in the middle of the winter?"

"He's a pet. Stays with me year round." The grin Duane flashed revealed two chipped front teeth. With his freckled nose and twinkling brown eyes, he was the image of Tom Sawyer.

"Put it away, Duane. I think we might come up with something useful along these lines. For instance, what do teenagers find attractive about..." It was somehow dismaying to see Duane squash his "pet" under his boot heel. However, Carly managed not to miss a beat before the bell rang.

As she was leaving, Carly bumped into a coworker, Ed McLaughlin. She flashed her friend a delighted smile.

"Doing anything exciting this weekend?" he asked good-naturedly.

"Not really. The crew from the club heads out early in the morning for Bismarck. We're going to buy groceries and maybe see a movie."

"That sounds like fun. Well, have a good weekend."

Have a good weekend. She would certainly try. During the week she let nothing interfere with her positive mental attitude. No teacher could afford to be without one; it was the key to success. But the missing ingredient in Carly's life became a nagging hole in her heart on weekends. That was when she missed seeing Rafe the most.

It was a hundred and fifty miles round trip to Bismarck, and the residents of the Employees' Club shared transporation for the monthly shopping expedition. It was Todd's turn to drive, with Carly and Donna the only passengers this time. The shopping chores were usually rounded out with evening entertainment, and the women had suggested a movie. Todd cast his vote for the high-school basketball game, but nothing had been resolved. They were still debating the issue as each one tugged on a handle to dislodge a grocery cart from the mass of wire on wheels. Todd's parting shot was, "I'm driving, remember," as their quest for food took three separate paths.

Backing out of the dairy case with the last two quarts of low-fat milk in the place, Carly's posterior met hard resistance. "Excuse me," she mumbled, but the body wasn't backing away as she turned, unfolding herself from her stooped-over position.

"Trying to crawl into the refrigerator, Miss Austin? I thought you didn't like the cold."

"Rafe!" He was wearing his butternut-and-cream sheepskin jacket and an off-white Stetson, a startling contrast with his jet-black hair and deeply tanned face. Surrounded by stacks of cracker boxes and sacks of cookies, he was a striking incongruity. Carly's pulse rate stripped its own gears. "What are you doing here?"

He let the foolishness of the question go unchallenged. "I ran out of macaroni and cheese."

She glanced at the cart behind him, which held, among other things, several boxes of macaroni and cheese. "Chalk dust," she said, laughing.

"You didn't leave me your recipe." His eyes flickered over the jumble of items in her basket, the things she would cook for herself, the things she would use on her body. There was the soap that made her smell lemony, and she was buying a new toothbrush, a blue one. He picked up a wedge of cheese and studied the cellophane wrapper as though the recipe for her macaroni and cheese might be printed there. "If you're almost done here, maybe we could—"

"C'mon, Carly! We're all checked out." Rafe and Carly twisted necks simultaneously in the direction of Todd Johnson's bellow. "Afternoon, officer. This girl pushing the speed limit for grocery carts again?"

"Todd, you know Rafe Strongheart..."

"We've howdied, but we ain't shook, as they say." Todd offered the unmistakable jock-in-front-of-the-camera grin along with a handshake. He pumped Rafe's arm for water.

"You're doing well with the junior high basketball team," Rafe said.

"Thanks. They're good boys. You don't mind if I hurry this woman long, do you? I'm starved."

"I'm going to see if I can talk Donna into taking my groceries home for me," Carly said, giving Rafe a corner shot with her eyes. "Rafe and I are going to stop over at my grandfather's. I don't want to hold you up, and Rafe's willing to take me home."

Rafe's hooded look didn't change.

"I, uh..." Todd's eyes darted from Carly to Rafe and back again. "You're not holding me up, Carly. You know that."

"I'm eager to meet Carly's grandfather," Rafe enjoined smoothly. "And to offer Carly a dinner she won't have to cook herself."

"So that just leaves you and Donna, Todd. You two have fun."

"Yeah, well, it should be a good game. Nice meeting you, Rafe." Todd backed away as he talked, shrugging. "I always like to see the girls home safely, but I guess it's okay to leave her with a cop. What could be safer, right? I'll wait for your groceries, Carly."

Rafe's mouth lifted at one corner. *Nice switch. I get the girl, and he's left holding the bag.*

* * *

Carly hopped into the Bronco, making no effort to suppress her satisfied smile. But the smile faded when her eyes met the flat blackness of Rafe's. "Now what?" he asked, his voice flat as well.

"Now? Now we do something together."

"I'm sure you've decided what."

The mandarin collar of her white wool coat chucked her chin, so she unbuttoned and rearranged it. Her shrug was innocent enough. "Whatever you were going to suggest when Todd interrupted."

The Bronco was slipped into reverse. Rafe's eyes slid past her on their way to the rear window. Carefully avoiding a young boy with arms full of groceries as he backed out, he said, "You're too presumptuous for your own good. I might have had something downright indecent in mind."

"If you did, you weren't going to say it. Would you mind stopping at my grandfather's for a little while? I really do want you to meet him." She focused her attention on the Bronco's square white hood, adding quietly, "Or you can just let me off there."

Rafe's chuckle was unexpected. "Is this a pout? Don't tell me Miss Congeniality likes to pout once in a while. Which way to Grandfather's house?"

It was an elm-lined street in a neighborhood of old houses, mostly pink, yellow, or white stucco. The early dusk of winter cast mellow shadows over the houses' motley colors. Carly pointed to a white one with a flat-roofed garage and a steep driveway. "Grandpa rented this house out and lived with my father and me for years. When my father remarried, Grandpa moved back here."

The Bronco swung into the driveway, tilting its nose skyward. "What happened to your mother?"

"She died, and my grandfather took her place."

"Funny," he mused, shutting off the engine. He gave her an almost apologetic look. "I figured you had all the necessary parts of a typical American family."

"Funny," she echoed. "You've never asked about my family."

Just inside the back door Carly unzipped her tall brown fashion boots and kicked them off, calling into the kitchen, "Grandpa, I've brought a friend. Can we come in?"

"What sort of friend did you bring?" The dry, gravelly voice echoed from another room.

"A gentleman friend," she shouted, and then, to Rafe, "Come on in." Her face was bright with anticipation—the child who'd come to visit Grandpa.

"The cop?" the voice wondered.

"Yes, the cop." Over her shoulder she warned Rafe, "Don't take anything he says too seriously."

Rafe expected someone tall and gray with the bearing of a decision-maker. The man who appeared at the kitchen doorway was not the man he'd pictured. Carly's grandfather was short, his gray hair neatly slicked back from his wizened face. The density of his body had fallen toward his belt, leaving his chest a little sunken. But he had the eyes of a young man, bright blue and alight with pleasure at the sight of his granddaughter. The top of his head came to her eye level when they embraced.

Rafe towered over the man, who offered a handshake as Carly offered her introduction. The old man gave Rafe an unabashed once-over and said, "First thing I'll say is that I'm glad to meet you, but you may not want to take that too seriously. Carly's told me a lot about you, mostly pretty high praise, but I don't take her too seriously, either. How about you?''

"I took her seriously when she almost frozen to death on the highway. That was very careless."

"Good man," Grandpa Austin said, patting a gnarled hand against Rafe's back. "That's your job. Carly says you're good at it. Come on in the living room. Carly'll put your coats in the front closet."

Carly took the cue to hold a hand out for Rafe's jacket. "Do I smell coffee, Grandpa?"

"You do, and you'll smell more than that soon as I get supper going." He turned to Rafe. "There's some whiskey in there if you'd like a drink."

"Rafe doesn't drink, Grandpa," Carly said quickly.

Carly got sharp looks from both men.

"The man has a right to answer the offer for himself, girl." The old man's eyes shifted to Rafe's face then and waited.

But Rafe was watching Carly, who'd reddened. It was the first time he remembered seeing her hang her head. His eyes softened. His heart stirred in her direction. "Carly's right, Mr. Austin. I don't drink." She looked up at him, and he caught the apology conveyed by her round eyes. He spoke with gentle patience. "I do like to turn it down myself, though. I've had lots of practice, and I'm pretty good at it."

Grandpa Austin put his hands in his pockets and rocked back on his heels, smiling. "Sit down, son. Carly'll get us some coffee, and we'll fry us up some fish pretty soon. You like walleye? Caught 'em myself last summer. Got 'em packed in the freezer."

"Yours will be *baked*, Grandpa," Carly put in over her shoulder on her way back to the kitchen.

The older man tossed a wink at the younger one. "She learns her lessons quick, and her spirit bounces right back. You're right, though. She takes too many chances. I haven't had a drink in twenty-four years. How 'bout you?"

"Eight."

"I've got the stuff around for my son. Offer it to company sometimes." The young eyes danced, unaffected by their wrinkled setting.

The three cooked supper together, and Rafe found himself enjoying Carly's grandfather with an ease he hadn't felt since his grandmother had been with him. The old man would have fit right in with a circle of Rafe's own people. He had a dry, understated sense of humor, and he was an inveterate tease.

"Don't set the table with that stuff, Carly. You made me buy sixteen boxes of Blue Down detergent to get those glasses, remember? Still taste the soap. Use the good stuff with the gold rings around the rims. That oughta give him an idea what we're looking for here."

Carly laughed, and put an arm around her grandfather's shoulder as he dug through the silverware, clinking forks against knives in his selection process. Her voice was a loud whisper. "Grandpa, this man's avoided gold rings for almost thrity-five years."

"That's why we use the glasses. Subliminal suggestion. They do it all the time with TV commercials. Read all about it in *TV Guide*."

"He doesn't have a TV," Carly whispered, flashing Rafe a grin over her grandfather's head.

Grandpa Austin gave Rafe his most convincingly incredulous stare. "No TV, boy? Best way to enjoy all the habits you've had to give up. Vicariously, you know."

"I read a lot," Rafe said, wondering whether he'd torn up enough lettuce for three people. "That way I can have anything I want vicariously."

"And without any risk to yourself," Grandpa Austin said, nodding thoughtfully. "Smart man. I'm living that way pretty much myself these days. Doctor says vicarious excitement is the only kind that won't kill me." Taking a handful of silverware to the table, he voiced an afterthought. "Good thing I don't live with Carly anymore. She has a way of livening things up."

"That she does," Rafe agreed, raising his voice toward the dining room. "You keep talking her up, you might get a pretty good price for her. Twenty horses at least." He watched Carly climb to the top of a step stool and reach into a high cabinet for three gold-rimmed glasses. The soft, winter-white sweater-dress hiked several inches above her knees as she reached, exposing a length of silky, stockinged leg. "Maybe twenty-five horses," Rafe amended.

Grandpa Austin stood in the kitchen doorway, grinning. "How many horses you got, boy?"

"Four." Rafe took the glasses from Carly and set them on the counter before offering her a hand down from the step stool.

"Four, huh? Well, I'm holding out for twenty-five. Got my granddaughter's honor to think of."

Dinner was easy and relaxed. Carly ate quietly and let the men talk, watching them grow to like each other. It happened almost visibly. Grandpa told fish stories, and Rafe responded to each catch with one of his own. Grandpa's interest in horses drew Rafe's attention. In his youth, Grandpa Austin had worked for a Thoroughbred trainer and had exercised race horses.

She'd known these two men would hit it off. It would have been different with Carly's father. He was a good man, but his values weren't Carly's. It was her grandfather who'd taught Carly to reach past the thorns of life and enjoy the roses. He'd taught her that the best roses weren't the ones cultivated in greenhouses and bred for show. It was the "serendipity rose"—the one you ran across by the roadside or in the middle of the prairie—that one was the sweetest. Carly had become a seeker of serendipity roses.

Rafe had a cigarette in his hand before he had a conscious thought of smoking. The coffee was on the table, the dishes pushed back, and having a smoke was automatic. Then he remembered that Carly's grandfather had had to give up smoking for his health's sake. Quickly he slid the cigarette back in its pigeonhole and tucked the pack back in the flapped pocket of his western shirt.

"Go ahead, son. It doesn't bother me anymore."

"No, I'm trying to quit. Cut down, anyway. That was a reflex."

"I know what you mean. Doctor told me if I kept lighting up those cigars I was bound to ruin my health. I tell you, I've paid that man a fortune over the years, and all he ever does it listen to my heart and tell me what I've got to give up. Well, I gave up lighting the cigars, but I carried one between my fingers for months. I still have a few around. They're old friends."

Carly reached for her grandfather's plate and stacked it with hers. "Grandpa, I'm going to do these dishes while you and Rafe have another cup of coffee. And then Rafe and I thought we'd catch the eight o'clock show," she added on her way into the kitchen.

Rafe caught Carly's glance and recognized the please-don't-object message. Following the old man into the living room and watching him ease into an overstuffed chair, Rafe knew Carly's concern. Her grandfather was exhausted. His body simply wouldn't keep up with his enthusiastic mind anymore.

"She doesn't *mean* to be careless, you know," Grandpa Austin began as though it were where he'd just left off. "She loves life, and she lives it, trusting that the world won't hurt her. There's no point in worrying about it. If she didn't stick her neck out, she wouldn't be Carly."

"She doesn't know how to calculate her risks," Rafe noted, deciding to let the old man assume he referred only to the blizzard.

"But you do," Grandpa surmised, and his eyes held an understanding that surpassed the need for any assumptions. "And I'll bet you've stuck to conservative wagers these past eight years. Remember, son, the greater the odds, the better the payoff." He winked and clucked, punctuating his assurance. "Some risks are worth taking, and some women are worth all the horses in Kentucky."

Within a few minutes the dishwasher started humming, the light in the kitchen went out and Carly glided into the living room with silent, lithe grace. Grandpa Austin watched the lights come on in Rafe's dark eyes as he drank in her every move. The old man sighed and settled deeper into his chair. This was the man to care for Carly, he thought. This man would be her rock. He'd be her gravity, and she'd be his levitation.

She went to the wall of shelves that surrounded the fireplace and selected a tape, which she slipped into a player. Soft music came from speakers camouflaged somewhere along the wall. Kneeling beside the big chair, Carly spoke quietly. "Grandpa, we're going to catch a movie. Dinner was wonderful."

"I like this boy, Carly. Like him very much."

"I knew you would." Carly planted a kiss on the loose fold of skin that drooped over her grandfather's cheekbone.

He returned the favor, patting her shoulder as he bussed her cheek. Then he pointed a finger at Rafe. "You come back and see me, son. I'd like to hear some police stories."

Rafe chuckled. "We'll have a visit next time I get up to Bismarck. My best stories would singe the delicate ears of our lady friend."

"Mine would, too." Grandpa Austin cackled. "You bring me some of that venison you were talking about and we'll trade stories."

They left him smiling, and Carly knew he'd doze off in his chair while the music drifted about his tired gray head.

"He won't forget your promise to visit him," Carly said, watching as an occasional snowflake dashed against the Bronco's big windshield.

"Neither will I. Would the venison be okay for him, you think? It's very lean."

Carly grinned and turned sideways in her seat. She had an urge to touch the two feathery flakes that glistened as they melted in Rafe's black hair. "He'd love that."

"Should he be living alone like that?"

"It's what he wants. A woman comes in to do the cleaning, and he takes care of himself very well. My father lives close by, and he sees that Grandpa has all the groceries and things he needs."

"How bad is his heart?" Rafe asked, his voice gentle.

"He's had two heart attacks. He probably wouldn't survive any surgery. I think one morning, probably fairly soon, he just won't wake up."

The traffic light ahead turned yellow. Rafe braked, easing the Bronco toward the signal as it became red. He swung his gaze toward Carly. The serene face calmly told him that her grandfather was dying. "You made your peace with that, I suppose—the fact that you'll lose him soon."

"I'll never lose him. He's part of my mind and part of my heart. I have his stories, his philosophizing, his love. I even have a mole on my back right where he has one. Only a corpse will go to the grave."

"That sounds pretty, Carly. You hang on to that and maybe..." The light turned green, and Rafe accelerated, clamping his mouth over words he knew were unnecessarily cruel. The only way to avoid losing someone you love is to avoid loving, he reminded himself. It had worked for him, but it probably wouldn't work for anyone like Carly.

"Where are we going?" she asked, realizing they were not headed west or south or home.

"To Kirkwood. You were planning on a movie, weren't you?"

They chose a comedy, which apparently wasn't going to be well-attended with only a scant twenty people scattered about the theater. Carly marched down the aisle toward her preferred place to sit—left aisle, two-thirds of the way from the back. She marched alone. An abrupt halt and an about-face. Rafe stood near the back of the theater. He tossed some popcorn into his mouth

and gave her a little come-back-here jerk of the head.
She closed the distance crisply.

"You meeting someone else down there?" he asked
quietly.

"No. I just like to get physically *into* the movie."

"I like to sit back and observe." He gestured toward
the empty row of chairs as the lights dimmed. "Wanna
sit with me, or not?"

Carly shrugged and sidled into the row. "You've got
the popcorn," she admitted, pointedly eyeing the big
paper barrel.

The movie was as irresistible as the popcorn, and
Carly laughed until her sides hurt. But while Carly
laughed, Rafe only smiled or chuckled. They stole
glances at each other when the other's eyes were on the
screen, and there was an unspoken agreement to allow
these alternating appraisals to appear unnoticed.

The color of laughter is sky blue, he thought.

Such reserve, she thought, but he can't keep his eyes
from dancing.

Then she felt his hand close over hers. The warmth of
it diffused throughout her body, and she swallowed
dumbly, watching his hand and hers slip over the arm-
rest wall and settle on his knee. Their eyes met, and he
smiled.

Carly's heart stuttered. She flushed, feeling foolish.

Rafe's eyes laughed at her. "If I buy the tickets and
the popcorn, I get to hold your hand. That's the deal on
these dates, isn't it?"

"That's the deal." His thumb teased her palm, and
she felt her stomach fishtail.

Slouching down in his seat, he swung his focus back
to the screen, murmuring, "Sounds fair."

With a heightened awareness of the hand holding hers, the film for Carly became disjointed snatches of dialogue and unexpected pratfalls. The side of her hand rested against Rafe's thigh, and her forearm drew heat from him. Tactile assessments of the length of his fingers and the hardness of his thigh were enormously distracting. By the time they left the theater, Carly's senses all throbbed in the palm of her hand.

"How did you like it?" Rafe's question seemed to reverberate inside the gray-white eggshell of a low-sky winter's night. A scattering of snowflakes drifted over the parking lot.

"What?" *Your hand? Your incredible thigh?* "Oh, the movie. I loved it! It was absolutely...absolutely *funny*. Didn't you think so?"

"Absolutely," he agreed.

"But you didn't laugh much."

He shrugged, reaching in his pants pocket for keys. "I never laugh much. Tough guys don't laugh, y'know?"

"Never?" She stepped close to him and slipped her hands into his open jacket, catching him off guard with teasing fingertips. "Not even when they're tickled?"

Rafe buckled in the middle. "Hey! Whoa!" He backed against the Bronco, stifling laughter, trying to protect his vulnerability with his elbows and fend Carly off all at once. The keys plunked at their feet as he caught her wrists. "Stop it, Carly, that's enough!" he insisted, straightening and looking around for witnesses to his moment of weakness. "Behave, now, people are watching."

"Who couldn't care less," Carly assured him. "Tough guys are always the most ticklish." Still manacled by his hands, she leaned against him. "Am I under arrest?"

"You oughta be." Unsmiling, his eyes arrested hers.

"On what charge? Illicit frivolity?"

"Being a public nuisance. You'd better hope I didn't lose those keys." He set her back from himself and bent to retrieve the keys, which glinted under the lamplight.

"Why don't we find some good dancing music?"

"Because it's snowing, and I don't dance."

"I don't dance..." She sang a choppy little tune, and he chuckled because she was flat. "And I don't laugh...don't ask me."

The door was open, and he growled, "Get in there."

The engine roared furiously at the cold night, and Carly's body shivered. Rafe reached behind his seat and drew out a folded car blanket, which he shook out and flipped over Carly's knees. "Thank you, Rafe. Tough on the outside, marshmallow underneath. I'll bet you're a good dancer, too."

"We're due for a lot of snow, Carly. If we both get stuck, who's gonna thaw you out?"

She smiled and gave him a saucy little tilt of the chin. "Maybe it's time for me to thaw you out."

South of Bismarck the snowfall became heavier, but the four-wheel-drive Bronco plowed boldly through the puffing pillow drifts. Carly talked about her grandfather, reminding Rafe that his promised visit would mean a great deal to the old man. Rafe indulged her with assurances, but he had no need of persuasion. He would keep his promise because he wanted to.

They settled into a comfortable silence, Rafe concentrating on his limited view of the road ahead, Carly letting herself be lulled by the monotonous whining and clicking of the windshield wipers. Her eyelids began to droop.

Rafe knew it was selfish, but he didn't want her to fall asleep. He wanted her with him. He was growing accustomed to her way of finishing one tale and launching into another, punctuating her prattle with sudden exclamations of wonder at things beautiful, funny, or somehow unusual. He liked the sound of her voice.

"Have you taken those hardcases of yours on any more educational excursions?" he wondered.

"Hm? Hardcases? You mean my devious dozen? I am planning something next week, weather permitting. I hope Frankie doesn't miss it. He's been pretty moody since his brother got sick. I hope he doesn't..." She glanced furtively at Rafe. "Well, I hope he doesn't try anything foolish."

"If he goes AWOL again, he'll be going to school from jail," Rafe said disgustedly.

"When did he go AWOL?"

"Several weeks ago. He managed to get a ride to Mobridge. That worthless old man of his was in the hospital."

Carly turned ninety degrees in her seat, suddenly wide awake. "It was his little brother," she insisted. "And he wasn't AWOL. He had a pass."

His glance was quick, incredulous. "*You? You* drove him to Mobridge, for God's sake? *Alone?*"

"Yes, alone. He seemed so distraught over his brother's illness, and I couldn't see...he *had* a pass."

"It was the old man who was in the hospital. Kidney damange after a fight or some damn thing. Kid must've written the pass himself." Rafe gripped the wheel, giving the road ahead a hard stare. After a moment he decided upon a controlled approach. "Carly, you're gonna get yourself fired. Worse, you're gonna get hurt. That boy *is* devious. And his father is even worse. The man has some kind of remote control over him. It won't be long before I have old Frank behind bars, and Frankie Junior seems determined to follow him.''

"You can't blame the boy, Rafe."

"I can't stop him, either. He has to make that choice.''

"Part of your job—and mine, too—is to try to help him see the choices for what they really are.''

Rafe's hardened look suddenly put miles between them. "You have no idea what his choices are, Carly. You don't know who he is or what he feels. He puts up a front for you, and you see what you want to see— what he *knows* you want to see. Don't meddle in it anymore.''

"Rafe, please, don't try to tell me how to—''

"I *am* telling you," he barked. "Don't meddle in it.''

The rest of the drive was uncomfortably silent. The snow was piling up, and though there was little wind, navigating the Bronco became increasingly difficult. Carly was relieved when the lights of Fort Yates glowed gray-white ahead of them.

"Maybe you shouldn't try to drive any farther in this," Carly suggested quietly when they pulled up to the curb at the club. "Maybe you should stay here." She caught Rafe's pointed glance and hastened to add, "Todd has a spare bed. I'm sure he wouldn't mind.''

"If I want to stay in town, I can find more hospitable arrangements than Todd Johnson's room," he clipped.

"Yes, I'm sure you can. Well, thank you for...good night, Rafe.''

Although she didn't mean to, Carly closed the car door with a loud slam. The falling snow slid past her cheeks and caught on her lashes, and as she watched the intensity of the red taillights diminish in the distance, Carly thought she hadn't meant to feel so completely empty.

Chapter Six

"**I** thought I'd make myself a b-i-i-g salad tonight." Donna's eyes widened as she spread her hands to emphasize the size of her plans. "You know—all kinds of vegetables and eggs and tuna and stuff. I can eat all the salad I want on this diet. Shall I make it double?"

"Make it triple if you can eat all you want." Carly poked at the burning logs in the fireplace with their makeshift poker—a piece of pipe. She leaned the pipe against the brick work and sipped at her glass of red wine.

"I mean enough for both of us," Donna offered.

"What I want is a huge plate of spaghetti with a loaf of garlic bread and a jug of Chianti. And then maybe a chocolate mousse. What do you think?"

"I think you're cruel," Donna groaned.

"I'm sorry, Donna. You're being thoughtful, and I'm being nasty. Maybe I'll just have the Chianti and skip the rest. I feel like drowning in..." She turned a bright-idea face on Donna, dropping in the chair next to her. Air whooshed insolently from the vinyl cushion as Carly wagged a finger at Donna. "You know what I'd like to be right now? I'd like to be an orange slice floating in a bowl of Sangria, bumping into lemon slices and lime slices and never having to say excuse me."

"What's gotten into you, Carly? You're positively morose lately."

"Mororse? I've never been morose in my life. I've never gotten drunk, either, and I just thought it might be an interesting experience." Studying the fire, she sipped at her wine again, watching the flames turn red gold as she looked at them in the bottom of her glass.

"You have a natural high. You don't need to get drunk. How 'bout that salad?" Donna urged.

"My natural high has reached a new low," Carly mumbled, ignoring the suggestion of food. "Do you realize what I've been doing, Donna? I've been chasing him. Never in my life have I chased a man. I didn't think of it that way until just now."

"How did you think of it?"

"I guess I just *assumed* that because I wanted to see him, he wanted to see me, too. I thought I was doing what we both wanted—making time to spend together."

"What makes you think he doesn't want that, too?"

"He's never called me. Not once."

"He enjoys your time together, though."

Carly looked up, amazement registering on her face. "He doesn't want to. He does enjoy being with me, but he doesn't want to. Why not? I know he's attracted to me, Donna, but he doesn't want to be. Why not?"

"Maybe he has other commitments."

"Do you think...Maxine's sister? What's her name—Carmen?"

"Oh, I don't know, probably not," Donna said on second thought. "He would have told you."

"But the other night when he let me off, he said—"

"He would have told you, Carly. He seems like the kind of man who wouldn't start up a new relationship without breaking off any old ones he might have."

Carly sighed. "I don't know if he's started a new relationship. I know *I* have. And I think he wants to. But there's something about me he doesn't like. Doesn't trust. I thought it was my background. I thought meeting Grandpa would change that, but..." She shook her head and sighed again. "He doesn't think I know what I'm doing with my students—doubts my sincerity." She frowned, folding her arms over her chest in disgust as the cloud over her grew blacker. "He calls me a *do-gooder*, of all things. Doesn't he know that do-gooders don't stick it out this long?"

Her satisfaction with this observation led her to another. "He accuses me of meddling where Frankie Fire Cloud is concerned, which is certainly *not* true. I think Rafe *does* have it in for that boy for some reason." She settled back, musing, "Maybe I've been as much of an inconvenience for him as Frankie has."

"Well, Carly, maybe you'll have to join the ranks of the average people. Most of us have been rejected once or twice."

Carly had to think about that one for a moment. *Rejected?* They were two people who were drawn to each other as surely as the opposite poles of two magnets. Lord, yes, they were opposites in so many ways. But they complemented each other; they were good together. And her need to see him, to be with him, had become compelling.

"I'm horrible at brooding," Carly said with a sigh. "What I need is a nice long drive."

What I need is to see Rafe. And what he needs is to stop denying himself what he really wants.

To the north the clouds were running across the sky in a swirl of erratic patterns, now hiding the full moon, now exposing it again. Rafe watched the sky as he drove over the frozen ruts in his long driveway. The road dipped and then angled toward the house, which became a purple silhouette against the bright night sky. A spark darted from the chimney. A little hatchback was parked by the pickup. She was here.

He parked the Bronco, steeled his senses against the impending assault, and went inside. He found her sitting on his sofa studying the fire in his wood stove. Her legs were tucked back under her bottom. Dressed in the same soft white sweater-dress she'd worn a week before in Bismarck, she looked like someone fine and fragile that had mistakenly found her way into his log house.

Turning her face into the shadow where he stood, she said quietly, "Hello, Rafe."

"What are you doing here?"

"Waiting for you. Isn't it nice to have a warm fire and a warm woman waiting when you come home? I've made you some coffee, too."

Peeling his parka off, he tried to inject his voice with some measure of patience. "Look, I've had a long day. I don't want coffee or cake or conversation. I just want to get out of this uniform and go to bed."

Her laugh was thin and taut.

He sighed. He had the feeling that no matter what he said it would be the wrong thing. "Carly, when people aren't home, you're supposed to go away—come back another time."

Shouldering his jacket, Rafe passed behind the sofa on his way to the bedroom. Carly heard the door close. Then she counted the opening and closing of each door and drawer as she lifted the bottle of Chianti from the floor and poured half a glass. She'd had two glasses before she came, and she wasn't sure why she'd brought the rest. To offend him, probably. It seemed easier to make him angry right from the start and go from there. He seemed to need to get some anger out of the way before he could feel anything else.

The door opened, and the light went off in his room. She wondered what he was wearing. "I'm still here," she said needlessly as he passed behind her again.

"I figured you would be. You say you made coffee?" The kitchen light went on. She heard no boot heels on the linoleum. "Did you get some?" he asked.

"No. I brought my own refreshment."

The kitchen light went off, and he joined her on the sofa, a half-eaten sandwich in one hand, a cup of coffee in the other. "Is that supper?" she wondered.

He nodded. "Hungry?"

She shook her head and sipped her wine.

"You figure I owe you another party or something?"

She shook her head again.

"Look, I don't care if you pass out in my living room, but if you get sick on that stuff, you're going outside."

She slid her hip to the right, letting her feet peek out from under her on the left and burying her right shoulder in the back cushion of the sofa as she turned toward him. He wore his jeans without a belt and his red plaid shirt hung open over a white T-shirt. She gave him what she believed to be a sultry look. "I have never passed out, nor have I ever gotten sick from drink. In fact, I've never been drunk."

"Good girl." He gave her an approving wink.

"But that's not to say I won't. Do you know—if you'd been on the ball tonight, you could have gotten me for driving with an open container."

He shook his head slowly and clucked. "Foolish girl. I'd have charged you, too. You know that, don't you?" She nodded. "Don't play games with me, Carly."

"You don't know *how* to play."

He eyed her over the rim of his cup. Swallowing, he concurred. "No, I don't, so I don't understand what you're doing here. What do you want from me, Carly?"

She set her glass down on the table. "I don't know why I'm drinking this," she said quickly. "I don't even want it. It tastes bitter. I guess I just...thought it would make you mad."

"Why would it make me mad?"

"Because you don't drink."

"I don't care if other people drink." He reached in his shirt pocket and handed her something wrapped in cellophane. "Here. This'll get rid of the bitter taste."

She unwrapped it and popped it in her mouth. "Butterscotch?"

"I've been chewing a lot of gum and sucking on these lately. Helps keep me from smoking."

"Have you quit?"

"Not completely. I could really use a cigarette right now."

Carly scooted closer and reached into the pocket that had yielded the first piece of candy, coming up with a second. Watching his dark eyes, she unwrapped the hard candy and slipped it between his lips. He sucked it back into his mouth.

"So what's it going to be tonight, *friend*? I've had woman friends, but you're my first *girl*friend. Did you want to run around in the snow, or break my horses, or what? What's your game plan, Carly?"

"What's wrong with doing those things?" She leaned back and waited for him to deny his enjoyment of the things they'd done together.

"Nothing. But it's late, and I want to go to bed."

"What do you do with your *women* friends?"

"I take them to bed," he said quietly.

Neither of them moved for a full minute. Carly stared hard into the fire, looking for words. Rafe unconsciously curved his fingers tightly into the palm of his hand and watched the firelight cast a burnished halo in the hair that framed her face. *Just say the word, Carly. Let me prove to myself that it's the same with you as it is with anybody else.*

"I came here tonight because I don't know where I stand with you," Carly began. Rafe leaned toward her slightly to catch every softly-spoken word. "But I know where you stand with me, and I thought I should just lay those cards on the table."

Her glance in his direction was uncharacteristically nervous. She shot to her feet, padded to the bookshelf, and whirled to face him, talking quickly from the shadows. "I know it's none of my business, but I wonder...have you been taking these women friends to bed since we've sort of been seeing each other?"

"No."

''Then why haven't you taken me to bed?''

There was a space of silence. ''Is that what you want?''

He heard a breathy sound and saw her hand come to her mouth in the shadows. ''Not unless...'' Her voice trembled, and she had to pause for control. ''What I came to say is that I'm in love with you. I wanted to tell you that because guessing at each other's feelings is not one of the games I want to play. I'm not a girl anymore,'' she went on quickly. ''I haven't *fallen* in love like a person *falls* in a hole.''

''Or over an outstretched leg,'' he injected quietly.

He was choosing not to take her seriously, just as he had chosen not to trust her. She looked down at her hands and felt a terrible emptiness. ''I've *grown* to love you, Rafe. I thought telling you that would be...easier than it was, I guess.''

His mental calculator had erred, and a wild fluttering in his chest overpowered him. He went to her and lifted her chin in the palm of his hand. ''Never hang your head, Carly Austin. You keep this pointed little chin up where it belongs.'' His hand ducked under the fall of hair at the back of her neck. Easing the tension from her neck with slow, circular caresses, Rafe touched her face with his free hand. He tested the softness of her lips with a gentle thumb, and his fingers found the crest of her cheek to be wet. Her tears stung his hand.

''You're not crying, are you? You're not going to say you're in love with me and then cry about it, are you?''

She shook her head.

He pulled her against him, slipping arms around her back. ''Good,'' he whispered, ''because I haven't had much experience with crying women, and I don't know what to do with them.''

"You're doing fine," she said, filling both hands with the back of his flannel shirt.

Her trust terrified him. "I don't know anything about love, Carly. You're the only person I know who uses that word much, and you love so many things."

"Let me love you, too," Carly pleaded, raising her mouth to the one she knew would descend for hers. It was a hard-driving kiss, lips and tongues sharing the sweetness of hot butterscotch. Rafe dragged his hands the length of her back, pressing them into the tapering V of her waist and over the soft swells of her hips. Filling his hands with her buttocks, he drew her tightly to himself and rolled his pelvis against her. He needed her more than he needed his own breath.

All senses diffused in Carly's head, darted about like moths at a lightbulb, and then plummeted, racing toward the pit of her stomach. All feeling converged where his hard body rotated against her. She moaned.

"I want you, Carly," he answered in a hoarse tone. "I can't remember a time when I didn't want you."

"Rafe..."

"Here in front of the fire. I want to see you in the firelight." He took a step back from her, holding her at arm's length. "Wait for me."

Carly wrapped her arms around herself and watched him disappear into the bedroom. *Wait for him?* She'd been waiting half the night, and longer, for him. He brought quilts from the bedroom and spread them between the sofa and the wood stove. She watched his hands, the hands that had held guns and restrained lawbreakers—the hands that had gentled frightened horses and had brought warmth back to her own frofpzen limbs—the hands that would soon touch her. She shivered and hugged herself tighter.

"You're cold?"

Standing in the shadows, she nodded. Even in the dark, the man missed nothing. He knelt before the fire to add a log, then brushed his hands on his pants before he stood and reached for her hand. "We'll make each other warm," he promised.

She went to him. He brought one arm up behind her shoulders and his other hand found her hip as he nuzzled her hair away from the tender spots around her ear. She smelled like a lemon tree—blossom-soft citrus scent, a little woody. He smiled, knowing he'd never smelled a lemon tree.

"I like this dress," he said, moving her hair to one side. The zipper buzzed along her back. "But if I'm going to warm you up, I'll have to take it off."

"That doesn't make sense," she countered quietly.

"Yes, it does. I've done it before—mentally. When I brought you in from the storm I wanted to undress you and rub your body to make it come alive again." He slipped the dress over her shoulders and pushed it down her arms very slowly.

"Would that have worked as well as a warm bath?"

"Oh, yeah...better. I had to go outside to cool myself off just thinking about it."

The dress swished past Carly's hips and plopped at her feet. He leaned back and looked at her, hovering on his next breath. "My God, you're beautiful," he mumbled, carefully running his fingertips along the top edge of her satin camisole. His eyes finally sought hers. "You look so damned delicate—like you might crumble in my hands."

"Have I before?"

"I haven't seen you like this before, looking at me the way you're looking at me now, knowing what I want, telling me you want it, too." His hands were warm on her shoulders, his thumbs tracing the breadth of her collarbone.

"I promise not to break."

He smiled, sliding his hands down her arms and taking her hands in his. "Lie down with me, then. I still don't believe you're really here for me." She followed his lead to the floor, and he pulled her across his lap. Balanced on one hip, she leaned into the cradle of his arms. "You're that snow angel who won't stay out of my dreams," he concluded, wondering at the perfection of that pink mouth.

"I'm Carly Austin," she whispered, wishing he would kiss her again.

"Not Carly Austin. I can't touch Carly Austin."

"Oh, Rafe," she moaned, straining toward his mouth, "I'll die if you don't."

His kiss was slow and lazy and hot. His tongue looked for all the places where her mouth might be hiding the candy he craved.

Carly moved one arm over his shoulder and held his back with the other. He felt hard and strong beneath the soft cotton of his T-shirt. She swept her tongue along his lower lip and stretched as she felt his hand ease its way up along the ladder of her ribs toward her breast. Brushing lightly against the satin, he made her breast swell inside its cup.

Somehow he knew, and he slipped his hand inside to unfasten the front closure, ease the tightness, and tenderly hold her breast in the palm of his hand. When he teased her nipple into a tight pucker, she groaned and arched her back, offering an open kiss. Accepting that offering, he gave more besides, his tongue dancing. He turned her into his arms and sat her up. His mouth left her last.

"This top, Carly...it's beautiful...soft... How do I get it off?"

"Over my head," she said, raising her arms like a provocative gypsy dancer. The camisole was whisked away. When he leaned toward her again, she stopped him. "I like your top, too, Rafe," she said, pulling his T-shirt up from the bottom, "but I think it poses the same problem." It came off quickly, leaving them both to admire the satin of human skin with wondering hands.

"Your skin is blue white, like..."

"You have no hair on your chest. It's smooth and..."

"Softer than..."

"Such gentle hands...oh, Rafe."

He lay her down, kissing every little shallow he could find—places where kisses should be left—at the corner of her eye, the indentation above her chin, the hollow at the top of her breastbone. Then he peeled her slip and panty hose away, smiling at the little satin panties she wore underneath all that, aroused by the length and leanness of her.

"What about yours?" she whispered, sliding a hand along the jeans over his hips as he slipped an arm under her shoulders and gathered her into his arms again.

"You take care of that...when you're ready for *mine*."

They touched as they kissed, coming to know each other inch by inch, building the heat in each other degree by degree, until Rafe dipped his head to taste the breast he'd known with his hand. Then the growing heat began to swirl, just as his tongue swirled over the cone of her breast.

Straying lower, his touch quickened a need more intense than any she'd known before. She arched into his hand, and he slipped his fingers beneath the satin cloth, into the warm nest he coveted for himself. Fingers curling in the thickness of his hair, Carly gasped his name.

"It's all right, baby," he crooned, his voice suddenly near her ear. She shuddered, burying her face in his shoulder, her chest heaving against his.

"Oh...Rafe...please..."

"More?"

She tugged at the snap of his jeans. "Lots more," she groaned, and in the end he helped her find him. And then he found her.

She was the warmth of woman waiting, and she took him inside and held him there, her body saying, "This is where you belong."

With each loving stroke his body answered, "This is where I want to be."

She was the fever of a woman needing everything a man has to give, her body insisting, "Take me with you."

With a quickening pace, his body answered, "Be with me... Be with me..."

They built the fire together, stoking its source until it leaped to a high-licking flame and sent them aloft like white ash. They hovered at the apex and then drifted together back to the quilt-covered floor.

His first thought was that he must be crushing her, and he levered himself away and rolled to his back, drained.

But Carly would have none of this separateness. Putting his arm behind her head, she applied the entire front of her body to the side of his. She found him wonderfully slippery and trailed a lazy forefinger from the heaving swell of his chest to the hard, flat plane of his belly. His skin was dewy mahogany, sleek, warm and touchable. She slid along the slickness of his side, maneuvering her mouth to the pillow of his breast, where she pressed an open kiss. The tip of her tongue tasted his saltiness, teased the small, dark nub of a nipple.

She heard a sharp breath, felt a slight quiver. "Cold?" she whispered.

"That wasn't a chilled shiver," he assured her, draping his arm over her shoulder. "That was a *thrilled* shiver."

She heard a smile in his voice, and she lifted her head to see if it were there. The underside of his chin obstructed her view, but she saw the stretched corner of his mouth. That lovely, rare smile. She reached to touch it, laying two fingertips at the edge of his mouth. The smile became a grin, and then his head came suddenly up off the floor. He tucked his chin, and she met his kiss.

"You taste like butterscotch wine," he said, chuckling as his head fell back again.

"I don't think wine comes in butterscotch."

"It does now. Potent stuff." He stretched his neck for another kiss, which she accommodated immediately. "Goes to my head faster than Southern Comfort," he said against her mouth, kissing her again.

"What are you like when you get drunk like this?"

He lay his head back in the palm of his hand, relaxing. "I've never been drunk like this," he marveled. "*Never* like this. I'll probably pay for it tomorrow, but it sure feels good tonight."

"You always worry about having to pay for whatever you enjoy," she noted quietly.

And I have paid, he thought. Surely I've paid all I owe.

"Tomorrow is Saturday." She laid her cheek against his chest. "Please tell me you don't have to work tomorrow. Even you should have a day off once in a while."

"I don't have to work tomorrow."

"Good. Then tomorrow we can play. Tonight we can—"

He cut off her suggestion, clutching her to him and rolling her over him, settling her down on the other side, near the wood stove. "Tonight we can be very close friends," he said. "I want you over here where I can see you better." Bracing his head in his hand, he leaned above her now, smoothing her jaw with the back of his hand. The firelight was kind to her skin, casting it in pale gold.

"Aren't we lovers now, too?"

A slight frown creased his forehead above his straight black eyebrows. "I don't know any more about being a lover than I do about...love."

"Yes, you do, my darling. I can attest to that." She returned his touch, stroking his angular jaw.

"I've had women, Carly, when I've had time for them. But tonight..." He couldn't explain tonight. He was afraid to look for the words.

"Tonight was different?"

He nodded. "It was different."

"For me, too."

Dark eyes sought sky-blue ones, questioning what he never would have asked. "I haven't had *men*, Rafe. There was a man some time ago—several years now— whom I loved for a time. We went our separate ways." She looked solemn, almost grave. "So you see, I didn't come to you on a whim. I'm not as whimsical as I seem. I came because I needed to be with you, and though you haven't said it, I know you care for me. That's why I had the nerve to come."

"I'm...glad you did," was all he could say before kissing her with as much tenderness as he knew how to give. His hand slipped to her slender throat, and then to the collarbones that, like the rest of her bone structure, gave her a look of such delicacy.

"Which side did you break?" he asked when he raised his head.

"Which what?" she whispered, eyes still closed.

"Which side of that little...collarbone?" His thumb and his middle finger spanned it, rubbing gently as though soothing remembered pain.

"The...left side, I think. I was only about seven. How did you know?"

"Your grandfather told me." He dropped a small, soft kiss on that left bone. "I took him some venison the other day."

Carly felt an internal rush of warmth as the image of Rafe visiting with her grandfather flashed through her mind. "I suppose he told you all kinds of embarrassing stories."

His eyebrows flicked teasingly. "He told me lots of interesting stuff. He likes to talk about his granddaughter."

"And he likes to tell tall tales."

"He'd probably kill me if he knew what I was doing right now. He wants his twenty-five horses."

"My father would *give* that much and more to see me properly married. By my grandfather knows what I'm worth."

Rafe grinned, sliding his hand over her breast. "I don't think so, baby. I don't think he's got any idea what kind of a price he could get for you."

Something burrowing under his armpit roused Rafe from sleep. For a moment he couldn't get his bearings. He swallowed furiously at that insidious, familiar fear. His head thrashed to his right, eyes wide, and the floor registered itself. To the right was the wood stove, fire out. Something stirred against him again, and he stiffened, dropped a hand over it, and found Carly. Several deep breaths helped him relax. His house. His floor, His...woman.

At least for now. She'd come to him. She'd wanted him. She'd said she loved him. But then Carly had no trouble loving. She loved a thousand things. He made a thousand and one.

She moved again, and he ran both hands along her. God, she felt cold. He'd pulled up a quilt, but her skin was cold. He didn't feel like starting another fire. She'd be warmer in his bed.

So he carried her there. She was a wisp of straw in his arms. When she woke to question the move, he whispered, "We're going to bed now, baby. It's warmer in bed."

"Time is it?" she murmured against his chest.

"It doesn't matter."

He had to lower her feet to the floor while he flipped the covers back, and she leaned against him with unconscious confidence. He tucked her in on one side and cralwed in next to her from the other.

"Rafe?" she mumbled, snuggling against him.

"Yes." He pulled her closer. "I'm right here."

"I love you, Rafe Strongheart. I really do."

"I know."

Carly found herself in a snug tunnel of covers bounded on one side by a hard wall of male chest. She wriggled a little closer, enjoying the feeling of waking up warm in bed. The arm that was draped over her waist tightened possessively.

"Good morning," he intoned over her head.

"I think so, too."

"You should have been born a prairie dog or something. You're a burrower. Is that a word? *Burrower*?"

"Probably." Undulating against the bedclothes, Carly stretched, surfaced, and smiled at the morning-soft face of the man she loved. "Some women are nesters. I'm a burrower. Hi, friend."

"Hi, friend." His eyes were liquid chocolate, warm and sweet. She'd never seen them that way.

"I'm usually cold. This niche in your arms is the warmest place I've ever slept."

"Sleeping next to you seems to drive my body temperature up," he noted. Carly grinned and hooked an arm over his neck, squirming up a little higher. "Uhh," he croaked. "Except when you get me with those cold feet. Good Lord, woman, what's wrong with your circulation?"

"Cold feet, warm heart. Shall I make some coffee?"

"Mm-hmm." She moved, but he held her, adding, "Later. First I wanna kiss an angel good morning."

His lips were warm and wet and flavored with butterscotch. "Mmm," she purred. "Candy before breakfast?"

"Better than a cigarette. Want another taste?"

They luxuriated in the lazy kisses and the lingering touches of two who'd come to know each other well and liked all they'd learned.

He pushed the covers down and cupped his hand over the curve of her cool shoulder. "Your skin is cream."

"And yours is coffee." Smiling at the pale fingers she splayed over his chest, she added, "There's really no need to get up, is there?"

"Not if we put us together."

Her lashes did a seductive flutter over bright blue as she rolled him to his back and herself over him. "I think the cream must be added to the coffee."

"Mmm...yeah. What a fool I've been, taking mine black all these years."

"It has to be stirred." Chest to chest and belly to belly, she rocked against him in slow circles. "Do you like being stirred?"

"It feels great to be stirred."

His hands were a warm current that swished up and down the length of her back as his body responded beneath hers. They settled over her hips, and he said, "Lift up, Carly. I want my cream from the source."

She braced herself above him on her arms and gave him access to her breasts. He suckled. She shivered, and she sighed. The heat between them grew moist and sultry. His lips moved to her shoulders and the curve of her neck, and his breath was hot against her. His hands held her hips against the rhythmic surging of his, and he whispered, "Is your body ready to drink from mine?"

She burned deep inside and needed more than anything to drink from him. "Yes...ye-e-es."

Done together, the morning rituals of showering and dressing became little pleasures in themselves. Morning chores, done together, were unlike the chores they'd always been. A fifty-pound bag of horse feed came out of the big, hinged storage box like a pillow. Rafe laughed at Carly's attempts to keep the sleeves of his big sheepskin jacket pushed back enough to allow her hands to fill the feed bucket.

Oats and corn flew from Carly's scoop when a big yellow cat leaped up to the edge of the box. "Oh! You scared me, kitty. I didn't know you had a cat." She scratched behind the cat's ears and drew a low rumble from its throat.

"I don't. Rusty has two of them."

"Rusty?"

Rafe nodded with a little pucker of his lips toward the sorrel. Carly shot to her feet with a delighted giggle, not so much a reaction to his teasing, but to that peculiar gesture. She caught his square chin in her hand and forced an exaggerated pucker with her fingers. "You find this lip position quite useful, do you?"

"Quite useful." He took her hand away and warmed it in his as he kissed her alluring smile.

On the way back to the house she pelted him with snow, darting around him and managing to land some in his hair. He played along until it went down his neck. Then he caught her, flung her over his shoulder, and carried her into the house.

It was fun to make pancakes for breakfast, something Rafe never made for himself. He didn't have syrup, so Carly improvised by heating jelly. The coffee was good, but he assured her it couldn't compare with the first coffee of the morning. She brought the glass server to the table and offered a refill. He chuckled, offering the same. Catching her free hand, he pulled her to stand between his knees.

"You like wearing my pants," he asked, filling his hands with her slim hips. She had tied the bottom of his T-shirt in a knot over one hip, and she wore a blue plaid flannel shirt over that. "Maybe I should give you a pair."

"Keep them here for me. I might need them again."

"You just might." He pushed the T-shirt up and slipped his fingers just inside the big waistband of his jeans. "They don't fit very well."

She set the coffee server on the table and rested her hands on his shoulders. "They would if my waist were the same size as my hips."

"But fortunately it's not." He made a belt around her middle with his hands, bringing his thumbs together in front. Then he laid his head against her belly, putting his arms around her to hold her to him.

His sudden tenderness was irresistible. Carly stroked the jet-black thickness of his hair and said the words that were, for her, a monumental statement: "I love you, Rafe."

He turned his face to her belly, and she felt a soft kiss.

"Do you believe me?" she asked quietly.

"Yes."

"But you don't put much stock in it, right?"

He tilted his head back and gave her a soft, sloe-eyed look. "I told you, Carly, I don't know what it means. If it's what brought you over here last night, I'm glad for it."

"What we've shared is special to you. I can see that, Rafe. You can't hide that from me."

"It's important to me, and I'm not hiding that from you."

She sighed, eyes closed, her fingers still laced in the back of his hair. "I wish you could trust me, just a little."

Rafe drew a long, deep breath, then moved her a step back and came to his feet. He took her hand and led her to the door across from his bedroom, the one he always kept closed. Wordlessly, he opened the door and led her inside.

He stood in the middle of the room, thumbs tucked in his belt, while she moved slowly among the canvases that leaned three and four deep in stacks against the walls. Much of his work reflected Indian themes and used geometric shapes and vibrant color. Some were straightforward statements of motion—movement and changing movement. Some of the work was angry, and its intensity shook her. Beyond, however, was a deeper confusion and a sense of loss.

"Rafe...this is—"

"Don't say anything, Carly. No one sees these because I want no judgments on them—no approvals or disapprovals. They simply are what they are."

"But people *should* see them. They're too good to..."

He shook his head. "This is something I have to do for myself. I won't be stripped in public."

Carly held a painting at arm's length. A group of Indian men were dressing for a dance contest. One rested his foot on the bumper of a dilapidated green sedan as he tied a beaded moccasin. Another leaned on the hood of the car, the feathers of his bustle fanning behind him in a splash of blue, yellow and red. Here was the contemporary powwow—its incongruities and its riot of color. "I don't have to tell you how good this is," Carly said. "You know it's good."

"Yes. I know it's good."

"It speaks of you...the part you guard so jealously."

"And you're not to *speak* of it to anyone else."

"Of course not. This is yours to share as you choose."

He took a large portfolio down from a shelf. "I *choose* to share it with you. These are watercolors. You'll find them to be very different from the oils."

Indeed, they were softer. They were studies of small things—leaves and berry bushes and birds and prairie dogs—and there were muted prairie landscapes abloom with yucca and prickly pear or swept soft with snow. And there was an old Indian woman whose gentle eyes found no fault with the paper her grandson presented her.

"You chose to share them with her, too," Carly said.

"Yes." He remembered being a six-year-old boy who'd presented the old woman with a paper smeared with purple paint in which his small index finger had made unidentifiable pictures of things he liked. "I paint dreams and visions and things that won't leave me alone unless I put them on canvas or paper."

Carly looked down at the old woman and the boy, and she swallowed hard at the burning in her throat. He did know the meaning of love. Words simply were not his medium.

"Is this door open for me now?" she asked quietly. "May I come in here sometimes...just to look?"

"You don't harbor any ambition to be an art dealer, do you?" There was a warning couched in his jest.

Sliding the crinkling sheets back into the portfolio, Carly answered quite seriously. "No. I want to look at them just for myself."

"For your eyes only, then," he said, and he smiled when he took the portfolio back. "Wanna take a ride this afternoon?"

"I'd love to. Where are we going?"

"Ever been to Bullhead?"

"No. What's there?"

"Roots, I guess. Some graves, and a little house. I was born there." He was putting things away now, and she watched every move, as though he were taking things away that she didn't want to give up. "You might want to put your dress back on. There's a feed at the community center. There'll be some dancing and a giveaway. They're honoring a local marine who's going overseas."

She nodded and then looked down into the studio once more before she closed the door. "Rafe," she said, taking in one more sniff of paint and linseed oil. "Is it Raphael?"

"Raphael David Strongheart. Hell of a name, isn't it?"

"Yes. You have quite a name."

Chapter Seven

The tiny community of Bullhead was nestled in a soup-bowl valley. Rafe pulled over to the side of the road at the rim of the bowl and let the Bronco's engine run. This was the town's best side. From here it looked like a postcard. The sun slanted across the hills, spinning gold in grass stubble and snow.

From here they could see the little rodeo arena and the circular pole frame for the bowery, where pow-wows would be held in summer. A little frozen river twisted around the town like a pale ribbon that lay as if it had just fallen from a child's hair. From here, there were no small houses; there were tiny colored boxes. From here there were no roads, no children without winter jackets, no sad-faced old people.

"Everyone who teaches at the boarding school in Fort Yates should visit Bullhead at least once—and Little Eagle, Wakpala, Cannonball—all the districts,"

Rafe told Carly, his eyes scanning the valley without readable expression. "New housing going up." His chin and his lips pointed to the south. "I suppose that'll be Bullhead's version of 'uptown.' Some federal program—HUD, I think. But you look at the little three-room houses there in the center of town. That's where your students came from."

"And you?" She wondered now whether this was homecoming for him or some kind of catharsis. She saw no sign of anticipation.

"We lived in the country. I'll show you the house later. But this was uptown for me until I was about nine years old. After my grandmother died, I lived here in town with an uncle for a while. Then I started playing musical foster homes."

Carly thought it strange that he should say that. It seemed a bid for something. Sympathy? Not Rafe. "Are you telling me this is where you really come from?"

"I'm a different breed." He shifted the Bronco into gear and eased out onto the road. "I started out here, and then fate decided I should see both sides."

Yes, he'd seen both sides. It showed in his paintings. He had vision, and knowing what he did of both worlds, he lived with the knowledge that he, alone, could do little to change things. "And you can't go home again," she assumed, knowing she couldn't either. She wasn't *their* Carly anymore, but only Grandpa understood that. Only Grandpa knew who Carly had become.

"I've worked every reservation in the northwest," Rafe reflected. "I swore I wouldn't work my own—not as a cop. But they needed me, and I knew there wasn't anyone else, and I came."

"Do you speak Lakota?"

"I thought I'd lost it, but it's come back to me. You don't hear it much in Fort Yates anymore, but the people out here in these isolated districts—they use it." He pointed to the right. "Downtown Bullhead. Store, post office, gas station all in one building. Couple of churches, elementary school, community building— that's it. The first time I saw a shopping center, I was terrified."

In her mind's eye Carly saw him, standing alone, surrounded by people in too much of a hurry to notice the young boy, and she felt that fear prickle in her own stomach for just a fleeting moment. It was a strange feeling. She'd known sympathy, but this wasn't that. It was *empathy*—a moment of real fear of not being accepted.

In her adventuresome career there had always been an enclave of teachers who brought their lives with them, much like the group in the club. They were there by choice, and they would leave when they chose to. Carly had come to her job knowing what was needed, bringing it with her, making the offer. The question of whether the people in the community accepted Carly simply had not troubled her. She had always been accepted—as far as she knew. *Here I am—Carly Austin. Now, boys and girls, with just a little work, a little education, you can be just like me.*

Now she would listen. Now she would learn. She would see through Rafe's eyes, the eyes of one who'd been a child without any choices.

The Community Center was the social hub of the little town. It seemed as if a lot of people fit into the small building. Rafe greeted some people in Lakota, others in English, all with a nod of the head and few words. He

introduced Carly to several men and women whom he
referred to simply as "my aunt" or "my uncle," and it
became obvious to her that the introduction was
enough. She was not expected to make small talk with
these people. A stern-faced woman indicated two empty
folding chairs, and Rafe and Carly sat down.

Without any understanding of the language, Carly
surmised that the speeches were in praise of a young
man with shorn hair, wearing a stiff-collared uniform.
He sat between his parents, all three solemn-faced and
dignified. There was no program, but three men in
VFW uniforms seemed to preside over the proceedings. People came forward to speak as the spirit moved
them. In one corner of the room stood a large drum
surrounded by men with big bellies and long, fleece-
wrapped drum beaters. Periodically they would punc-
tuate something that was said with a couple of booms
on the drum.

Carly recognized the young men preparing to dance
from Rafe's painting, not by their faces, but by the
feathered finery they wore. There were four of them,
each with a double fan of colored feathers attached to
his back. Porcupine quill roaches were perched on their
heads like cock's combs, and bells, fastened at their
knees and ankles, jangled with every movement. These
were "fancy" dancers, Rafe explained, and the single
"traditional" dancer was the one whose bustle of natural pheasant feathers and beaded buckskin reflected
the old style.

There were two young women, dressed in red and
royal-blue satin dresses, shawls with long fringe, and
bright, beaded leggings. The dancing was a kaleido-
scope of color—feathered Ferris wheels and spinning
centrifuges of shawl fringe. The singers' voices sounded

low in their throats, rose through their noses, and became the baleful wail of the wind. And always there was
the drum, a steady rhythm, the heartbeat of man.

The dancing stopped. Gifts of quilts and blankets
were then presented to a number of people, whose
names were called in succession. There was no fanfare,
no speech, no thanks—just a handshake with the young
Marine and his parents. Rafe's name was called, and he
received a star quilt, a burst of red, yellow and orange
cotton pieced together in one great star. Carly watched
the solemn proceedings, remembering Rafe's discus-
sion of respectful handshakes.

Honoring songs came next. The drum music accompanied a slow procession of the Marine and his parents
followed by dancers and guests. In his turn, Rafe
handed some money to one of the drummers in spon-
sorship of a song.

Through it all, Carly watched, quelling the urge to
ask a string of questions. When food was served, Carly
waited in line with Rafe for soup and frybread, potato
salad and fried chicken. Most of the guests had brought
their own tin plates and bowls, but there were paper
plates for the few who were unprepared.

Now there was visiting, and there were more intro-
ductions. Carly remembered not to press her handshake. Giggling children raced among the folding chairs
and snatched pieces of food from the serving table. The
combination of Lakota and English teased Carly's curiosity. She understood enough to keep her attention,
but missed each point and punch line.

"Now's your chance to dance with me," Rafe offered, taking her hand.

Carly saw that only a few couples joined the cos-
tumed dancers in the middle of the room, but she was

delighted for the chance to participate. She flashed a bright smile up to Rafe. "Show me the step."

"Very simple. Two steps forward, one back, in time with the drum."

"A two-step!"

"Rabbit Dance," he countered. He indicated with crossed wrists that she was to cross hers, too, and take both of his hands. They danced abreast, moving gradually about the room in a solemn circle. The heavy drum beat stirred the blood. Later they joined in a Round Dance, becoming part of one circle, which, as in folk dances from across the world, symbolized communal unity, the circle of life. Carly directed her smile, bright with enjoyment, at each person in the circle opposite her, and it was returned in kind. One older man raised his eyebrows over a knowing grin and did an extra-fancy little shuffle, which Carly tried to imitate. Then they laughed with one another across the circle, and Carly felt Rafe's hand squeeze hers.

When they left, Carly's head was swimming. For a time she said nothing. She hardly noticed that they'd left the main highway and were bumping along a roller coaster track of road. They stopped at a post-and-wire gate.

"I'll get the gate. You drive through," Rafe suggested.

Startled out of her revery, Carly clambered into the driver's seat. There were three such gates to be traversed before they reached the small log house that stood in a grove of cottonwoods. It was river-bottom land, though the river here seemed too narrow to deserve the name. In spring it would be a different story, and the house stood a respectable distance away in deference to that fact. Now in late winter's pink-streaking blue-gray dusk, the house stood stark and quiet in the shelter of bare trees.

Rafe took out a key and opened the padlock on the simple hardwood door. The step over the threshold was like a step back in time. Carly stood just inside the door while Rafe went to a small wooden table and lit a kerosene lamp. Then he set to work building a fire in the little potbellied stove. Wide-eyed, Carly crept to a doorway, craning her neck through the opening. If there were ghosts here, she wanted to see them before they spotted her.

The other room was a tiny kitchen with cupboards, dry sink, and an old-fashioned wood-burning cookstove. A window over the little kitchen table was boarded up. Turning back to the main room, Carly continued to assess: a metal frame bed with a mattress, but no bedding, a small sofa, the table with the lamp on it, a steamer trunk. The house smelled of earth and wood. She looked down at the floor, then knelt to touch it.

"Rafe, this is—"

"Dirt. Hard packed. You sweep it, it stays clean."

"And the bathroom?"

He closed the door on the stove and stood, brushing his hands against his thighs. "Out back. It'll warm up in here quickly now." Then he flashed her a light-going-on-in-the-brain look. "Oh. Here's the flashlight if you want to..."

She shook her head, smiling. "Just checking. Rafe, this is absolutely...it's absolutely nineteenth century."

"It's twentieth century Standing Rock," he assured her, taking her hand, drawing her to the sofa. "When I first came back here after I took this job, I found it still standing, which surprised me. But the sod roof had caved in. Seeing it like that—it came back to me then. I remembered feeling that way after she died. I felt just like that roof."

"After your grandmother died?"

Rafe leaned forward, planting his elbows on his knees, and he stared ahead. "Yes, my grandmother. I was so damned young. I'm surprised I even remembered."

"I'm not."

He said nothing for a moment, the memory, the vision too vivid. Then he snapped his head back, chasing at his thoughts with a sigh. "Anyway, I put a new roof on it, cleaned it up, replaced a few things. Great hunting out this way. The place is mine. Why not make use of my inheritance, right? I come out here to hunt."

Carly rolled her eyes in an arc from wall to ceiling to wall, whispering, "It's like being in a time warp."

He gave a short laugh, laying an arm behind her along the top of the sofa. "Much of the world's population, living without electricity and running water, would say you were exaggerating, Carly Austin." He gave her chin a little tap with his forefinger. "This is the lady who's seen it all?"

She glanced away. "Being with you makes it different somehow."

Rafe studied her soft profile, running his gaze from the top of her hair to the tip of her chin and back to her downcast eyes. What was she thinking? What seemed different? Did he seemed different to her now? Or did she see the differences between them more clearly, and did that make all the difference? "What did you think of the party?" he asked quietly.

She wasn't sure she wanted to answer that. She was confused. But, being Carly, she was open about her confusion. "When I was in Alaska, I went to celebrations, watched dancing, admired the costumes. But I always went with a group of teachers. We watched—we ooed and ahed..." Her eyes darted away and then back to his. "We were like tourists, weren't we? That's why I didn't feel like an outsider then. It was like going to a movie."

"And today you felt like an outsider?"

"I wanted to be part of it this time, not just a watcher, but I didn't understand much of what was said. I didn't fit in—except when we danced. But then, you didn't exactly fit in, either."

In the flickering shadows cast by the flame, he saw that she understood now. In the yellow glow of the gaslight, his eyes told her, yes, it's true. You can't go back.

"If I fit in, I couldn't do my job. I'd lose my objectivity." He shrugged out of his parka and tossed it behind him on the sofa. "I have to sit back from the screen. And you—you get as close as you can and imagine you're right there in the thick of things. But the screen's still there, Carly. You're safe. There's still a place for you uptown."

"And there's a place for you, too," she realized. "Here—uptown—wherever you want to make it. You're not stuck here, any more than I am. You're here because you want to be."

"That's true. But I don't make any pretense of being part of the community. I have my job and my house and this haunted cabin."

"And you use them all to set yourself apart," she observed. *But not from me.* She lifted her hand to touch his smooth jaw.

"Maybe." Her soft eyes forced a smile at one corner of his mouth. "I can't afford to lose my objectivity."

"The objectivity is there in your paintings, but the empathy is there, too. Did you study art in college?"

"Um-hmm. Took all I could get. Here, let's take this off." He was dispatching the buttons of her coat with one hand. "It's already warm in here."

"The color and motion of those dances—you captured that so perfectly in some of your paintings. The dancers are..."

"Peacocks confined to a zoo. That's what they remind me of. Things meant to be wild." He perused her face as he slipped the coat behind her shoulders. She, too, was a thing meant to be wild. She'd flung open the doors to her gilded cage long ago. Ironically, it was he who was the settled one, set in his ways. Her face was open, waiting.

He shrugged, deciding on a metaphor. "Every time I see a pheasant lying on the road, I think 'He had wings. What was he doing *walking* across the road?' And then I remember those wings don't take them very far. And it's hard to avoid roads these days. So they strut across the road as though there wasn't any break in the grass at all. You protect yourself as best you can, but there's a primal memory of wildness, and every once in a while you have to try to recreate a piece of it."

Carly nodded. "Controlled wildness. We kill things off until they're almost gone, and then we say, 'Hey, wait a minute. Pretty soon there won't be any more of these. We'd better save what's left.'"

Rafe patted his shirt pocket, where weeks ago there would have been cigarettes. He caught himself and chuckled. "Old habits are hard to break. But we keep the vestiges of the old ways around—the feathers and the drum—so we can take them out and look at them once in a while. We know they were once connected with something important, but damned if we can remember exactly what it was.''

''Oh, that drum, Rafe—you don't have to *remember* anything to understand that. You *feel* that drum. It's the human heartbeat, and the connection crosses time and space and culture. Could there be a drum at the center of the earth, do you think? A pacemaker for all of us?''

He slid down and dropped the back of his head against the sofa, rolling it back and forth. ''There's no going back, Carly. Things change, and you can't go back to where you were before the changes came. I remember being part of something once. Even that doesn't exist anymore.''

''Yet you keep this place the way it was.''

His head rolled in her direction. ''For the one vestige of wildness in me. I use it for hunting.''

''That's not all, my friend.'' She touched his square chin with a forefinger, returning his gesture of a moment past. ''This is your connection with the past. There are vestiges of other things here, things you don't want to lose.''

Rafe caught her wrist. She was making him out to be some sentimental fool. ''I come out here three or four times a year to hunt.''

''Why did you bring me here?''

''There are things I thought you needed to see.''

''Can't you say that there are things you need to share?'' Her eyes were hard blue crystal, glinting in the gaslight. ''Can't you tell me that you wanted to share this with *me*?''

He sat up. He gave himself the advantage of looking down at her. ''I don't want to share poverty and isolation with anyone, Carly. I just wanted to open your eyes."

"My eyes are open. You're not poor, and your isolation is self-imposed. You brought me here for the same reason I took you to see my grandfather. It's part of you."

Her words were quietly clipped, and he almost laughed at her. "You're seeing things that aren't there, Carly."

She caught his face in her hands. "You're here. I want to see you. I want to know you. Every bit of you fascinates me—past, present and future."

"There's only the present," he insisted. But he was drawn. He was leaning closer.

"Share that with me, then. Make love to me...here."

His mouth came down in angry pursuit. But she was too soft, too vulnerable. As he kissed her the anger melted away. He luxuriated in long moments of kissing, just kissing. Then he entreated, "Stay here with me tonight."

She tightened her arms around his neck, smiling. "If you're not leaving, I guess I'll stay with you. I can't see myself walking back."

"I'll take you back if you'd rather."

"I want to stay."

They got blankets from the Bronco—the quilt he'd been given and the two blankets he carried throughout the winter—and they put them on the bed. For light he pried the boards off the two front windows. Then, with flashlight in hand, he took her for a walk. He pointed out the places she knew to be his best memories, places preserved in the cold, blanketed by snow.

The starry, black velvet sky was as timeless as the little log house with its smoking chimney. It was as timeless as a man and woman, walking with arms about each other. It was as timeless as a favorite climbing tree, a sandy knoll, a place in the river where it was shallow enough to wade when late summer slowed the current. And, like all women who love, Carly cherished every vision of her man as a young boy.

Rafe pointed to a little hill, and there time became immaterial. There, enclosed in a little chain-link fence, were the graves of Rafe's mother and his grandparents. A brother was buried there, too, and Rafe would say only that he died very young.

Rafe added wood to the stove, and Carly hung her coat on a peg, wondering at the efficiency of the little wood burner. The cabin was toasty. The soft white light from the windows and the dim yellow light from the lamp cast long shadows across the floor.

She stood in front of one of the little windows, and he came up behind her, slipping arms around her waist. The knit dress accentuated her slimness. "Hungry?" he asked, laying his chin against her hair.

"No."

"Good. I've got nothing to feed you. I'll take you to McLaughlin first thing in the morning for breakfast."

"First thing?"

He drew his hands up her arms and gripped her shoulders for a moment. "Among the first things." The zipper descended the middle of her back, and then the dress. "Mind if I undress you now?"

"Be my guest."

It was a gradual unwrapping, a whisking away of satin tissue paper, a search for a precious gift. Bared to the waist and bathed in winter starlight, she was blue-white dresden. She was a figure too delicate for a man's hands to touch. But his lips and his tongue were soft enough, and they loved the taste of star-glow on citrus-orchard skin.

Carly's breath caught when his kisses reached her breasts, and she used that breath for all it was worth, unable to exhale until his trail of kisses wended its way to her midriff. He was on his knees in front of her, snatching her slip away and then rolling the rest down her legs—the nylon, the satin—all of it at once. He kissed her stomach and then nestled his head on its soft roundness.

"My grandmother would laugh at this little body of yours, and then she'd try to stuff it with frybread and molasses cookies," he said, finding her small, round buttocks in his hands and kneading gently.

"And you?" she asked, her voice husky.

"I'm not laughing." He turned his face to her belly and nuzzled. His tongue dipped into her navel, and she braced her hands on his shoulders, groaning. "Be patient," he whispered. "I know how to take care of you."

His kisses fell, and he moved her thighs to make way for their descent. The world went soft for Carly. Her legs went soft, and she swayed, unsure of her footing. Then his tongue touched her softest secret, and her mind melted on the utterance of his name.

He lifted her into his arms and whispered into her hair. "It's crazy, but I've always wanted to do this."

"What?" Head against his chest, she suddenly realized that he was fully clothed, and she was fully naked.

"Carry a quivering woman to my bed." He laid her in the shadowy corner of the room on the quilt he'd been given that day. The pearl snaps on his shirt opened quickly beneath his eager hands.

"Carly's never quivered quite this way," she assured him. Watching him shed his shirt, she rose to her knees, muttering, "This is something I've always wanted to do." She unsnapped his jeans and offered a seductive smile up to him as she dragged his zipper down.

Rafe's grin was delightfully wicked. When she touched him, he bore it only a moment before he growled, shucked his pants, and enveloped her in a passionate embrace. Unhurried exploration gave way to urgent fondling and hungry kissing. She undulated beneath him, wanting to be filled with him, but he kept himself just beyond her reach. His need was great, but he wanted hers to be desperate.

She ached for him, arched to him, and he met her with hands and teeth and tongue, and all that was just short of what she needed. He filled himself with the taste of her, the scent of her. She called his name, but that wasn't enough. He would hear more than his name from her.

She clung to him, hands full of the flesh of his back, and she growled deep in her throat. "I need you, Rafe. I need you inside me, deep inside me."

And he was there on a thrust of quicksilver, mixing his passion with hers. On a gulp of air, Carly drew the moment into the core of her brain—the earthy smell of the cabin, the quick sound of Rafe's breath, the pressure of his body on hers, and the flurry of sparks deep inside her. She had a fleeting mental picture of passion as matter—a hot, combustible liquid. And then her passion exploded with his in the dark.

Carly woke to a half-empty bed. There were no pillows, and she'd somehow managed to become cocooned in blankets. She rolled her head toward the room's light source—the fire in the little wood burner, which stood with its mouth open while a naked man fed it fuel.

The fire fed, he sat back on one heel, his forearm draped over a thigh. His face was bathed in red-brown warmth. Black hair fell over a corner of his forehead, and flames flickered in his eyes. Primal man—fire provider, hunter, protector. Potential energy. Power in repose. A statement of possibilities, both beautiful and dangerous.

When he started to rise, she stopped him with a sleepy command. "Stay there a minute. I want to take a picture of you."

In the shadows he could see her braced on an elbow, her lion-colored hair all atumble about her face and shoulders. His mouth widened in a smile. "A picture like this could be very incriminating."

"It could. But I don't want to incriminate you. I just want to remember you this way. I wish I could paint."

"Maybe you'd like to pose for me," he suggested, closing the door on the stove and plunging the room into darkness. He moved silently, but she knew he was coming to her.

"Since no one sees your work, I guess my secret self would be safe on your canvas." She held up the blankets for him when the weight of his knee made the bed creak. "But when you die and become famous, I'll be exposed."

He gathered her against him, pillowing her head on his shoulder. "When I die and become famous?"

"Great artists aren't appreciated until they're dead. Then your paintings will be unveiled, and the world will wonder about the beautiful lady wearing a satisfied smile and nothing else." Hooking a leg over both of his, she snuggled into his side. "You will make me look beautiful, won't you?"

"I already have. I've given you the satisfied smile."

"Mmm, yes. But you could add a little cleavage, give me smaller feet—maybe with an arch so I can wear frivolous shoes—pinch my waist in a little."

"I can take care of that right now." He did, and she squealed. "How 'bout if I shorten your nose, too?" Another pinch. "And take about an inch off your bottom?" She shrieked in protest.

He hugged her to him, and she gasped, "Could plastic surgery be this much fun?"

"Only when it's done by an artist," he assured her, and even in the dark, she knew he was grinning. "I do great mouths. Want me to rearrange that silly little mouth of yours?"

"Silly little mouth!"

"Mm. Come here." He cupped the back of her head in his hand and leaned over her for a kiss. "This lip down here..." A brush of his tongue indicated the lower one. "Too round, too pink." A slow stroke traced the outer edge. "Let's just fix that with a little magic paint. There. Now this other little kewpie doll lip, we'll just..."

He had Carly giggling and returning his kisses. Burrowing into the hollow of her neck had a quieting effect. She sighed, knowing she'd never been as comfortable as she was at that moment. Then she heard a distant howling, a high-pitched wail that shattered the night's quiet.

"Listen," Carly whispered.

A moment of stillness—another plaintive yowl. "Coyote," Rafe said. "Sounds lonesome as hell."

As if on cue, there was a duet of wails. "He's not alone," Carly noted. "He's got family."

Several more coyote voices joined in, some harmonizing with fancy trills and yaps. Rafe chuckled. "It's the whole Coyote Tabernacle Choir. How's that for a lullabye?"

"Is that what woke you?" she asked.

Rafe shifted her back into the pocket of his shoulder and held her close. "No. Sometimes I wake up at night, and I don't know where I am. After all those years of waking up in strange places, you'd think I'd have gotten used to it."

"Does it scare you?"

Damn right, it scares me. "I just have to wake up completely to get my bearings."

But how did he *feel*? Would he ever admit to having emotions? "Why were you shuffled around so much?" she asked.

"I guess there were lots of reasons, but I didn't understand any of them. After a while I perfected meanness, and then nobody could stand to have me around for very long. I just figured: be mean to them before they have a chance to be mean to you. That way when they threw me out, at least I knew why."

"You must have dropped out of school for a while."

"Twice. The police caught up with me the first time. Then after the second time, the Smiths got hold of me. He was a minister, and I was his mission."

Rafe remembered the stern face, the quiet lectures. He remembered cleaning the church and taking care of its lawn, under duress at first. He wasn't going to end up in any state training school, which was just a euphemism for reformatory. Later, he took pride in the job he did, and when he was sixteen, he got a part-time job in a gas station besides his caretaking chores.

"He was strict with me, especially at first, but when I got into trouble, he'd pray with me and give me another chance. He changed my mind about school, and he let me stay there in his home until I finished high school."

"He sounds like a good man," Carly said.

Rafe's hand stirred absently on her back. "He was. By the time I graduated from college, he was dead. I felt bad about that—him not being there. It was his doing."

"It was *your* doing, but he faciliated it. He must have loved you, Rafe."

"He never said anything about love except when it had to do with God. But he stuck by me, and that's what counts."

"What counts. Yes, that's a big part of it," she mused, her lips brushing his flat nipple. She felt it tighten. *Trust me, my love.*

His hand traced the swell of her hip and strayed down her thigh. "You're easy to talk to, Carly."

That's part of it, too. "The more you touch me, the more difficult it becomes to listen," she murmured.

"I know." He shifted toward her and pulled her hip against him. "You're lying here naked in my arms, and I'm telling you my life story." He kissed her forehead, whispering, "How's that for socially backward?"

"I think this has gone beyond a simple social engagement." Her breast swelled to fill his hand. "Ah, yes...*far* beyond. Make love to me, Rafe."

He watched morning's gray light caress the contours of her sleeping face. Whenever he moved, she scooted closer. She was a snuggler. He could probably get used to being snuggled. He could certainly get used to going to sleep in her arms. Something remarkable had happened when he'd awakened this time. He saw her face, her cheek resting against the mattress, her hair tossed back from her face. He saw her first, and, for once, it didn't matter where he was.

The little booth-and-lunch counter café in McLaughlin was gearing up for the Sunday brunch regulars. At the counter two old farmers sat on shiny red vinyl stools nursing bottomless cups of coffee and recounting the difficulties they'd had with frostbitten udders and snow-covered haystacks after the last blizzard. Each detail was repeated for emphasis, and both gray heads shook slowly in acknowledgment of shared troubles. It was an event that could be milked for stories at least until a good drought came along.

Eggs and bacon would ordinarily have passed under Carly's nose without exciting much response, but this morning the aroma was irresistible. Before excusing herself to the ladies' room, Carly ordered "the ranch hand's special." When she emerged from the little washroom only a few moments later, she was surprised to see a whithered man taking her place in the booth across from Rafe.

The man's face was puffy and purplish, and he blinked his red eyes slowly but often. His old trench coat was buttoned over his chest, and the flap on his plaid scotch cap was pulled down over his ears. Carly's appearance seemed to confuse him for a moment as she slid in the booth next to Rafe. The old man looked at her as though he wasn't sure what she was. Then he mumbled, "Uh, I didn't know. Sorry, cap'n. Sorry, ma'am."

"That's all right," Carly said. "I'm fine over here."

"I told you already this morning to leave the customers alone, Tommy." The waitress's brown sweater curtained Carly's face for a moment as the woman plunked a plate in front of Rafe. "I'm gonna call the—" Carly's plate plunked, and the woman straightened, laughing. "You *are* the cops. You can throw him out any time."

Rafe wasn't laughing. "Bring another special, Mrs. Mueller, and coffee. I'm not on duty this morning."

Mrs. Mueller glanced sympathetically at Carly. "You want me to serve him at another table?"

"No," Rafe answered. "I want to see that he eats." Mrs. Mueller had already brought another mug and was pouring coffee. "You don't mind if we go ahead and eat, do you, Tom?" Rafe asked as he sliced into a fried egg.

"No...sure. I just...a coupla dollars..." The befuddled eyes pleaded with Rafe as Tom opened a stiff old hand on the table in front of himself.

"It's Sunday, Tom. You need to eat."

Tom gave that idea a few seconds of consideration. Then he turned a funny little spacy-toothed grin at Carly. "The cap'n saved my life 'bout a month back. I passed out cold back in the alley in a snowbank." The wave of the stiff hand apparently indicated the location of the alley. "And I mean *cold*. Cap'n pulled me out. I'da froze for sure if he hadn'ta come along."

Carly gave the old man a warm smile. "He did the same for me during the blizzard. And now he's buying us both breakfast. Can you believe he's really a cop?"

"How long were you locked up?" Tom asked, warming up to Carly. "I only got three days after I got out of the hospital that time."

"Three days?" Carly asked.

"In jail," Rafe supplied. "For public intoxication. Carly's car was stuck during the storm, Tom. I can't put people in jail for being stupid. Not enough room."

Tom's laughter was a papery crackle. Carly slanted a frown at Rafe, and he answered with an unobtrusive pat on her knee as a third plate of ham, eggs and hash browns clattered on the table.

Tom gave the two egg yolks a return stare and then a bleak look at Rafe. "Cap'n, I don't feel...I don't think I can—"

"You're going to eat, Tom. I do lock people up for wasting my money." Rafe watched Tom reach reluctantly for a fork. His face was reminiscent of a guilty basset hound. "Eat," Rafe repeated. And Tom did.

When all plates were empty and coffee had been refilled, Rafe asked, "How do you feel now, Tom? Still a little shaky?"

Tom glanced at Carly and then drew himself up. "That was a good meal, cap'n. It's settin' pretty good."

Carly's stomach turned when Rafe bought a can of chewing tobacco, what the boys called "snuff," as he paid the bill. *He's getting desperate.* Then he handed the can to Tom, and her stomach righted itself again. "Will this help you get through the day, Tom?" Rafe asked.

"By God, that'll do it, cap'n." Tom's grin brightened his face for a moment. "Think I'll go see my daughter. Tell her I had breakfast with the cap'n and his lady friend. Hell, I bet she won't even believe me."

"I'll drop you off, Tom. Then she might believe you."

Tom nodded vigorously. "She'll think she has to try 'n feed me, and I'll just say, 'No, thanks. I just ate.' Heh, heh." The gnarled hands broke the seal on the green can, and Tom thrust it under Rafe's nose. "Have a dip, cap'n?"

"No, thanks. I just ate."

"Isn't there any help for Tom?" Carly asked as the Bronco bumped over a set of railraod tracks on the way out of town.

"We dry him out once in a while, but he's been at it too long. He's got no reason to quit. He'll die drunk." Rafe's mouth was a grim line, and his eyes were hidden under his dark glasses. "But I won't."

"It's a problem everywhere, Rafe, not just—"

"It's a very acute problem among Indians, Carly. You know it, and I know it. I've heard every theory, every excuse, every snide remark, and every joke in the book, and I'm tired of all that. We don't know why it hits us so hard, but it does. We need to face it, and we need to fight it. Alcoholism is killing us. Old and young alike. I get so tired of pulling smashed kids out of wrecked cars." He seemed to study his knuckles as he gripped the top of the steering wheel and added quietly, "We took a twenty-five-year-old heart attack victim to the morgue last week. Twenty-five, and his circulatory system was shot. Five years ago that kid was dazzling the sports announcers in four states with his incredible ball-handling on the basketball court." He shook his head. "It's such a terrible waste."

"My grandfather says that each person has to throw off his own monkey."

Rafe smiled, remembering the expression as it had

come from her grandfather's mouth to him, too. "As always, your grandfather is right."

Ah, good. He's smiling. "Rafe, you were wonderful with Tom. You made his day."

"And you made mine," he said quietly.

Chapter Eight

Carly had made a commitment to Rafe, and she couldn't understand why he let days go by without a call. She decided that he was not comfortable using the telephone. When an unexpected call did come one evening, she was not surprised that it wasn't Rafe, but she noticed the caller's voice sounded like a young version of the one she'd hoped to hear. She thought her ears were playing tricks on her.

It was Frankie, and he needed help again. He'd lied to Carly before, and he'd probably do it again. But she knew Frankie was telling the truth when he'd said there was no one else to turn to. Whatever he'd done, he deserved to have someone in his corner. Carly decided to do what she could.

Unfortunatley, that meant going down to the police station. Unfortunate, too, was the fact that Rafe probably carried the only key to Frankie's cell in his pocket.

She had decided to wait for him to come to her, and for her to go to the police station on Frankie's behalf would surely mean a confrontation. He'd say she was meddling again, and that was an argument she wanted to avoid. Still, a fifteen-year-old boy should not have to face police trouble alone.

"I didn't steal the car, Miss Austin. Carol White Horse let me drive it while she was at the clinic. I might have squealed the tires a little, and I guess I went through that stop sign, but I didn't steal anything."

Carly listened as the boy pleaded his case to her through a four-inch hole in a Plexiglas window. She believed the part about Carol White Horse. The girl would do anything to get Frankie's attention, and she usually drove a car to school.

"Why do they think you stole the car?"

"Her mother saw me driving it and reported it stolen. She hates my guts," Frankie reported glumly.

"I don't see what I can do, Frankie."

"They'll release me in your custody. I'll go back to the dorm, and that'll be it. I swear. Tomorrow I'll have to go to court. Carol will have to tell them I didn't steal the car, won't she? I mean, you can't lie in court, right?"

A promising assumption. "That's right, Frankie. And you shouldn't lie to people you ask to trust you. Like me."

"I ain't lying, Miss Austin. I swear." His handsome young face looked open and honest.

"You lied to me about your brother being ill," she reminded him.

Frankie hung his head. "It was my father. I didn't think you'd give me a ride to the hospital if you knew it was my father. Strongheart's got it in for him. Probably told you all kinds of lies about him.'' His chin snapped back up, eyes wide with convincing innocence. "I didn't know the boots were yours, Miss Austin. I got 'em back as soon as he told me. That was just...kind of a prank. You know—somebody dared me.''

"That's one too many confessions, Frank.'' Carly turned toward the voice at her back. Arms folded over his chest, Rafe leaned against the doorjamb, looking through the window at his young prisoner. "I didn't tell Miss Austin who it was that stole her boots.''

Carly glanced briefly into Frankie's apologetic eyes and then back at Rafe, whose nod beckoned her to follow him to his office.

"Carly, I won't release him in your custody," Rafe repeated. "If he ran away, I'd have to come after you, too.''

"He won't run away.'' Carly sighed in disgust. She shifted against the gray vinyl upholstery in the office chair.

"If he thinks he's really got his butt in a sling this time, he will," Rafe assured her, sliding his fingers toward the point of a pencil before reversing the pencil and sliding toward the eraser.

"Does he?" she asked.

He shook his head. "He didn't steal that car.''

"Then why—"

"The mother signed a complaint on him. She wouldn't let us talk to the girl. She hasn't let the girl admit she gave him the car, but it'll come out in court.'' He gave Carly a hard look, his eyes glittering like shards of onyx. "But he has to be stopped. I can't pry him loose from the old man, and he's bound to—'' He cut himself off. There were times when he had to remind himself that he was a cop, not a social worker. He saw a look in Carly's face just then telling him she'd caught the slip, but she chose not to chide him. "Rafe, I just want to help the boy."

"The only way you can help him is by teaching him English." Rafe swung his chair away from the desk and catapulted to his feet on a sudden push of frustration. He snatched his jacket off a wooden hanger in a gray frame coat rack.

"Where are you going?" Carly demanded.

"I haven't had supper yet, so I'm going over to the café. And you're going home."

"I'm not leaving that child in jail." She was on her feet, too, blocking the path between the desk and the door. "If I were someone else from the school—any other teacher, a dorm matron, *anybody* else—you'd let him go."

In a stare-down, he'd lose, and he knew it—because she was right. He didn't like the idea of keeping a teenager in jail overnight—not if there was a responsible adult on hand, a parent who would take him home and talk things over. No chance of that for Frankie. All he had was Carly, standing up to the big, bad cop like some avenging angel. And Rafe knew damn well he'd end up spending the night here at the station as long as he had the kid locked up.

"Why didn't you tell me it was Frankie who stole my boots?" she asked.

Rafe avoided her eyes by watching his hands align the two sides of the zipper on his jacket. "You got your property back." He shrugged, admitting, "He asked me not to tell you. It seemed important to him. At the time,

I figured the kid need a friend." Raising hard eyes to hers, he amended, "But he's a user, Carly. I don't like the way he's used you. I want you to back off and let me handle him."

"He'll end up in reform school," Carly countered.

"Probably. He might get the help he needs there. We don't have anything for him here. The church used to run a boarding school for troubled kids, but they got out of that business. And the BIA boarding school can't handle cases like Frankie. They need...I don't know..." He cast his eyes about the room as though looking for answers. An open-handed gesture expressed dissatisfaction with those that came to him. "Counselors, psychologists, mind readers."

"A minister named Smith," Carly supplied.

"Contrary to what you read in the phone book, there are too few Smiths," he said quietly.

Carly allowed the quiet moment to calm them both a bit. Then she called upon her most reasonable tone of voice. "They need a lot of things, Rafe, but not jail. Let him go. I'll see that he makes his court appearance, and then I'll be done with it. Please."

"All right," Rafe agreed. "I'll take him back to the dorm. You go on home."

"Thank you," she said, letting him turn her toward the door. "Will I need to sign anything?"

"I'll take care of it," he promised. "From here on out I'll take care of it."

The wheels of justice turned quickly for Frankie. He would be heard in Tribal court the following day. It meant taking a couple of hours of leave from school, but Frankie had asked that she be there, and Carly had said she would. He's used the phrase that always got to her: there was no one else. Frankie seemed to accept the fact that his father wouldn't be there when a father was needed.

The courtroom was part of the Law and Order building, and on days when court was held, it was a busy place. People milled around in the hallways. A young couple stood in one corner arguing, and another couple sat beside each other on a bench in stony silence.

Carly had one eye on the reception area, watching for Frankie. It was Rafe who appeared there, though. He returned Carly's gaze for a moment and then turned to hand a folder to another policeman. She smiled when Rafe again glanced her way, but he only nodded stiffly before turning away, leaving her smile to fall softly from her face as he disappeared through a door.

He thinks I'm meddling again. But I didn't say I'd be done with it until after... He thinks Frankie's a lost cause. But he's not, damn it. Come on, Frankie. Don't you dare not show up.

Frankie came in with Carol White Horse, and Carly felt a moment of triumph. Her faith was justified. Carol's mother appeared minutes later. When they were called to the courtroom, Frankie whispered to Carly, "You'll talk for me, won't you?"

"What do you mean?" She wasn't prepared for anything beyond the moral support she'd promised.

"Say something good about me." Frankie had an engaging, slowly spreading smile, which reached his eyes last. It reminded her of Rafe's.

"If they ask me, I'll try to think of something. Did they appoint an attorney for you?"

Frankie shook his head. "I'll just tell my story, and the cop who picked me up will tell his. When Carol backs me up, I should get off okay."

"Except for the reckless driving," Carly reminded him. "And you're not even old enough to have a license."

"I've got a permit," he assured her, taking a seat in the dark, richly paneled courtroom. "At least, I had one."

Police officer Merle Horse Soldier testified that Mrs. White Horse had reported her car stolen, that Frank Fire Cloud Jr., had been driving it, and that he'd cited Frankie for exhibitionist driving and failing to stop for a stop sign.

"What's exhibitionist driving?" Frankie whispered to Carly.

"Impersonating Mario Andretti" was the answer.

And Frankie came back with, "Yeah, but those stop signs can get away from anybody, can't they?"

Carly cut him a mock-scowl and shushed him with a forefinger to her lips. From the corner of her eye she noticed that Rafe had taken a seat in the back row. After Frankie had told his story, the judge asked Carly what her relationship to the boy was. She explained her presence, adding that Frankie had a good attitude in her class and that she liked him personally.

Carol White Horse corroborated Frankie's story, and Mrs. White Horse admitted that Carol had permission to drive the family car. The judge dismissed the theft charge, and Frankie was fined thirty dollars. Before leaving the courtroom, Carol's mother turned a stormy face on Frankie, wagging a finger at him. "You stay away from my daughter, Frankie Fire Cloud. Next time I'll take care of you myself."

Carly's wide eyes expressed her surprise, first at Frankie, and then at the retreating woman's back.

"I told you. She hates my guts," Frankie complained as he followed Carly toward the door.

"Apparently. Well, Frankie, I'll see you in class. I hope you'll—"

Frankie's hand caught her elbow. "Miss Austin, I—uh...I don't have thirty dollars."

"Then how are you going to...uh-uh, Frankie." Frankie glanced past Carly's face, and he dropped his hand. She continued with, "You still owe me ten dollars from the last time I helped you out. I'm not *that* big a—" Carly felt Rafe's presence at her back. She didn't have to turn around. She knew what caused that tingling sensation in her stomach.

"Not that big a what, Miss Austin?" His drawl challenged her to admit it or prove otherwise.

She'd do neither. Rafe was wrong about Frankie, and she'd stand by her judgment. "I'll pay the fine, and you'll pay me back," she announced stiffly.

"I'll take care of the fine," Rafe said. He leveled a dark glare at Frankie. "Go on back to the dorm, Frankie. You're restricted to the dorm, school and police station, where you'll work off your fine."

Frankie returned the glare. Getting the money from Austin would have been easier. "You're not to drive anybody's car," Rafe continued. "You're not to be a passenger in anybody's car. You are not to go anywhere except those three places." Rafe shifted his eyes to Carly. "I'll make sure the matrons and all your teachers understand that, too, *especially* Miss Austin."

"And when is this sentence supposed to be up, *Captain*?" Frankie growled.

"When I say it's up, Frank. Now go on back to the dorm. The matron will expect you within five minutes. And remember: you can't afford another screw-up. You're out on borrowed time as it is."

Carly could almost smell the animosity simmering behind Frankie's eyes.

"Move," Rafe ordered, and Frankie did, but with deliberate casualness and a pointed, "Thanks, Miss Austin."

Rafe turned to Carly. "If you have a moment, I'd like to see you in my office."

Rafe closed the door behind him and gestured toward one of the two chairs that faced his desk. Mentally she refused to let him get the better of her, and she turned down the chair with a shake of the head. She was not a kid in the principal's office, and she would not let him make her feel inferior.

"Please sit down, Carly. We need to talk."

An unintimidated adult would sit down, she told herself. She chose the chair he didn't indicate, pulling the coat she held over her arm into her lap. She watched Rafe open a file drawer and withdraw a folder, which he tossed open on the desk.

"This is the story of Frank Fire Cloud, Carly." Carly cast her eyes in the direction of the folder. "If you ever want to cause a lot of trouble for me, just tell someone I showed you that." She looked away from it quickly as though it stung her eyes. "No, I want you to look at it. Shoplifting, vandalism, truancy. Look at all the slaps on the wrist, the court-order placements, the social workers' reports. This is one very troubled kid."

Carly nodded toward the file. "This is none of my business."

Rafe scraped the other chair across the floor as he turned it to face her. Then he sat down, leaning toward her with the earnestness of what he had to say. "No, it shouldn't be your business. It wouldn't be if you'd draw the line with him at school. You, my friend, are an easy mark. You're a gullible young woman whose heart bleeds at the mention of a motherless kid. Well, this kid's got you figured, and he's a whole lot more than you're equipped to handle."

Carly glanced warily at the file again. She couldn't read it at this distance. She didn't want to. The fact that it lay there made her uneasy. "I know better than to become too personally involved with my students," she said, but there wasn't the conviction she intended in her voice.

"Then why have you allowed yourself to become involved with this one?"

"Because he needs a little moral support, and if he doesn't get it from someone like me, he'll look to his father, a man we both know is—"

"A man *neither* of us knows." As soon as he'd bit out the words, Rafe clamped his teeth together and rolled his eyes ceilingward on a sigh. Shaking his head to clear the murky steam that had suddenly filled it, he reminded himself that he was nothing if he was not objective. "You don't understand this situation. You don't have a chance against his father's influence. Carly, you're playing out of your league. You're the girl from uptown who doesn't believe the boys from across the tracks are as bad as people say."

Carly stiffened, and her eyes iced over. "I thought we'd exploded that myth."

"I thought so, too, but here you are doing the bleeding heart number again. You're too trusting. That kid could hurt you, Carly."

"Oh, Rafe." Carly sighed, dropping her head into the nest of her fingers. Rubbing her forehead, and then her temples, she said, "We shouldn't predict the worst."

"We have to be prepared for the worst even while we're trying for the best." He leaned forward to touch her shoulder. "You okay?"

She nodded and lifted her head to show him that she wasn't falling apart over this. "I'm tired, and I have a headache. Look, Rafe, I know you know your business, but I know mine, too. Part of the reason I'm good at my job is that I relate well to kids—kids like Frankie."

"That's fine, Carly, in your classroom..."

She sat up straight in her chair, gripping its arm. "In my classroom and out of it, too. I have almost ten years' teaching experience, Rafe. I don't need a policeman to instruct me in dealing with teenagers." No need to get upset, she told herself, consciously curbing her indignation, changing her tone to a lower key. "You're looking at this from a policeman's point of view, but I'm looking at it as a teacher. Can't we just admit that our methods have to be different and leave it at that?"

Rafe threw up his hands in surrender before levering himself out of the chair, exasperated. He snatched the folder closed and stuffed it back in the file cabinet before turning back to Carly, who'd risen from her chair. "Frankie Fire Cloud is restricted to the dorm, the school and the police station," he reminded her. "*I've* paid his fine, and *I'll* see that he pays it back—in honest sweat. You, Miss Austin, may bring all your meth-

ods and experience to bear in this case and teach the kid
some English. We'll leave it at *that*."

Carly swallowed an angry retort and called upon a
quiet, controlled voice. "Am I dismissed, Captain?"

His eyes bored through hers, his biting tone incon-
gruous with the words. "Certainly. Have a nice day,
Miss Austin."

Nice days were on the way. Warming temperatures
and brisk March winds had eaten away at the prairie
snow blanket, leaving the high ground brown and barren. Catches of snow clung tenaciously in the sheltered
spots—the draws, creek beds, and the occasional clusters of trees. If the wind had its way, the prairie would
have its greening in another month, with a little help
from the sun and rain. But a fickle wind in this country
could just as quickly bring winter back to the plains.

The hour's drive to Bismarck rolled this prairie car-
pet by Carly's car window with hardly a break. Then the
small city rose up suddenly ahead of her, the break in
the skyline signaled by the city's single skyscraper—the
state capitol building. It was a signpost that said
"home" to Carly.

"Hi, Grandpa!" It was an old man who appeared on
the porch in his shirtsleeves, shading his eyes with his
hand, but the years fell away as Carly's quick steps
splashed in the snowmelt on the front walk. "It's a
gorgeous afternoon, isn't it? Think we'll be able to plant
potatoes on Good Friday?"

"Yes, ma'am, I do. I think we'll have crocuses up
soon, too." The old man took his granddaughter's
hand, just as he had in years past, when her hand had
been much smaller and his more supple. "It's just you
and me tonight, girl. Your dad can't make it."

"I'm just as glad, Grandpa. We can't really talk when he's around, and I really need to talk."

"You, too? I think I'll hang out a shingle."

Carly let her coat slide off her shoulders as she pulled the closet door open. "Is someone horning in on my territory, Grandpa?" she teased. "I won't have it. I spent too many years winning you over to my side."

"Seems I've earned a reputation for my fine cup of tea and sympathy."

"Oh, really?" Carly led the way into the kitchen. "Who's been bending your ear, Grandpa?"

"Does deer sausage for supper tonight give you a clue?"

Carly's hand froze on the teakettle. "Rafe? Has he been here lately?"

"Yep." Grandpa had the sausage out of the refrigerator. Bouncing it in his hand a couple of times he added, "Brought this by yesterday."

Carly registered the information with a lift of the brow as she resumed the tea-making process. "Thoughtful of him," she acknowledged.

"We're becoming pretty good friends, your policeman and me. He's stopped by three or four times since he first came here with you." Grandpa leaned his hip against the counter, crossing his arms over his chest with his hands under his armpits—a stance that said he knew a good deal about the subject at hand, and he was prepared to talk if Carly wanted to do her share of listening.

"Wonder why he keeps coming around," Grandpa continued. "I must be a pretty fascinating old cuss. We've swapped some tales, but I do most of the talking."

"About what?" Carly asked, handing Grandpa a steaming cup of tea.

"Army stories, horse tales...reminiscences. He never seems to tire of the stories about my granddaughter."

"I don't understand that man, Grandpa. I really..." Carly sighed and put the coil of sausage in the electric skillet. "And I don't think this sausage is good for you." She knew the remark wouldn't be well received even as she said it.

"It's good for my morale," he said, taking a carton of milk from the refrigerator and pouring a shot into his tea. Carly took hers to the little kitchen table, and her grandfather joined her there, smiling. "He's good for my morale. You're good for my morale, and the two of you together would—"

Carly shook her head. "I don't think so. Every time he opens a door for me, even just a little, he regrets it later. He doesn't want me in his life, Grandpa."

"You're wrong, Carly. You're very much part of his life. More than you realize—more than he admits. Do you love him?"

Carly glanced at the ceiling. Water suddenly pooled along the rim of her eyelid, and her throat burned. She saw Rafe's face in the round ceiling light fixture. "Yes, I love him. I love him so much, I... Oh, Grandpa, I think the emptiest feeling in the world must be the one that comes with waiting for a man to say, 'I love you, too.'"

"You're waiting for him to say it your way, Carly. Meanwhile, he's said it *his* way, and it's gone right by you."

Carly swiped at her eyes with the length of her forefinger. "When we're together he seems to care for me— that's true enough," she sniffed, and then she drew a deep breath. This was Grandpa, after all. She could snivel now. "But he won't take that telling step; he won't commit himself. He won't say he loves me." Her sad eyes reflected the hopelessness she felt. "He doesn't *want* to love me...because he doesn't trust me. I've always prided myself on my honesty—always thought it shone through like a beacon, but Rafe...he can't love me if he doesn't believe in me, can he?"

The old man reached across the table for his granddaugther's hand. "I'm going to show you something that might help you find your answers, Carly."

He'd brought a simple frame and hung the painting in his bedroom—his private place for this very personal gift. Carly stood away for a moment and then took a step closer, amazed. There was no mistaking the identity of the woman in the painting—the tawny hair, blue eyes, pale skin. She wore an oversized sheepskin jacket—Rafe's jacket—as she held a bucket below the horse Rusty's eager muzzle. A prickling rose from Carly's stomach to her throat as she noted the soft treatment of her hands and face. And there was his jacket, his horse. His vision of her included pieces of himself.

"He gave you this?" she asked, touching tentative fingertips to the "Strongheart" signature.

"He knew what it would mean to me, but I believe he also knew you would see it here. The gift was for me, but there was a gesture in it for you. He wants to tell you, Carly."

Carly felt the familiar weight of her grandfather's stiff hand on her shoulder.

"He says he doesn't know what love is," she reported, her eyes affixed to the painting.

"What he denies in his head, he feels in his heart. Here's his declaration."

Words were not his medium.

Gratefully, Carly gave her grandfather's hand a squeeze.

Rafe's brush said "Carly." When he abandoned the brush for a pencil, that said "Carly," too. He went back to the brush and let it have its say. He saw her in the warm tones of fireglow—the copper glints in her hair and the flush of loving in her cheeks—the way she'd looked that first time.

Staying away from her didn't help. He was on the verge of admitting to himself that he needed her— needed her badly. And then what? Admit it to *her*? Hardly. He'd handle it. Rafe Strongheart didn't believe in handling other people. He believed in handling himself. That he could do. That he had down pat.

Banishing her from his mind would be a futile effort. Control the image, he told himself. Don't dwell on its presence. Accept it; let it diffuse throughout the gray matter and carry it comfortably. He warmed her hair with burnt sienna. *Control the image.*

On the canvas he brought the warm gold of the firelight through the cool blue of her eyes. The moment he brought life into those eyes, he knew he'd given the image control of some vital piece of himself.

Carly stood back from the arrangement of cutouts and pictures she'd stapled over a third of the surface of her huge bulletin board. It would do. It was upbeat, at least. She snatched the staple puller off the desk. It was stupid. "Swing into Spring," for heaven's sake. It was nonsense. More to the point would have been four-inch red letters warning: "Get Your Research Papers Done or Else..."

Green. She wanted to see green outside; she'd use it inside. Her stance on the padded seat of her chair was precarious. Stretching beyond her reach, she turned an ankle and stapled her finger.

"Ouch! Damn!" The stapler clattered to the floor, skittering toward the open doorway. Carly shoved the stinging finger into her mouth.

"If this thing's loaded, you shouldn't be so careless with it."

Carly's eyes followed the brown hand that carried the stapler from the floor to her desk. Then they slid to Rafe's face.

He shrugged, offering a one-sided smile. "I saw the light. The janitor's gone. Thought maybe someone was stealing your answer keys."

The finger popped from her mouth with a sucking sound. "Always the suspicious cop," she noted, leaning toward the hand he offered. He took a step closer and surprised her by settling his hands at her waist. She thought he meant to steady her as she jumped down, but he took her full weight in his hands and lowered her to the floor in front of him.

"It's good for my image." He pressed his fingers into her waist at the back and extended his thumbs to trace the curvature of her lowest ribs. "What are you doing here this time of night?"

"I don't log hours," she answered, echoing an old comment of his. Her heart pumped a hard, steady celebration of his proximity. His gray sweatshirt was soft contrast to the hard shoulders underneath.

"You didn't mean to leave the side door open, either," he surmised, one eyebrow admonishing her.

"No," she said with a sigh. "I didn't. What is it with you?" She pulled a pinch of sweatshirt away from his shoulder, frowning. "Obviously you're off duty."

"I told you—I saw your light on, and then..." He lifted one shoulder, his face softening. "My pickup stalled right there in the street. Figured I was supposed to come up here and see..."

Her eyes responded to the need in his, and kissing became a necessity. He hadn't intended to let her know it had been too long, that when he'd seen the light in what he knew to be her classroom window, his chest had tightened. He'd been like a man controlled by a post-hypnotic suggestion. The light had been his cue. *Go to her. Pull her body against yours. Kiss her. Without that kiss tonight your heart will feel empty inside.*

"See if you were okay," he breathed against her lips.

"So now you see," she whispered, and then pressed a soft kiss of reassurance to his lips. "I'm okay, you're okay."

"Amazing, isn't it," he began, nipping at the sweet resilience of her lower lip, "what a kiss can do for a person's well-being?"

And the next kiss was deeper. It brought their arms tightly around each other, brought tongues and lips into agile undulation against each other, and brought their mingling breaths pressing harder and quicker upon the last ones. It was Rafe, taking a deep breath, who finally drew back.

Bright fluorescent light gave Carly's eyes a rude sting as she blinked up at him. "I take it our friendship is still on," she said quietly.

"Looks that way."

"I've missed you."

Oh, God, I've missed you, too. He smiled past the strain in his throat. "You don't happen to have any molasses cookies on you, do you?"

"I haven't made any lately. Didn't want to end up eating them...oh!" She pulled her cut finger back from his shoulder. "I'm bleeding a little." She snatched several tissues from the box on the desk, and balled her fingers and tissue into a fist.

"Here," he said, the word suggesting an offer rather than a direction as he reached for her hand and pulled the tissue away. Blood flowed from two pinholes, which he staunched with a fresh tissue and then clamped with his own thumb and forefinger. "I'm good at putting the pressure on."

"Mmm-hmm," she agreed, eyeing the first-aid process, "so Frankie tells me."

"That's a topic we don't want to get into tonight," he warned. "This isn't a professional call."

"No?" She nodded toward her finger as she leaned a hip against the edge of the desk. "If you're not qualified to do this procedure, you'd better let me bleed. I might end up suing."

He considered that for a moment and then shook his head. "Naw, you wouldn't do that. Too softhearted."

"I've gone from 'bleeding heart' to 'softhearted.' Is that a step up in your book?"

She caught a slight smile as he ascertained the condition of the wound. "It's sort of a lateral move on the scale. This must be pretty deep. Hope you've had all your shots."

"Why? Are you planning to bite me?"

"Where you're concerned, things aren't planned. They just happen."

Her eyes found his. "Was that kiss planned?"

"That first kiss was as much of a surprise to me as it was to you." He added with half a chuckle, "The second one was no surprise at all."

"Then the third one shouldn't be, either," she murmured, cupping her free hand over the back of his neck. She laced her fingers in his thick hair and pulled his unresisting mouth to hers. Her mouth was soft and seductive, her lips parted just slightly, her tongue beckoning his.

She drew back, let her eyes drift open, and caught him smiling at her. "I went to see my grandfather last weekend," she said.

"How is your grandfather?" Rafe asked.

"He's feeling very well, as you well know."

"I made a promise to visit him."

"You've more than kept it."

"I like your grandfather, Carly. Almost as much as I like you." He glanced at the stapler and the papers scattered over the desk top. "You about finished here?" Carly wrinkled her nose in disgust at the stapler and nodded. "How about going for a drive?" he suggested.

"Sounds entertaining."

Rafe draped an arm over her shoulders and nudged her toward the door. "Maybe do a little snipe hunting, catch the submarine races." He flicked the light off, and Carly locked the classroom door.

They walked toward the security light above the fire door, and Carly remembered then that she hadn't come empty-handed. She made a quick dash back to the room for her purse. Returning to the landing where she'd left him standing, her rubber soles squeaked on the newly waxed floor, echoing down the dark hallway as she turned the corner to the gym lobby. All else was quiet.

"Rafe?" she called softly.

There was no answer.

An outside floodlight cast its dim shadows into the lobby. Carly noticed the Bronco's big white hulk parked at the end of the sidewalk, and she pivoted in that direction. But a hand grabbed hers from behind and reversed her motion. Her purse flew from her other hand as she was pulled behind a set of tall lockers. His kiss came hard and quick, like one stolen in a brief and unexpected moment of privacy. Carly gasped his name when he freed her mouth.

He answered with a deep, satisfied chuckle. "I always wondered what it would be like to sneak a kiss from you behind the lockers." His arms settled around her as he leaned a shoulder against the brick wall.

"Really? Was it all you thought it would be?"

"Mmm, pretty much. I imagine the danger of getting caught by old Mr. Pross would've added to the excitement."

"For you, maybe. He used to call kids' parents if he caught them necking in school. My father would have grounded me for a month."

"Yeah, but your grandfather would have seen that you got off with a week. And I'd have spent several hours on my knees after my foster father got his call."

"Asking forgiveness?"

"Giving thanks." He dropped a kiss on her forehead. "Maybe asking for another shot at it. You'd better keep your eye on this spot, Miss Austin. It's a good one." He levered himself away from the wall, taking Carly with him as he moved toward the door.

"My purse seems to be on the floor again," Carly observed. The pen that had fallen from it caught both their eyes at once, and they laughed together as they picked the things up off the floor.

"Are you sure snipes are in season already?" Carly teased. "I hear the police are very tough on snipe poachers."

"I hear you've got a friend in the department."

Carly leaned on the glass door's push bar. "Uh-huh. I think that's his vehicle right there." She imitated his pointed lip gesture, and he laughed at her attempt, taking her chin in his hand and gently shaking her head.

"Funny lady. That doesn't look like a police vehicle to me," he protested.

"I know; it's very misleading. But my friend looks unmistakably like a policeman, I can assure you."

"Good. It's taken a long time to perfect the look. I'd hate to think it might still be mistakable." He gave her an appraising look. "But you'll have to work on that lip jerk. Let me see it again." Carly tried, but her giggle overpowered the first effort. She got it on the second attempt, and Rafe stole another kiss from the irresistible pout, afterward judging, "That definitely needs more work."

Chapter Nine

Carly unloaded books and bag on the living room table and pried one shoe off with the toe of the other. The word *Friday* escaped her throat with a sigh, and she planned to ignore the contents of her tote bag at least until Sunday afternoon. She'd just sunk into the whooshing cushion of a vinyl chair when the back door slammed. Todd wheeled in on a cloud of furor, threw his canvas bag and jacket in a chair and mumbled a curse.

"I thought you'd left for Bismarck with the basketball team," Carly said.

Todd threw himself into the chair next to hers. "Can't get in or out of town. Cops have the causeway blocked off."

"What for?"

"How the hell do I know what for? Some show they're putting on. Stick your head out the door. You can hear the gunfire from here."

"Gunfire?"

"Yeah, gunfire. They're probably taking pot shots at stray dogs or something. God knows what these cops'll do." He cast her an innocent-eyed glance. "No offense."

Carly felt a queer tightening in her throat. "They have the whole causeway blocked off?"

"That's what they said. I can't believe this. The State Tournament is no time to play games, for God's sake."

"Something's wrong." She was rebuttoning her jacket, her feet fumbling with her shoes even as she headed for the front door. "I have to find out what's going on."

Carly was skipping down the porch steps when Todd shouted after her, "They won't tell you anything!"

The man was dead. A janitor at the elementary school. Donald Sees The Enemy, age fifty-one. Probably on his way to work, just like on a thousand other afternoons. Only some crazy had decided to spend *this* afternoon taking pot shots at cars on the causeway. Donnie Sees The Enemy, who had played Santa Claus every Christmas for the past fifteen years, would not haul the flag down the pole in the elementary school's front yard this evening.

Rafe had to hand it to the ambulance crew. They were scared, but they'd gotten both victims off the road—a wounded woman, whom Rafe judged would be all right, and Donnie Sees The Enemy, who was on his way to the morgue. There'd been life signs when Rafe called for an ambulance, but the man was gone when the ambulance got there. Shot through the neck.

With a deadly *ping*, a bullet glanced off its bumper as the ambulance sped away, siren wailing. Thank God, it was soon out of range. Those guys weren't paid for hazardous duty. Arriving at the scene, Rafe had seen the gunshot victims and called for the ambulance immediately. He hadn't known exactly what he was facing until, moments later, a shot rang out, and then another. He tried to turn the ambulance back, but they were already on their way, and they knew Donnie was hurt. And now Rafe knew what was out there. Across the road, behind two derelict cars, lay a sniper, with an abandoned house and another car body at his back. Rafe got on the horn again.

"This is Police Captain Strongheart. We have the causeway blocked at both ends. You've wounded some people, but they're getting help. If you give yourself up, you'll be treated fairly." No mention of murder. Give him a chance to cool off, maybe even come to his senses. Don't let him know he's already committed the ultimate crime.

But the answer was another bullet, which ricocheted off the pavement to Rafe's left, two feet in front of the patrol car. Rafe slammed the patrol car door shut and walked down the embankment that sloped away from the road and down to the backwater. Fort Yates was nearly surrounded by water—the Missouri River on the east and the river's backwater, which coddled the town on the north and south. The causeway, which connected the town with the highway, was flanked by water on both sides for half a mile. The sniper had dug himself in on the northwest bank of the backwater. Rafe and four policemen held the south side of the road.

A chilly western breeze lifted Rafe's hair away from his forehead. He adjusted his sunglasses on the bridge of his nose and watched Dale Lone Bull trot down the slop in his direction. Dale was young, eager—the best marksman in the department, next to Rafe. The look on his face said that he was about to volunteer for something. Rafe knew exactly what it would be.

"Somebody has to get behind him, Captain." Dale squinted, one eye closed against the sun. His grin was so broad that it stretched his lips tight against this teeth, and a silver-crowned molar winked at Rafe in the sunlight. Rafe wished for five more Dale Lone Bulls—with just a little more experience.

Rafe nodded. He'd already thought it out. Now he calculated the risks aloud. "Somebody has to take a covered position from behind. He's got all kinds of cover where he is. We've got to get a man behind him, let him know he's trapped. It's likely he'll surrender. He doesn't know he's killed a man."

"I can do it, Captain."

Rafe towered over Dale, but he didn't see a young policeman. He saw an eager second-string halfback, confident that he could run the ball all the way from the fifty and make the winning touchdown before the clock ran out. Too young. Too eager. A wife and two kids. Rafe looked past him at a heavier man, who hung back, dreading the moment when Rafe would give him an order. Merle Horse Soldier. Older. Hardly eager. Couldn't shoot worth a damn.

"I know you can, Dale, but—"

"It's you or me, Captain. You know that. And you have to stay here and call the shots. So it's me."

Rafe managed a confident smile as he clapped a hand over the young man's shoulder. "It's you. And you're on foot, and that means you hustle. Stay on this side of the road. Don't cross over until you're at least half a mile down. We'll keep him occupied.''

Dale's head bobbed as the instructions continued. "Pick your spot. Be sure you've got a clear shot at him before you tell him to throw his weapon down. But you're covered. You got that? No movie stunts.''

"No stunts,'' Dale agreed.

Rifle in hand, Dale trotted through the crusty remnants of snow cover at a good clip. Lean and wiry. Part antelope. Rafe remembered watching Carly bound through the snow, shrieking with laughter as he chased her. *God, go with him. He's got a wife and two little kids.* Now Rafe would draw the sniper's attention, and he would wait.

Crouching behind the hood of the patrol car, Rafe had drawn a couple of pot shots. Those were the sniper's only responses to Rafe's repeated warnings. Now, through the scope on his rifle, Rafe spotted Dale Lone Bull. He'd maneuvered behind the house and positioned himself along the west wall.

Dale shouted his warning, his rifle ready to have its say if words failed. Rafe watched through the scope, his finger curled around the trigger of his rifle, the sweat on his forehead chilled by cold wind. The next moments became a slow motion film with Rafe sitting too far back from the screen. Or maybe he'd let himself get too close. Two shots were fired, and Dale Lone Bull went down. Like a clay duck in a shooting gallery, the sniper's back emerged above the old car. Rafe Strongheart leveled his rifle for another shot, and then he blew the back of the assailant's head away.

* * *

"I just want to know if Rafe is out there." Carly stood her ground, her eyes pleading through the Plexiglas window at a woman in a blue shirt, who was also standing her ground.

"We can't release any information at this time, Miss Austin," the woman's emotionless voice reported.

"You can tell me whether he's out there. You can tell me that much, at least." She clutched her unbuttoned coat to her breast, trying to ignore the chill that ran through her intermittently like any icy current.

The woman's black eyes were cold, too, but they were all business. "If you know the captain, you know where he'd be."

Carly's hand trembled as it went to her mouth. "Yes. Of course," she mumbled. "He's out there, and someone's shooting at him." She turned away from the window. A wall supported her back, and she stood there trying not to cry. Two slow, deep breaths and a swallow. The pins and needles in her throat would go away in a moment. Someone was shooting at him, but he was shooting back. She fixed her mind on the marksmanship plaque she'd seen in his office. He would defend himself.

"Hoo-wee! They got him!" It was the dispatcher. He was the only other person behind the window. Carly froze. "Captain Strongheart shot him. But Lone Bull's down, too."

"Oh, God. Is it bad?" the woman asked.

"I don't know. I'm calling...yes. Send an ambulance back out to the ambush site. Two down, but it's all over."

It's all over. Carly slumped against the wall. Two down. Lone Bull and the sniper. Rafe's all right. It's all over.

The knock on her door came after Carly had turned her light off. Eleven thirty, according to the lighted face on her alarm clock. Out of bed, she switched the lamp back on and fumbled with her robe, squinting against the rude light. "Who is it?"

The voice was low, barely audible. "It's Rafe."

She dropped the ends of her sash. The doorknob and the knob on the deadbolt lock refused to cooperate with her impatient fingers. When she swung the door open, it was as though she were angry with it.

They spoke simultaneously in hushed tones.

"I'm sorry to wake you. I thought—"

"I'm so glad you're all right. I was afraid—"

He lay a forefinger over her lips. "You people forgot to lock the back door again," he said quietly.

"Door? Oh, I hate locks. They get in the way." He looked tired. Worse, he looked worn—older somehow. "Come in."

"I walked down from the police station. I didn't want to leave the Bronco parked—"

"It's all right. Please come in." He seemed unsure, a little disoriented. She reached for his hand. The hand that always warmed her was cold. She took it in both of hers, and he allowed himself to be drawn over the threshold.

"I wanted to walk," he said. "I needed the air."

"I knew it wasn't a good time to bother you with calls, so I stayed away from the phone. But I've been thinking about you...worried about you." She unzipped his jacket for him. "You're really all right?"

"Fine. Not a scratch on me."

"I've never been so scared."

"They shouldn't have told you anything until—"

"They didn't. I went down there."

"They told me you'd come."

She pushed her hair back from her forehead, shrugging. "All kinds of rumors were flying. First that four people had been shot by a sniper. Then seven. Then four civilians and three policemen. I only knew what I overheard when I was standing by the reception window. When I knew you were safe..."

She wanted to take his jacket off, but he'd have no more of that. He grabbed her wrists, held them to his chest. "I need a friend," he said quietly.

"I'm your friend."

"Then don't flutter around me. I want you to listen...no, I want you to *look* at me. People have been tiptoeing around me, lowering their eyes. Do I look different? I want someone to *look* at me, so I know I'm still—"

"Rafe," she said, her eyes unflinching. "You're still Rafe."

He looked down at her hands, afraid he'd lose control right there in front of her. "It isn't the first time I've had to..." His voice dropped, became very quiet. "But never a kid. Today I killed a kid."

Carly's heart hesitated before it wedged itself in her throat. *Be still,* she told it. "Come sit down. Tell me what happened. Can I get you some coffee?"

Two chairs flanked a lamp table. He took the closest one. "No. I've had enough coffee." Slouching in the chair, he laid his head back and stared at the ceiling. "He was sixteen, Carly. He could have been one of your students."

Oh, God. "Who was he?"

"His name was Charles Kills The Fox. Know him?"

"No."

"We don't know much about him yet, but he was from South Dakota. He killed the janitor from the elementary school. Donnie Sees The Enemy. You know him."

Carly dropped into the other chair. "Donnie. Yes, I know him. His grandson is one of my students."

"Some woman from Montana was wounded. She'll be okay, though. He hit several other cars. I guess we were lucky it wasn't any worse. The kid was quite a marksman."

"Does anyone know why?"

Rafe sighed, shaking his head slowly. There was no explanation painted there above his head. He'd seen nothing in the black velvet night sky. He kept thinking he'd look up, and something would be there to explain it all way. "The answer to that question will go to the grave with Charles Kills The Fox. I'm sure we'll find out that his father beat him, or he had a history of psychotic behavior. He probably needed help, and he'd probably been pleading silently for it for years, and nobody paid any attention. One thing he didn't need...a bullet in the back of his head."

"Neither did Donnie Sees The Enemy."

"No. Neither did Donnie Sees The Enemy. Nor the woman from Montana. Nor Dale Lone Bull—another kid."

"Is Dale the policeman who was hurt?" Rafe affirmed her question with a nod. "How is he?"

"I saw him before they took him to Bismarck. He was conscious. The bullet missed everything vital, and they say he'll be all right." Unbidden, the whole scene played across Rafe's mind again. "Dale said he had to step away from the house to get a clear shot. He's a damned good shot, but under fire...it isn't the same when the target shoots back. The kid hit Dale and then stood up, ready to take a second shot."

"Which you prevented," Carly pointed out.

"Permanently. *Dammit*. Sixteen years old."

She wanted him to think about Dale Lone Bull instead of Charles Kills The Fox. "Is Dale married?"

"Yeah. Two kids."

Carly went to him, knelt by his knee, and looked up to Rafe's troubled face. "You gave those children their father back—a wife her husband. You did what had to be done."

"I know," he said. "I know." But the image of that boy with the bullet in his brain was all Rafe saw.

"Rafe, look at me." It took a moment, but he did. "I could have been out there about that time, but I canceled a dentist appointment for this afternoon."

Rafe sat up a little straighter. The thought of Carly at the end of a rifle's sights chilled him. His stomach twisted in a knot. "Why did you...what made you change your plans?" he choked out.

She smiled, unconsciously rubbing his knee as she had so many nights before in the club basement. "Fear of the drill."

"For once you weren't in the wrong place at the wrong time, Carly Austin." He touched her cheek, and that was all it took. She reached for him, and he pulled her into his lap, taking her head in his hands. Their kiss was a joyous celebration. They were both alive.

When she drew back, it was to look at him, touch his face, his hair, as though making sure he was all there. "They wouldn't tell me whether you were out there, but

I knew you would be. I wanted someone to tell me you were all right, but...I imagined all sorts of things, Rafe. Terrible things.''

"Terrible things? Did you imagine I'd killed a man...a *boy*? What did you think when you heard that?''

There was such pain in his eyes, and she thought she could feel him trembling beneath his jacket. How could she ease this awful burden for him? "My first thought? Thank God it wasn't the other way around. And then I thought how sad you must be and how alone you must feel. I wanted to run to you, to be there with you.''

He laid his head against her breast, the silkiness of her nightgown cool against his face. He put his arms around her waist, and she began to weep.

"Don't, Carly. Please don't.''

"They're yours, my love,'' she whispered, letting the tears roll freely. "They're the ones you can't shed. I've started them for you.''

"I have no tears,'' he rasped.

"Yes, you do. They burn inside you. Let them go.''

"I...have...no...tears.'' Each word was wrenched from his throat.

She would not look. She would hold him and stroke his hair, but she would not look. "I know you, Raphael David Strongheart. Your sorrow is too heavy for one heart. Share it with me.''

"No. It's part of my job. *My* job.''

"Of course it is,'' she whispered. "Of course it is. It hurts, doesn't it?''

She felt the shudders that wracked him, and she absorbed the pain of his terrible groan into her body. For half an eternity she held him without saying a word. She waited while his ragged breathing became quiet, even.

When he lifted his head, she saw through her tears that, indeed, he had none. His unsteady hand wiped her face.

"I got sick," he said at last. "We got Dale to the clinic first and then...then the boy's body. I went to the clinic, talked to Dale, talked to God knows how many people—the whole time with my gut churning. When I got back to my office, I went in the bathroom, and I...I was sick. Some tough cop."

"Your feelings will have their way with you, Rafe Strongheart, one way or another."

"I may have a strong heart, but I guess I have a weak stomach." And he gave her a weak smile.

"Oh, Rafe." She shook her head in wonder at the man. "You saved a man's life today. You put us all out of danger. The whole community was threatened, and we depended on you. No matter what his age, no matter what his problems, Charles Kills The Fox became a killer today."

"Like a wounded bear," he mused.

"Yes. Purely destructive wildness is an awful thing."

His eyes delved deeply into hers. "I couldn't stop myself from coming here tonight."

"You shouldn't have tried."

His eyes slid away. "Yes, I should have. But I didn't. Not very hard. I needed...just to see you."

"Then stay with me tonight."

"I don't want any talk going around about—"

"The front door is right at the foot of these stairs," she reminded him. "You can leave by it very discreetly. Anyway, the people who want to talk are going to talk, just because we're seeing each other. Fishbowl, remember?"

"You could get hurt," he warned, knowing full well that he wasn't going anywhere for a while.

"Not as long as I'm with you. You won't let anyone hurt me." Her hands held his cheeks, forcing him to look at her. "Will you, Rafe?"

"Never," he promised, hungering after her lips. "Never."

Moving Carly from the hollow of his shoulder caused her to stir only slightly before she settled deeply into her pillow. After they'd made love, she'd tried to stay awake, and though she said nothing, he knew she was waiting to respond to whatever his needs might be. It made him uneasy. She anticipated his needs and responded so readily. She made it too easy to give in and admit needs he knew were better denied. He'd loved her with a desperation, a driving need to feel life throbbing within himself, and he'd held nothing back. Afterward, he'd felt exposed. He'd shown her everything he felt, and she lay quietly there beside him, waiting for him to betray himself further. Finally, he'd closed his eyes, suffering the images beneath his eyelids long enough to allow her to go to sleep.

It was partly because the bed was too small that he couldn't sleep. It was mostly because of the images—because of Charles Kills The Fox. Charles Kills The Fox and Roger Strongheart. In a way, cops had killed them both.

Rafe pulled his pants on and fished a pack of cigarettes out of the pocket of his shirt, which hung over the back of a chair. Someone had handed him the cigarettes down at the police station. He pulled out the book of matches he'd stuck under the cellophane wrapper and shook out a cigarette.

"Rafe? Are you leaving?"

With his back to the bed, he lit his cigarette and fanned the match. Imagining the damage he was doing himself, the first lungful of smoke brought him a perverse feeling of satisfaction. These days people didn't cut their own flesh and tear at their hair when they mourned. There were quieter ways. He blew a stream of smoke at the streetlight below the window.

"Rafe?"

He watched the street. "I didn't mean to wake you," he said quietly. "I'll get out of here and let you get some sleep."

"There's no need for you to go."

"I can't sleep in that little bed." He dragged deeply on the cigarette, trapped the smoke in his mouth briefly, and then let it go. "I can't sleep."

She crept up behind him, laid her breasts against his bare back, and slid her arms around his chest. His body was warm, hard, and his velvet skin smelled faintly of musk. "We'll stay awake together, then," she said.

He tucked a thumb in his empty belt loop. He had to hold on to something or he'd end up turning around and holding on to her again. "We didn't pull that trigger together, Carly. You can't help me with this." He crushed his cigarette in what looked like an ashtray on the dresser right next to the window.

"I know, Rafe." She turned a brief kiss to the plane between his shoulder blades. "Nothing I say will change what happened. But you shouldn't be alone now. You need me—you said that yourself. You need a friend."

Yes—God, yes. I need you more every day. When this "love" of yours runs its course, and I've completely lost my perspective, then where will I be? "I needed you in bed. Now that that's done, I need to be—"

She stiffened. "Now that *that's* done?"

He turned and took her shoulders in his hands and saw her face in the light from the window. Her eyes glistened, and her mouth was a tight line. For the first time in his life, his stomach tightened with the knowledge of the hurt he'd caused—not physical hurt, but emotional hurt—the kind he wanted nothing to do with, neither in the giving nor the taking. He yanked her to his chest and buried his face in her hair.

"My needs were simple before you came into my life, Carly. Now I hardly know myself. I don't know what brought me over here tonight. I started walking, and the next thing I knew, I was watching my fist pound on your door."

She turned her face to the warmth of his neck. "Now you know how I felt breaking into your house."

He'd shown a weakness, and she'd taken it as an apology. He had to remember that it was a weakness—a fatal one for him. The same inclination in her was not a weakness. It was innocent whimsy. She did things on the spur of the moment. He did not. But he told her honestly, "I'm glad you were home. If you hadn't been, I might have gone looking for you tonight."

"Well, I'm here, so there's no need for you to go anywhere. Not tonight. I'm sorry about the bed, but it's all I have."

Running his hands down her back, he found her skin to be growing cold to the touch. "I don't know why I'm complaining. It just means we have to curl up together a little tighter. Let's get your back under these blankets."

He moved her in that direction. She scooted under the covers and made room for him, but he hesitated. He didn't want to close his eyes again. He knew what he would see.

"There's more than one dead boy haunting you to-night, isn't there?" she guessed.

"What makes you say that?"

"On our tour of the police station when one of the boys asked what made you decide to become a cop, you said 'a dead boy.' Who was he, Rafe?"

His sigh echoed through the deep passageways of the past. He sat on the bed and leaned his back against the headboard. Carly sat up beside him, bring the blankets up to her shoulders. He knew what she wanted. She wanted him to talk. She wanted to hear about the part of his life that had nothing to do with her genteel up-bringing. How could be dredge all that up for her, for Carly Austin? But he was talking before he had an an-swer for that, and she was listening.

"He was my kid brother. His name was Roger. My mother died not long after he was born. I was four years old then. Roger and I were together until I was about nine. He stayed in Bullhead while I moved around, so I didn't see much of him after that. I was at the univer-sity when I got a call from some priest. Roger had been arrested for open container, driving under the influ-ence, contributing—the usual list. They threw him in a cell and found him dead the next morning. He'd used his shirt to hang himself. It was his eighteenth birth-day."

Nothing else was said for some moments. "Eight-eenth birthday" hung in the air like the echo in a can-yon. Carly lifted Rafe's arm over her shoulders, slid her arms around his waist, and pillowed her head on his chest. She listened to the air rush in and out of his lungs on a sigh and to the *thump-thump* of his heart.

His voice rose on a sardonic note with his conclu-sion. "So I became a cop and made the jails safe for kids. Close monitoring procedures, closed circuit TV—the works. Now I just have to learn to keep 'em alive long enough to lock 'em up.''

Carly sucked in a breath through her teeth. "Don't, Rafe. You've got to stop tormenting yourself.''

His arm was draped over her shoulder, and he shifted his hand now to cap her head, rubbing a tendril of hair between thumb and fingers. "I should go home and let you get some rest.''

"I'm resting right now.''

"You're not going to give up, are you?'' he whispered.

"No. I'm going to hold you through the night.''

"There's a penalty for detaining a police officer,'' he warned, unbuttoning his pants. If he could cheer her with a little teasing, his sadness might not be so much of a worry for her.

"Another one of your tickets?'' she asked, lifting a smile to him in the near darkness.

"Just the ticket for a bossy woman.''

She slid her hand along his belly, and he kissed her upturned mouth. "Is this the penalty?'' she whispered, her hand dipping below the waistband of his pants.

"Yeah. Scared?''

"It's a pretty stiff penalty, all right.''

He groaned and sat up to remove his pants. "You've got it coming, woman. Any woman as determined as you are to hold a police officer against his will—''

"Against his will?''

He slid under the covers and reached for her. His feet hung past the foot of the bed, so he cocked one knee over her legs. "Should feel the full measure of her punishment.''

"Is it the long arm of the law that I'm supposed to fear?" She began rubbing herself against him like a hungry cat.

"My arm isn't the part of my anatomy most anxious to reacquaint itself with you." He kissed her temple, then her cheek.

"Mmm...think I can...roll with the punches."

"Oh, God, that's good."

"What, Rafe? What's good?"

"The way we..."

"Love...the way we love."

"This is where...ah, Carly...this is my place...deep, deep in your...love."

"Yes, Rafe. Your place. Yours...because I love you so much."

Carly turned her alarm off before it sounded. Carefully lifting Rafe's arm from her shoulder, she sidled out of the bed. Smiling as she watched him sleep, she slipped into her robe. One side of his face was buried in the pillow, which rested on a outstretched arm. She had fit nicely into the curves of the S his body made. Lying there peacefully in his sleep, he could have been a teenager still trying to make do with a youth bed.

It was hard to turn away from the beautiful face nestled in her white sheets, the thick black hair falling over his forehead. He was so tired. He hadn't stirred at all when she got up. She wanted to make breakfast for him, but she knew he needed more sleep. Moving quietly, she got ready and left for work.

He was gone, of course, when she came back to her room at noon, but he'd made the bed and left everything in order. He'd even emptied the little carved soapstone dish he'd used for an ashtray. Carly caught herself fantasizing over a damp towel he'd left hanging by the shower. She laughed at herself. At seventeen, she'd been much too sophisticated for this. Now a perfectly sensible grown woman daydreamed over the very towel that had rubbed *him* dry. Perfectly sensible grown woman. *Sure, Carly.*

It wasn't just the shooting that had him tied up in knots. It was Carly. It was his *need* for Carly. Before she'd started wedging chinks in his armor, he'd have handled this thing alone, without spilling his guts about it to anyone. The minute he'd left her apartment, he'd started thinking about excuses he might make to himself for seeing her again that day. If he weren't careful, one of these times he'd start talking crazy to her, and then he'd be lost. He wanted to say things he had no business saying, suggest things he knew couldn't be. He wasn't entirely his own man anymore.

He arced the Bronco's front wheels and hit the long, graveled driveway. He'd take a day off. He'd paint. When the shooting was investigated, he'd have his perspective back. He'd denied himself a lot of things in the interest of keeping his perspective. He knew well enough what had to be done.

The receiver felt like lead in his hand. "Carly, this is Rafe."

"Hello, Rafe. How are you doing?"

"I'm fine. I took the day off. You were right. I needed some rest."

"Good. I'm sure it'll take time, but now you can begin to put all this behind you."

"Not quite." He took a deep pull on a cigarette, silently cursing himself for needing it when he dialed her number. "There's always an investigation. It's routine, but it'll keep me tied up for a while."

He'd withdrawn again. She sensed it. "Which means..."

"Which means I won't have much time for myself."

"Or for me."

"Or for you." *Play the dating game with some else, Carly. I'm too old to play.*

"I see." *You're not going to let your voice crack, Carly.*

"Listen, Carly, the other night...I was wrong to lay all that stuff on you."

"Were you? Which 'stuff' are you apologizing for, Rafe?" she bit out.

"I said too much. It was *my* problem, and I shouldn't have burdened you with it."

"*Burdened* me? My God, don't you know how I felt even before you came? You didn't have to say a word. You didn't have to tell me anything. You couldn't have kept it from me even if you hadn't come to me at all."

Like hell. Put a tourniquet on the bleeding heart, baby. But something inside him chided his mental cynic, and harsh words that he would have said easily weeks ago wouldn't come now. "All I'm saying is, it isn't my way to go to a woman and cry on her shoulder."

"And you're embarrassed about it?"

"Yeah. Something like that."

"Well, you needn't surrender your Clint Eastwood fan club card, love. Your single indiscretion will remain a secret—a secret between friends." *And I won't have you being disgusted with me for saying too much.*

Angrily, he ground the cigarette into an ashtray. He was getting nowhere fast, and pulling away from her made him hurt inside. He wanted desperately to backtrack, to start over, to tell her how much he wanted to see her that very moment. But he dammed up that stream of weakness and worked to get the old well-spring of indifference flowing. "For the sake of our friendship I'll let that pass."

"And you'll be in touch when things let up a little," she said as crisply as she could manage, summing it up for him.

"I guess I just need some time, Carly."

"Take all you need. 'As long as the grass grows and the rivers flow.' Isn't that what they say?"

"What?"

"The treaties. The ones that say you get to keep your hunting grounds if you'll just give our wagons the right-of-way."

"Oh, hell, I don't know what they say. I know I can't talk to you if you're going to be sarcastic."

"Sarcasm is a defense mechanism for me," she said quietly. "I don't carry a shell on my back. As I said, take all the time you need. I'll be around."

"Fine. Good night, Carly."

The trembling in Carly's hand betrayed her bravado, and she couldn't make the receiver fit its cradle on the first try. She had been close to him last night—closer, she knew, than anyone else had been allowed in a very long time. She'd had a glimpse of the place she wanted in Rafe's life. He'd needed her, trusted her, and, though he hadn't said it in so many words, he'd given much of his heart. *I can wait, Rafe Strongheart. Those words that stick so stubbornly in your throat—they'll come. They'll come, and...oh, my love, when they do...*

Rafe stared at the phone. He hadn't gotten his message across. What was his message, anyway? He unclenched his fists and studied his sweaty palms. Telling her anything but that he wanted to go on seeing her—that and much more—was a lie.

Chapter Ten

The tall white post, bearing a basketball hoop and backboard, was the shrine where young pilgrims gathered on Saturday morning for a boisterous ritual. Challenging shouts and rebounding retorts, punctuated by rubber thuds and rubberized footfalls, made sleeping in impossible for club dwellers.

Carly sipped at a cup of tea as she watched the play on the elementary school court across the street below her bedroom window. She'd opened the window, letting an early spring breeze chill her bare arms and chase the room's heated air to the ceiling. While she watched, a white Bronco drew up to the curb and parked near the court. Recognition of the driver made her tense up a bit as she drew a long breath. The weeks since she'd seen him had been measured, minute by dragging minute, in her conscious mind.

Stepping onto the sidewalk, Rafe turned to catch the ball and tossed it back to a grinning twelve-year-old, who urged him to join the game. Rafe shook his head, waving to the boys before he turned to cross the street. Carly knew then that she was about to have a visitor; and she dashed to the dresser for a decent pullover and a look in the mirror.

The pounding at her door threatened to rattle that barrier off its hinges. Carly slid the bolt and peered out into hot onyx eyes.

"Where is he, Carly?"

"Who?" she managed, blinking in surprise at his brusque tone.

"Frankie," he answered, reminding himself to stick to the questions and forget about how damn good she looked. "Did he con you into driving him somewhere again?"

"Frankie? No, of course not. Come on in." Carly pushed the door open and gestured her welcome. "What's wrong?" she asked, thinking little about the question as she opened the door for a better look. Rafe leaned against the doorjamb on one outstretched arm, the leverage apparently giving him better pounding power. His white V-neck sweater was pushed up at the sleeves, and the faded blue jeans looked soft and Saturday-morning comfortable. Carly wished to indulge her initial happiness at the sight of him, but he was all business as he walked through the door.

"Frankie Fire Cloud's gone again," Rafe announced. "Apparently he took off last night. The matron called me this morning. Did he say anything to you?"

Carly shrugged. "He was in school yesterday. I don't remember any talk of—"

"Has he said anything lately about his old man?" Carly shook her head. "About needing money or a ride?"

She shook her head again, more slowly as she tried to think. "He wrote about wanting to go to Canada in an essay last week. Said he dreamed of being a lumberjack. But I'm sure he didn't mean it."

Rafe snorted impatiently, hooking hands at his hips. "Lumberjack. What a pie-in-the-sky notion that is."

"It's a boy's dream, Rafe. He's just a boy."

"A boy who's about to become a man real quick if he's up to what I think he is. Kids grow up fast in reform school."

"Where do you think—"

"I think he's with the old man. And if he is, Frank's putting the kid up to something, sure as hell."

"Do you know where 'the old man' might be?" Carly asked.

Raking his hand through his hair, Rafe strode to the window and seemed to study the street below. "I know where he lives," he answered finally.

"Maybe we should start there."

"Who's *we*?" Rafe demanded, an eyebrow arched back over his shoulder at her.

"You and me. The Society for the Preservation of Frankie Fire Cloud. I think we're the charter members."

With another derisive snort, Rafe turned back to the window. "The only preservation I can manage is my own," he mumbled. And it doesn't look like I'm doing such a hot job at that, he thought, disgusted with the awful urge he felt just to touch her. "I can haul the kid's butt back here. That's all I can do."

"Who's going after him?" Carly asked quietly. "The chief of police...or Rafe Strongheart?"

"They're one and the same," he told the window.

"No, they're not." She moved closer, within two feet of his back. "The chief of police once told me quite matter-of-factly that Frankie would probably end up in reform school. Now here's Rafe Strongheart, pounding at my door at nine o'clock on a Saturday morning, anxious to find the boy—'haul his butt back'—before he gets into trouble again." He faced her, his eyes softer now. "I think you've developed a soft spot in your chest, too, my friend," Carly concluded.

"I knew it was a mistake to hang around you too much. It's infectious."

"A temporary condition, I'm sure. You haven't been hanging around me very much lately."

Her shoulders felt slight in his palms. "It's serious, Carly. One more charge, and he's on his way. Remember that record I showed you?" She nodded. "I *killed* a boy a few weeks back who had a police file just like Frankie's at another reservation." With the word *killed* she felt the quick pressure of his anguish transmitted in the grip on her shoulders.

"Frankie isn't dangerous," Carly assured him.

"Neither was Charles Kills The Fox until he got hold of his uncle's rifle and some bad drugs. And the old man—Frankie's father—is mind-altering in his own way." Rafe dropped his hands, his mind seeming to focus on a distant scene for a moment before he thrust his hand in his pocket and drew out his keys. "You're right," he said with a resigned sigh. "I'm not out to arrest anyone today. I just want to bring the kid back here so you can get him through English." Then a raised eyebrow accompanied the afterthought. "Is he passing?"

"Frankie's doing quite well for me, actually."

Rafe's smile warmed his face, and the little wink he gave her sent a warm rush of feeling through Carly. "Kid's got a good eye—and *some* good instincts. Maybe he's worth the effort."

Carly's eyes followed him to the door. "Don't give me the casual cop act," she admonished. "You know darn well he's worth *both* our efforts."

At the door Rafe turned to her again, rolling his keys so they chinked softly in his hand. "You coming?"

Carly snatched her purse from a chair and hurried after him.

The search for Frankie took them to Little Eagle, a tiny town south of the state line. It looked much like Rafe's home town of Bullhead, boasting the same unremarkable landmarks—store, post office, church, community center and similar clusters of small houses.

A rutted hard-pan road took them to a small house at the end of town. The little box of a house, surrounded by its yard of winter-worn buffalo grass, had one distinguishing feature: several sets of bleached-white deer antlers were tacked above its windows and door.

Rafe cut the Bronco's engine with a swift, impatient turn of the key. At the same moment a tall man emerged from the house. The leathery face peered toward the vehicle, the full head of gray hair glistening in the sunlight.

"Is that Frank Fire Cloud?" Carly asked.

"That's him."

"He doesn't look so sinister."

"No," he said quietly, pushing the door open, "he doesn't, does he?"

Approaching the old man with any kind of request was like walking the gangplank for Rafe. He had to tell his legs to move as he took pains to conceal the tension he felt. *Hands loose, jaw relaxed, face expressionless. Meet the bastard's vacant stare with one of your own.*

"Where's Frankie?" Rafe asked. Greetings were for friends. Rafe had business with this man—nothing else.

"Up there in Yates at the school, far as I know." The older man shaded his eyes with his hand and looked up at Rafe. "What's he done?"

"Run off."

"Didn't come here. What makes you think he'd come here?" the old man bristled.

"I know you sent for him," Rafe said. "And he'd like nothing better than to help you pull something off. You'll be his daddy then, right, Frank? If Frankie runs the gauntlet for you, you'll favor him with a little fatherly affection, won't you?"

It wasn't that he'd said more than he'd planned, but he'd let more emotion creep into his voice than he'd intended. He took a deep breath. "Why don't you tell him who you are, *Captain* Strongheart?" Frank injected a note of bitterness into the title. "Maybe he'd turn over a new leaf. Maybe you could get him into the Boy Scouts or something."

"I'm nothing to that boy that isn't an accident of birth," Rafe said.

"Me neither. So go on." The old man waved an impatient hand. "Keep him locked up there in that boarding school. I got no use for kids."

"You never did." At his back the thud of a car door cut off Rafe's sardonic chuckle. He watched the light of mischief grow in Frank's eyes as he listened to the swishing footfalls approach from behind.

"Hello, Mr. Fire Cloud. I'm Carly Austin, Frankie's English teacher." Carly extended a soft handshake. "You don't know where Frankie is, either, I take it."

"Haven't seen the boy since I was laid up in the hospital. Understand you're the one helped him get to visit me that time."

Carly glanced quickly at Rafe. His face was impassive. "Yes, well, I wasn't supposed to...that is, *he* wasn't supposed to..."

"It's all right, ma'am. I know the boy's no angel, but he's not really a *bad* boy. I don't suppose the police chief here told you about Frankie's older brother, did he?"

"He's dead," Rafe snapped. "And if I start thinking about how he died, I'm liable to run you in just on principle, old man."

"I had nothing to do with that," Frank protested, staring Rafe down with stubborn defiance. "Like I said, I got no use for kids. And the one you're lookin' for isn't here."

"You won't mind if I see for myself." Rafe shouldered past Frank and headed for the little house.

Frank followed, hesitating as Rafe reached the door. "You got a warrant, Strongheart?" he challenged.

Turning slowly, his eyes smoldering with unmasked scorn, Rafe growled, "No, I don't have a warrant. Why don't you try and stop me right here, Frank? Come on...try."

Frank's back stiffened for a moment. The reflex was still there, but there wasn't much left to back it up. His shoulders slumped, and his voice was hollow with aged resignation. "The kid's not here, I told you."

"The kid has a name, old man," Rafe said. His tone was quiet, ominous. "They all have names. This one should be easy enough to remember since he's the one who got yours."

Frankie was not at his father's house. Without a word to Frank, Rafe stalked across the yard to the Bronco, Carly in tow. In response to Rafe's impatient shifting of gears, his tires' toothy tread flung a message of disgust into the little prairie-grass yard. The Bronco devoured the rutted strip of road, quickly putting Little Eagle in its wake.

In deference to Rafe's heavy mood, Carly let long moments pass in silence. "He might have gone somewhere with some kids," she suggested finally.

"Carol White Horse is at home. I checked. No one else is missing from the dorm."

"Any other possibilities?" Carly asked.

"Yeah. Lots of possibilities. There must be fifty ways to run, Carly." Rafe cast her a short glance. "I should know. I tried forty-nine of them myself."

"What can we do?" she wondered anxiously.

"Nothing." His eyes held the road, remembering. "He has to decide for himself."

"But he's too young to understand what—"

"He's fifteen going on fifty," Rafe supplied quietly. "In the old days young men fasted and prayed, looking for guidance—a vision. Nowadays they run. The vision comes, and they're lucky if they don't run right by it."

"Did you run past yours?"

"Several times. You do that when you run in circles."

"What was your vision when you finally saw it?"

He didn't answer right away. He knew his vision had come in snatches, and some of the pieces were foolish notions that he refused to claim as his own. But the clearly sensible pieces—those he would own. "I saw myself in control of my life, and I saw what I had to do to gain that control."

"And that you've done," Carly acknowledged.

"Yes, I have." *Almost.* There were still those foolish notions teasing his brain with images of laughing, sky-blue eyes, and those images evoked feelings he knew now he'd not subdued.

It was noon, and the dorm students were on their way to the school cafeteria for lunch. The matron shook her head at Rafe as they crossed paths in the hallway. Carly watched the stout, gray-haired woman mount the stairs to the dorm's second floor without a word.

"I guess I could make a couple of calls," Rafe told Carly as he pivoted through the doorway into the matron's tiny office. "There's a chance..."

The whack of the screen door brought both their heads erect in anticipation. Within a moment, Frankie Fire Cloud appeared in the anteroom hallway. There was no surprise in his expression; he'd seen the familiar white Bronco parked outside. If there was surprise, it was the expression flickering in the faces of the two adults.

"You call out the National Guard yet, Strongheart?" Frankie's voice held only an echo of defiance. He looked worn and defeated.

"They wouldn't be interested in your escapades."

Carly squeezed caution into Rafe's arm, adding, "But we are, Frankie. We've been looking for you."

Frankie shored up his tough front with a wide, defensive stance. "So where do you want me, Strong-

heart? Spread-eagle against the wall?'' He cocked hi
head in the direction of the stairway. ''Locked in m
room? Or do I draw a 'Go to Jail' card?''

''Did your old man have anything to do with this?
Rafe asked.

Frankie tried to effect a cocky smile, but he couldn
quite pull it off. He shifted from one foot to the othei
blinking glistening eyes. ''He had nothin' to do with it,
Frankie snapped. ''*Less* than nothin'. I went dow
there...told 'im I hadda get outa here because I couldn
take any more.'' Swallowing furiously at the urge to cry
Frankie turned a reddening face toward Carly. ''H
thought it was funny!''

''We went there, too, Frankie,'' Carly offered, he
heart tight with sorrow for the boy. ''He didn't tell u
you'd been there.''

Frankie rolled his eyes, and his voice cracked wit
hollow laughter. ''You mean he didn't sell me out
That's a switch.''

''Where did you go after that?'' Carly wondered.

Stuffing hands in his pockets, Frankie shrugged. ''N
place else to go. It's a long walk to Canada.''

''The old man's never gonna change, Frank,'' Raf
said, his voice soft.

Frankie's eyes blazed suddenly. ''You don't kno
that. You've always been out to get him, Stronghear
He told me. He told me how you're always watchin
always waitin'.''

''Always waiting,'' Rafe echoed, and he glance
down the hall as though in expectation even nov
''Yeah, I waited. Waited a long time for that old ma
to make a move.'' *Why don't you tell him who you ar
Captain? Maybe he'll turn over a new leaf.* Maybe. Ra
looked down at Frankie, dark eyes to dark eyes, ma

ture chiseled face to younger, softer version. "I waited for a word from him, for just a sign of recognition. It never came, Frank, not one word of concern. You and I were blessed with the same father." He glanced away, dissatisfied with his choice of words. "I should say, we were sired by the same...individual."

The younger eyes widened. "You're lyin', Strongheart."

Rafe shook his head slowly, looking directly into Frankie's eyes now. "He never married my mother."

"But..." Frankie sputtered, unsheathing the hands from his pockets and curling them at his sides. "That makes you... You're no brother of mine!"

Rafe's hand settled tentatively over Frankie's shoulder. "I haven't been," he admitted sadly. "But maybe we can change that."

Jerking his shoulder away, Frankie resumed his defensive, wide-legged stance. "The hell you are! I ain't havin' no cop for a brother. You wanna put me in jail for runnin', go right ahead. But I don't want your pity, and I sure as hell don't want *you*."

Carly looked at Rafe for evidence of his reaction, and what she saw was understanding. He turned from them quickly and left the building without another word.

"He *is* lyin'," Frankie mumbled. "It *is* a lie, isn't it, Miss Austin?"

"I'm sure it must be true, Frankie. You know he wouldn't have said something like that if he didn't mean it."

"Somebody—my dad woulda told me." His dark, defiant eyes were swimming as he jerked a thumb toward his own chest and his trembling mouth puckered around the words, "*My* dad. Not his."

Carly gazed down the empty hallway for a moment before her eyes darted back to Frankie. "You need time to think this thing through, and so does Rafe. And then you need to sit down quietly, the two of you together, and hear each other out. But right now, you go upstairs and give it some thought. One thing you ought to think about is whose word you're going to trust." Frankie's eyes gave no hint of which way he might be leaning, so Carly concluded with, "I don't know your father, but I know Rafe Strongheart. He's a fine man, Frankie."

Rafe leaned against a pillar on the dorm's porch and watched several children playing on the swings across the street. He wanted a cigarette. He wanted to go home and shut the door on troubled kids and worthless fathers, and there'd been a time, not long before this, when he would have satisfied those wants straightaway. But now he waited for Carly. He wondered what she thought of him now.

At the sound of her footsteps he stood up straight and turned toward the door. Emerging slowly, her eyes sought his, and he looked for pity or disgust or detachment, but he found none. There was only love. Rafe recognized it as love and noted with surprise that the word had entered his vocabulary. It had real meaning.

"Is he okay?"

Carly nodded. "I asked the matron to look in on him, but I think he needs some time to himself. Letting us see the hurt he was feeling bruised his pride pretty badly."

"I know," Rafe acknowledged quietly. "I know all about that kind of pride."

"Then you know he didn't mean what he said. It came as such a surprise to him, but you know he couldn't really mean—"

"He meant every word."

Shaking her head, Carly lay a hand on Rafe's arm. "He'll change his mind after he's given it some thought."

"How about you?" Rafe's dark eyes were intense. "Will you change your mind after you've given it more thought?"

"About what?"

Indicating the Bronco with a jerk of his chin, he suggested, "Let's go for a ride."

"Where are we going?"

"Someplace where we can talk."

Corduroy clay roads south of town brought them to a hill overlooking the wide expanse of the blue-gray Missouri River. Rafe parked the Bronco, and Carly smiled when his briefly thrust lips indicated the direction of the river as he suggested, "Let's walk."

The slight breeze was snappy with spring chill. Old grass swished against their jeans and fresh new sprouts bent easily under their feet. Budding trees on the riverbank below promised the prairie's renaissance.

The hill gave way to a cut bank—a thirty-foot vertical slice of barren brown clay. They stopped at the edge and surveyed the driftwood that littered the water's edge. These were the bones of what had once been groves of river-bottom trees—willow and cottonwood—before the Oahe dam miles to the north had claimed large chunks of reservation land with its Lake Oahe backwater. Now the tops of the trees reached above the water's surface like the splayed fingers of the drowning. The river moved quietly past, unconcerned.

Standing at his side, Carly knew Rafe's concerns, and she shared them. Frankie was more special than Carly had realized or Rafe had admitted.

"What's going to happen to Frankie, Rafe?" she asked quietly.

Rafe shoved his fingers into the pockets of his snug jeans. He directed his gaze across the river, to the hill that could have been this one's twin. "I'm going to see that he tows the line, and you're going to see that he makes it through school. At this point it might be too...but maybe not. Maybe between us we can help him learn to look forward to waking up in the morning."

"I think he'll be more receptive now that he knows..."

The hill seemed to hold some fascination for Rafe, or some remembrance. "I stopped thinking of Frank Fire Cloud as my father a long time ago, Carly," he said.

"So you never thought of Frankie as your brother," she concluded for him.

He shook his head. "Maybe there was some good in him once for my mother to... But then, I hardly knew her, either. My grandmother said our father was dead, and we never knew any different until after she died. He never showed any interest in me, but Roger got in with him when he was about Frankie's age. Roger was in and out of trouble, too, but I had problems of my own." He lifted his face to the sky. High-sailing wisps of white urged him to tell whatever he had to because it would feel good to be free of it. "When they threw Roger in jail, he got word to Frank that he needed thirty dollars for bail. The old man never showed. I can see him laughing, just like he laughed at Frankie. A lousy thirty bucks.''

''Did Roger try to get in touch with you?'' Carly asked.

''No. By then we'd lost touch completely.''

''But you paid Frankie's thirty dollar fine,'' she reminded him. *You've paid in a hundred ways, my love.*

Rafe stooped to pick up a small rock and then tossed it into the river. He shrugged. ''I'm a good cop. I know how to deal with hardcases like Frankie. Paying his fine and making him work it off was just what he needed. You can't baby a kid like that—let him think he's getting away with all that stuff.''

''You can love him, though,'' Carly suggested quietly. ''He needs that, too.''

''I know that now,'' he answered, avoiding her eyes by picking a spot across the river again.

''And you need it as well.''

She watched his unflinching profile, the wind lifting his black hair away from the hard planes of his face. He squinted, seemingly absorbed by the distant bluff. ''I guess I had a lot of reasons for not wanting you to get involved with Frankie. I didn't admit them all to myself, but they were there all along.''

''I wish...'' She floundered, her throat filling with debilitating emotion. ''I wish you could learn to trust me.''

''You asked about my vision once, Carly, and I told you only part of it. I've had another vision for as long as I care to remember...of a girl with tawny hair and laughing blue eyes—a girl bathed in a box of light, playing out a fantasy in a high place, a place where I could never reach her.''

Carly wanted to protest, but her throat constricted around the words.

"Knowing I couldn't have that girl made it easy for me not to feel anything." He faced her now, and his soul was bared in his eyes. "But you've come here, to my world, and you're not a girl in a box. You're a flesh and blood woman, and I'm back to square one. I feel something I can't control, and I'm scared...because I need you."

She leaned into his arms, and he crushed her to him. "It'll be all right, Rafe," she whispered. "I need you, too."

Trembling with the need to give and short of breath from the desire to receive, they sought each other's kisses. "Don't keep yourself from me anymore," Carly begged when his mouth allowed. "I miss you too much."

"And I can't stop thinking about you, no matter what I tell myself," he rasped. He slipped his hands beneath her pullover and smoothed them over the softness of her back. "Oh, God, what a feeling...having your skin under my hands again."

She buried her hands in this thick, coarse hair and kissed his jaw. "You said you needed time," she reminded him.

"So I did," he murmured, his fingers sneaking round the satin cups of her bra.

"How much more time do you think you'll need?"

"About a minute before I have us both undressed."

With a sigh and a soft kiss on his neck she managed to squeeze out sensibly, "And another ten before you get us to a more...private place?"

He groaned, stilled his hands, and rested his forehead against hers. "I can do it in five. We'll use the siren."

"Is this an emergency?" she asked with mock innocence.

"You'd better believe it is," he growled.

They drove to his house over a shortcut that was little more than wheel ruts in the prairie sod. Carly had a sense of homecoming. The meticulously neat, sparingly decorated little house seemed to enfold her as she went inside. It smelled of wood smoke and linseed oil and spoke of Rafe in an intimate way. Carly walked to the sofa and hesitated for a moment, feeling a bit awkward. She hadn't been rescued from a blizzard or invited for dinner this time. She hadn't come to "lay her cards on the table" this time, either. The cards were out now, and she knew where the bedroom was, and this man, whom she loved, had brought her here to make love to her...because he needed her. He'd admitted that much.

Rafe closed the door and shortened the distance between them, his hands gathering her shoulders, melting awkwardness away. "Is this private enough?" he asked.

She drew a deep breath. "I love this house. It feels like a strong pair of arms around me."

Smiling, he drew her close. "No, *this* feels like a strong pair of arms around you."

"Have you been painting?" she wondered, laying her cheek against his soft, white sweater.

"Some. Why?"

"Distinctive smell, that linseed oil. Is that door still open to me?"

"They're all open to you," he said, sliding his hand down to hers and indicating the way. The big easel in the studio held a nearly finished painting. "My vision has matured," he explained. "She has a great deal more depth than I ever gave her credit for. This is my way of...of learning about her."

It was her face, pale as winter sun, her hair glinting copper in a fire's backlight. She wore a soft satin camisole and the unmistakable knowledge of love in her eyes.

"Oh, Rafe, you *did* make me beautiful," she breathed, drawn into the room by her canvas reflection.

He followed, stood behind her, and slipped his arms around front of her waist as she stood before the painting. "Not as beautiful as I will in the next one. I'll undress you," he promised, slipping warm hands under her pullover to caress her midriff, "and you'll pose for me."

"You'll be kind to my body with that brush of yours, I hope."

Rafe smiled to himself. "I promise."

"Because there isn't much to brag about, you know. I'm pretty ordin—"

"That's right. You're pretty," he assured her quietly near her ear. "And I'm going to paint every last inch of you." Without releasing her, he reached for a jar of brushes and carefully chose a fat sable. He stuck the wooden end of it between clenched teeth like one of the cigarettes he still craved, and he talked around it. "I want that Mona Lisa smile."

"You'll have to put it there," she said.

He unhooked the fastener between her breasts and filled his hands with soft flesh. And then with gently teasing thumbs he teased her nipples until they were round and hard. She gasped, and he grinned to one side of his brush. "Is it there yet?"

She dropped her head back against his shoulder and showed him liquid eyes and languishing smile. "Good," he whispered after plucking the paint brush from his mouth. "Perfect. That mouth is perfect."

"You once said it was silly." Her right breast was feeling drastically cheated at the moment.

Between light kisses he whispered, "Perfectly silly...but perfect."

At last his mouth took hers in earnest, and she turned in his arms to help make that much-needed deep contact possible. Carly reached behind his neck and sank her fingers into his hair, pressing herself tightly against him. He slipped his hands into the back pockets of her jeans and aided her efforts. She whispered his name into the promise of his open kiss, and he answered with a feathering of his tongue.

"We'll have to go in the bedroom to do this painting," Rafe said, his mouth a scant space away from hers.

"This room has...better lighting," she reminded, dreading any separation.

"Not for what I have in mind." Arm around her shoulders, he kept her close against his side, moving slowly. "I want to put your creamy skin against my sheets."

"What will you call it? 'Study in White'?"

"'Nude on Blue.' I got new sheets just for this!"

The bedroom surprised her. The large, thick area rug was new, as was the fluffy blue and rust-tone comforter on the big bed. The blinds were closed on the room's single window, and Carly noticed that he'd hung blue curtains. An arrangement of watercolors above the massive oak headboard included some she'd seen— some small ones of wild animals and larger land- scapes—and some she hadn't. There was one of a cal- ico cat with her kittens on the front seat of an old car, and one of a woman skating on a frozen stock dam.

"It's beautiful," Carly declared, gesturing palms up at her surroundings. "I just love it."

"You love so many things," he reminded her, watching her close in on the paintings he'd had framed because she'd admired them.

"But I express it so feebly," she said, touching the glass over his name in the corner of the skating scene, a quiet statement in muted colors.

"And I can't find the words," he said.

Her heart thumped wildly, and she turned to find that he'd bared his chest and his feet already. His belt slid quickly from its loops. In the darkened room his body looked like warm, rubbed wood. Carly slipped out of her shoes, but his hand stopped hers from removing more.

"Don't, Carly." His eyes caught hers, and he en- treated, "Let me. Let me take every step I need to take...to come to you."

The wooden brush clattered when he dropped it on the nightstand and reached for the bottom of her pull- over. He whisked it over her head and watched her hair flutter to her shoulders, some wisps straying over her face. That softness he brushed aside for her with one hand as the other slipped straps off her shoulders. His need grew harder when he saw her rosy nipples, al- ready round and tight. He bent to kiss them and knelt as he trailed his kisses to her belly and slid jeans over her trim hips.

Caressing her satin-covered bottom, he nuzzled her belly, teasing her breasts with the coarse thatch of his luxuriant hair. "I like your clothes," he murmured. "Especially the little satin parts. You smell lemony, but you taste—" his tongue chucked the underside of her breast and made something warm swirl in her stomach "—sweet. So sweet."

The satin fell to her ankles. "I'm losing my artistic perspective here," he grumbled, "and I have to get started on my painting before I lose the light."

Carly groaned as Rafe reached over to flip back the covers. "This light can't be good enough for—"

"The light is perfect," he insisted as he piled two pillows against the headboard and drew her to the bed. "Let me get you comfortably situated here."

"But Rafe...oh! Satin sheets?" She squirmed against them, smiling, and smoothed them with her hand. They were dark blue and certainly satin.

"I thought it might feel like being close to you," he explained, shaking his head as he leaned over her. "Poor substitute." Bending closer, he cupped his left hand over the top of her head and stroked her forehead with his thumb as though soothing a child. "Close your eyes and relax, now," he murmured. "Turn toward me just a little and think beautiful thoughts."

She complied, wondering, "Will that make me a more beautiful subject?"

"You are a beautiful subject. I just want you to feel as beautiful as you look."

"How shall I pose?" she asked, mesmerized by his touch. "What shall I do with my hands?"

"I think I want this one right here," he said, and he placed her palm high on the inside of his thigh. "Hush, now. I'm going to start with your face."

Carly felt the stroke of a soft bunch of hair down the length of her nose, and she opened her eyes. "Waht are you going to do?"

"Close your eyes, Carly." She did, and she felt a brush stroke across her eyelid, followed by a gentle kiss. "I'm going to make love to you," he whispered, "the best way I know how."

The brush and his lips took turns appraising the features of her face and then stroked their magic along her jaw, down the column of her neck, and to her straining breasts. The alternating wetness of his tongue and tickling dryness of the soft brush brought all sensation to those two taut points. When next he touched his tongue to one of them, Carly caught his head in her arms and pressed the aching nipple into his mouth, groaning with pleasure. He kneaded her hips with his hands and teased her sensitized belly with his thumbs.

Hearing his name on the end of a hungry moan, Rafe lifted his head, pulling her hands from his neck and returning the one hand to its original assignment. "You distract me from my work, Carly. I'm coming to the part that only your lover can paint."

The brush stroked around her navel and tantalized the caradle between her hipbones. "Oh, Rafe," she whispered, "Rafe, my wonderful lover."

"Your only lover," he insisted.

"My *only* lover."

The brush caressed the insides of her thighs, and his kisses followed.

"This painting is very personal, Carly. In time I might consider sharing some of the others, but not this one." His kiss became intimate. "Never this one."

The eddying drive that spiraled throughout her body swept away all thought but the one Carly voiced: "This one is yours."

The brush had done its work now, and Rafe had no more patience with props. He quickly shed his pants and went to the arms that reached for him. "Rafe, my darling, I want you so much," Carly told him as he slid his hard length against her. "You do need me, don't you? Tell me again."

"You know I need you, Carly. You've known it all along."

"I want to give you everything you need. What can I give you first, my love? What can I give you now?"

Rafe lifted himself above her and looked down, the desperation in his eyes completely unmasked. "At this minute, as much as I ache with the need to fill you with my body, I need something else more. Will you give me a place to put my love, Carly?"

"I gave you that long ago. You told me you couldn't—"

"I was wrong. I have a need for you that just doesn't let up."

"That's good." The words rumbled deep in her throat, as though uttered by a thoroughly stroked cat. "I hope it never lets up." Touching him seductively, she heard his breath catch. "Because there's nothing better than the best way you know how."

"The best is yet to come," he whispered, finding his passage. "The painting isn't finished until the artist..."

"Oh...Rafe..."

"Signs his name..."

His signature was a bold claim, one powerful stroke after another, inscribed within the soft folds of her cherished body.

They lay in each other's arms long after the heat in their blood had cooled and they wanted only to touch and taste and quietly celebrate the beauty they'd found. Carly braced herself on one elbow and watched her fingers rake furrows in Rafe's black hair. With his eyes closed, he smiled, enjoying the touch of her hands wherever she would put them. She could use him as a tactile playground forever, and he would lie there and relish the attention until she...stopped giving it. He caught her hand and brought it to his lips, kissing the center of her palm.

"I can't go on with you like this, Carly." She frowned slightly, not understanding. "I meant it when I said I need you, and I didn't mean just once in a while in bed. There was a time when I thought sure that would cure me—put you in perspective for me—but I was wrong about that, too. I don't want to have an affair with you."

Carly stiffened. "I told you I loved you, Rafe—the night we first made love. That's *why* we...why *I* made love with you. I'm not interested in an affair, either, whatever that is."

His eyes, deep-set and dusky, searched hers out. "What are you interested in?"

"Love," she said steadily. "Yours in particular, now that you admit to knowing the meaning of the word. You know it, Rafe. I know you do."

Rafe lifted himself above her, lowering her shoulders back to the mattress and smoothing her hair back from her temple. While he bared his soul, he would have at least one advantage—he would look down into her face. "I thought it meant trusting someone else with enough dynamite to blow your whole foundation right out from under you. I thought it meant disappointment and heartache, and I didn't want any part of it." She opened her mouth for rebuttal, but his single finger on her lips asked indulgence. "But I know I can't live without it anymore. I've never been loved like this before, Carly."

"And what are *you* interested in, Rafe?" she asked, tracing his full lower lip with a forefinger. He pointed quickly thrust lips in her direction, and the gesture, as always, made her giggle with delight. "What's *that* supposed to mean?"

"We don't point with our fingers; it's rude." But he tapped her breastbone with one anyway, translating for her. "It means I'm interested in *you*, Carly Austin. I always have been. I don't want you to stop loving me, and I want to spend the rest of my life learning the best ways to love you." His voice dropped to its lowest, quietest tone, and there was a look of love in his eyes. "I want to look after you, keep you off the road when the weather's bad. I want to be able to come home to you, and I want you to come home to me. And I want to keep you from ever getting cold in bed again."

She smiled up at him. "I want to be the first thing you see when you wake up."

"And then it won't matter where I am."

"You're home when you're with me," she promised solemnly.

He didn't trust himself to tell her what that promise meant to him. The dream they'd conjured together was one he'd practiced denying himself for so long that just allowing the image to form was like stretching long unused muscles. There was an awful stinging in his throat. He lay quietly and stroked her shoulder. "At home with you," he mused at length, his voice sounding rusty with the first of the words. ''What I want to know is...what's your stand on...kids?''

''What kids?'' Carly asked, stretching, extending herself down to her toes and then cuddling closer.

''Your own kids. I've thought more than once that having kids of your own might give you a more objective perspective of other people's...kids.''

Carly felt her smile spreading from the inside out. ''I've thought more than once that having kids would be the ultimate positive experience. How would you suggest I go about doing it?'' She leaned way back to look into his face.

His smile was warm, and there was an engaging proposition in his eyes. ''I suggest you let me help you with it.''

''Just like that we start making babies to improve my perspective?''

''Not exactly. I thought we'd get married first. I thought there were major differences between us, Carly, but now they seem minor...compared with this...this...''

''This what?'' she prompted. She knew his difficulty, but she wanted all the words he'd not given her before.

In its wanderings, Rafe's hand had rolled itself in a hank of her hair. Savoring its fragrance gave him an excuse to take a deep breath. ''This major lump in my throat.'' He chuckled self-consciously. ''Never thought I'd turn to jelly if I ever proposed.''

''You thought you were different from other men, didn't you? What did you think you'd do?''

''Thought I'd say two crisp words around a cigarette clamped between my teeth—kind of slit-eyed and steel-nerved.''

He demonstrated the look, and she giggled. "But then you gave up smoking and blew the whole scene."

"I know one scene that could turn even Eastwood's cool into jelly."

"What's that?" she prodded, grinning.

He smiled back, and his dark eyes glistened. "The prospect of being loved by you. I'm so damned hopelessly in love with you, Carly Austin, and I think we can make it together. I know we—"

She bracketed his face with her hands. "You did say 'love'?"

He caught her about the waist and rolled to his back, holding her tightly. "I said 'love,' and I said 'marry me.' I've said it all. Now it's your turn."

Tucking her hair behind one ear, she braced her hands on his chest and perused his face with studied consideration. "How many horses you got, boy?" she clipped in her grandfather's gravely tone.

"I have four fine horses, Grandfather," Rafe recited in practiced Hollywood Indian. "But your granddaughter is worth many more. Name your price."

"Four hundred horses," Grandfather's voice demanded.

"Four hun—"

"But your credit's good."

Laughing together, they rolled in each other's arms from one side of the bed to the other, wrapping themselves in satin sheets as they went. And their hearts sang with the sound, for none of Rafe's doors were closed to Carly any longer.

* * * * *